Mediterranean
NIGHTS™

Diana Duncan

FULL EXPOSURE

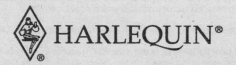

HARLEQUIN®

TORONTO • NEW YORK • LONDON
AMSTERDAM • PARIS • SYDNEY • HAMBURG
STOCKHOLM • ATHENS • TOKYO • MILAN • MADRID
PRAGUE • WARSAW • BUDAPEST • AUCKLAND

ISBN-13: 978-0-373-38967-4
ISBN-10:   0-373-38967-1

FULL EXPOSURE

WHERE DREAMS COME TRUE

The Daily Cruise Letter/The Daily Cruise News

Welcome to our final cruise of the Mediterranean!

Elias Stamos, the owner of Liberty Line and *Alexandra's Dream,* has chosen a special itinerary for this final trip of the season before we head for the Caribbean—a sail through his beloved Greek islands. Our cruise is a short one, but you'll experience the islands at their best. The summer crowds are gone, and these jewels of the Mediterranean are yours alone to explore.

While on board, be sure to take advantage of all our ship has to offer. Join one of Father Connelly's final library lectures on the ancient glories of Rome and Greece before setting off to visit the ruins yourself. Discover the gastronomic delights of our onboard restaurants and dining room. Indulge yourself at the Jasmine Spa. Check out the end-of-season sales for the fine offerings in our onboard boutiques. Climb a rock wall. Or you can always just dance under the stars.

DIANA DUNCAN'S

fascination with books started long before she could walk, when her librarian grandma toted her to work. Diana crafted her first tale at age four, a riveting account of Perky the Kitten, printed in orange crayon. The discovery—at age fourteen—of her mom's Harlequin romance novels sparked a lifelong affection for intelligent heroines and complex heroes. She loves writing about men and women with the courage to dive into the biggest adventure of all—falling in love.

When not writing stories brimming with heart, humor and sizzling passion, Diana spends her time with her husband and children and their two cats and very spoiled puppy in their Portland, Oregon, home. Diana loves to hear from readers. She can be reached via e-mail at writedianaduncan@msn.com.

Dear Reader,

Our lives sometimes take unexpected detours. We craft a carefully plotted road map, and then, *wham!* Circumstances beyond our control make things turn out far differently.

Years ago I spent several months exploring the Mediterranean. Three things still ring clear in my memory: the sparkling sapphire water, the wonderful savory food...and the overpowering charisma of Mediterranean men. Those handsome, dark-eyed heroes embody the intriguing combination of confident alpha male and gallant charm. Their tough exteriors disguise such tender hearts.

No wonder sensible librarian Ariana Bennett can't help but fall under the spell of Italian mystery man Dante. When their lives veer in a surprising direction and he's forced to kidnap her, *nothing* goes according to plan. I rode an emotional roller coaster as I lived their joys and their setbacks, and I hope you will, too.

Enjoy the journey,

Diana Duncan

ACKNOWLEDGMENTS

From the bottom of my heart to my dear friends, Serena Tatti and Josie Caporetto: You have my undying gratitude for many patient translations, oodles of advice and constant cheerful encouragement. *Grazie mille* for being my navigators on this bumpy journey that was transformed into a completely different destination than we planned or anticipated.

Vi voglio bene, belle!
I could never have survived it without you.

DON'T MISS THE STORIES OF

PROLOGUE

Philadelphia, Pennsylvania
February 14, Eight Months Ago

THE FAT LADY HAD SUNG, the curtain had dropped and Ariana Bennett had been unceremoniously fired. Sleet needles lashed her face as she trudged through snowdrifts. Frigid weather was the perfect encore. She flipped up the collar of her brown cashmere coat and turned on her iPod—two indulgences not yet paid for on her credit card—and not likely to be soon.

Administrative furlough due to budget cuts. Her department head hadn't summoned the nerve to make eye contact while delivering that fable. And the weasel had waited until the end of the day to oust her.

Ariana stomped her feet to warm them as she reached her bus stop. The coward didn't have the backbone to admit she'd been "furloughed" because the academic community was shying away from guilt by association. Her father's museum had shared fundraisers with the university and he had guest-lectured on campus. The Bennetts' battered credibility might affect public trust and alumni donations.

Thank you Pennsylvania University for rewarding my seven years of loyalty. She blinked back tears. She'd done enough crying the past months. Anger hurt far less than sorrow.

She peered through the stinging haze. Cars crawled bumper to bumper, but no sign of her bus. One advantage to being unemployed. She wouldn't have to choose between traffic or mass transit. And she'd never again feel duty-bound to wear a purple sweatshirt emblazoned with the initials P.U.

Huddled under an overhang, Ariana clapped her gloved hands together and listened to the dramatic power of Verdi's *Aida* soaring through her earbuds. Was any place more wicked miserable than Philly in February? Maybe the Arctic Circle. At least in Philly she wouldn't be mauled by polar bears. She grimaced. If she counted the FBI, the press and her ex-bosses, she did have wolves snapping at her heels.

She turned her back to the wind, and a poster in an employment agency's window snagged her attention. A cruise ship glided through sun-washed islands dotting the cobalt Mediterranean. "Get paid to travel in style. Greece, Italy, the Caribbean. Liberty Line has positions available for qualified personnel."

Ariana stared longingly at the inviting picture. She imagined standing on deck, looking over the railing at white beaches bathed in sunshine. Sailing to Greece and Italy—countries whose cultures and artifacts she'd loved and studied her entire life.

Shuddering, she spun and faced the street. *Right.* A cruise line was the perfect employer for a librarian. Especially a librarian who couldn't swim. She'd have a better chance at hitting bestseller lists with the fantasy stories she'd scribbled in her teenage journals…now in FBI custody. Another humiliating personal intrusion. She gritted her teeth. She hoped the Feds were bored to screaming by her secret girlhood dreams.

Her bus chugged into view, a sluggish dragon billowing steam, and Ariana clambered aboard. The packed interior smelled of soggy wool and overheated bodies. *Eau de wet terrier.* A baby's scream wailed from the rear seats, and she grabbed a pole and then cranked up her iPod. At least she *could* stand. Although slightly breathless after her sprint through the gale, she'd outgrown the asthma that had crippled her until late adolescence. Enforced inactivity had cultivated her adoration for reading and writing. Bored with kiddy drivel, she'd devoured Greek and Roman myths, an interest shared with her father, who had loved his job as a museum curator.

Until the FBI's relentless persecution killed him.

Her fingers clenched the pole, and she forced herself to concentrate on her music. *Aida* was a tragedy, but it was beautiful and romantic. She glanced at traffic snarled in the blizzard. Unlike real life, which was either humdrum or messy.

Humdrum would be welcome about now.

By the time she arrived home, she had resolved to put the setback behind her. There were other jobs. She still had a special dinner to anticipate. Still had a future with a nice guy. Compared to the past few months, getting fired wasn't the apocalypse.

Her mom pounced the millisecond Ariana swept breathlessly inside. "You're late. Is everything all right?"

She shut down her iPod. "The storm snarled traffic." If you looked up *overprotective mother* on Google, Sadie Bennett's picture popped up. Ariana had temporarily moved back in with her parents last fall after the FBI arrested her father. When he'd died three months ago, her mother had begged her to stay. From the moment Ariana drew her first uncertain breath, Sadie's focus was centered on her only child's welfare. Ariana didn't have the heart to leave her mom alone in the big old house. Yet.

She brushed a kiss on Sadie's cheek. "Geoff has reservations at Le Bec-Fin tonight. Will you be okay alone?" It would be the first Valentine's Day without her father. Although Derek's quiet, dreamy nature combined with frequent career travel had made her parents' marriage seem more like a business partnership than a great romance.

"Of course." Sadie's blue eyes twinkled, a paler reflection of Ariana's deep sapphire hue. "Le Bec-Fin, hmm? He's been jittery lately." She clapped her hands. "Finally, after seventeen months…the moment every woman waits for."

This was supposed to be the highlight of her life? A strange thought. "I suspect so." Geoffrey Turner was a professor of literature at the same university that had fired her this afternoon. Several months before her father's sudden death, Geoff had subtly questioned her receptivity to marriage and children. The university was about to offer him job security in the form of tenure.

Annual day of romance, check. Reservations at Philly's most prestigious restaurant, check. Exquisite food, superb wine and a tasteful ring served with the crème brûlée, check.

Ariana bit her lip. Their relationship wasn't exactly hot. But they enjoyed each other's company, shared common interests and didn't make one another crazy. She may not be delirious with rapture, but unlike passion, contentment wasn't disturbing. Or messy. She knew where she stood with Geoff. Many lasting marriages—including her parents'—had been founded on such secure principles.

She gathered her long, damp chestnut hair away from her face. "I'm a walking disaster. You know how the professor dotes on punctuality. I'm going to grab a coffee, run upstairs—"

The doorbell pealed. Geoff had probably sent a dozen predictable…ah…classic white roses. Ariana flung open the door. It wasn't flowers.

It was the police.

After six months of harassment, she recognized the FBI's second-in-command. Ariana scowled. "Unless you have another warrant, forget it. You people have already turned our house and our lives inside out." She blocked the doorway, shielding her mother. "I doubt you'll find America's most wanted by rifling through my closet again."

The solemn Agent indicated a U-Haul being unloaded by two movers. "After your father's demise, the government's case against him was officially terminated. The paperwork is complete, and we're returning personal effects held as evidence."

"Giving back our own possessions. Thank you." She stepped aside so the men could enter. FBI search teams had shown up one day in the middle of Sunday brunch and torn apart their home. Cops had poked and pried and violated every inch. They'd taken the antiques, her father's computer and research books and every scrap of paper, including her journals. The travesty had continued at his museum office. "Everything better be in perfect condition."

"Nothing has been damaged." Agent Thomas nodded stiffly. "Our experts didn't have time to dig too deeply before the case was abruptly concluded."

Hurt by his clinical description of the events that had destroyed her family, she pressed trembling lips together. "Is *abruptly concluded* the police-approved definition of ruining an innocent man's reputation and persecuting him into an early grave?"

The Fed's eyes glinted as cold and gray as the winter twilight. "Mr. Bennett was charged after brokering stolen antiquities to an undercover officer. The arrest was legitimate, as was the search."

Talk about professional detachment. Maybe the FBI confiscated agents' hearts when they entered the Bureau. For the second time in an hour, she let anger burn away pain. "Dad never so much as ran a stop sign. He didn't know the antique jewelry was stolen. It was entrapment. If your 'undercover officer' had listened to him, my father would be alive today."

"Everybody we detain is innocent, Miss Bennett." His level tone didn't negate the sarcasm. "Until proven guilty in a court of law."

"He didn't get that chance. He was convicted by the press and the museum's board of directors." Her father had been forced into a leave of absence. All because of the FBI and their gestapo tactics. Nobody would ever convince Ariana that the strain over the loss of his job combined with the impending trial hadn't precipitated her father's massive coronary. "In the public's eyes, he died a guilty man."

"Ariana." Her mother's quiet appeal made her turn around. "Don't let this spoil your evening." Sadie handed her a labeled box. "Why don't you take your journals upstairs and get ready for tonight?"

Ariana squelched her temper. Her mother hated confrontation. According to Sadie, a lady never raised her voice, never lost her poise. A woman with class practiced avoidance. That method had worked for Ariana...until injustice had struck down her father.

But Sadie had already been through the wringer, and Ariana wasn't about to twist the handle. She accepted the box and marched upstairs.

She dropped the carton on the blue organza bedspread, which matched the bed canopy and frilly curtains. Her room remained unchanged since she'd left for college years ago. Dad wasn't the only parent who liked museums.

She opened the box and began to slot journals in her bookcase according to year. She preferred order, in her surroundings *and* emotions.

Memories assailed her with each volume. Her first date. First kiss. First broken heart. A newspaper article fluttered out of the book dated Summer 1981, and her mouth softened. Even as a girl, she'd been a romantic. Charles and Diana—the Royal Wedding. She had set the alarm for dawn to watch the proceedings. A real-life fairy tale.

The grandfather clock downstairs chimed seven, and Ariana jumped. She had sixty minutes to prepare for "the moment every woman waits for." She dropped the journal and sprinted to the shower.

THREE HOURS LATER, she shakily let herself back inside the house. Sadie didn't ambush her, and Ariana tiptoed into the living room and found her mother asleep on the sofa.

A small boon in the day from Hades. She wouldn't have to break the news until morning. The sadness she'd held at bay flooded her eyes.

Instead of a diamond with the dessert trolley, Ariana had received a quiet brush-off. A "better for both of us if we go our separate ways" swan song. Her courtly, dependable literary professor had politely retreated from their relationship.

She swiped her wet cheeks as she trudged upstairs. Of course, she hadn't made a scene. Tantrums weren't her style. She was her mother's daughter. The goddess of get along. The countess of compromise.

And the Fates had compromised her out of a father, a job and a fiancé.

At least Geoff had possessed the decency to stop waltzing around the truth when she demanded a real explanation. He'd finally admitted Derek's tattered reputation and Ariana's "furlough" might threaten his tenure.

She tripped over the journal on the floor and snatched it up. *A real-life fairy tale.* In real life, the princess had been hounded to death…like Ariana's father. So much for romance. So much for loyalty and undying love.

So much for happily ever after.

Ariana hurled the book aside and it thudded to the floor, the binding torn. Newspaper clippings littered the carpet, and something shiny glinted at the tattered edge of the journal. With trembling hands, she extracted a computer CD. The thin disk had been sealed between the embossed leather cover and cardboard backing.

Tears dried on her face as she booted up her laptop and inserted the CD. Over forty scanned pages of ancient Greek script and cryptic personal notations in her father's spiky handwriting shimmered on the screen. She had enough rudimentary knowledge to discern that the information concerned antiques and Derek's international brokerage.

Her breath caught. Why had her father secreted the CD in her journal? Had he suspected he was being set up? Thought he was in danger? Had he put the CD where he knew she would find it…in case something happened to him?

Her mother would have said, "We can't change the past, let it go."

She used to agree. Now an old Chinese proverb sprang to mind. If you cannot succeed, then die gloriously.

Compromise hadn't worked out so well for Ariana, or her loved ones. Perhaps it was time to try a new tack. Her father's reputation would *not* perish in ruin and be buried along with him.

Heart pounding, she directed her Web browser to libertycruiseline.com. The police had stolen her family, her reputation and her future.

All she had left was a crusade.

She grimly hooked up her iPod to the computer and began to reconfigure and download files. Fed up with being tossed around by the whims of the Fates, she was taking her life back.

After all, how much worse could things get?

CHAPTER ONE

Alexandra's Dream
Mid-October

FATHER PATRICK CONNELLY aka Michael O'Connor dropped the benevolence he forced himself to wear in public and crossed the confines of his cabin in three impatient strides. Scowling, he unbuttoned his black shirt. The stiff white collar was penance for buying him credibility. He impatiently yanked off the torture device and tossed it aside. *Penance.* Now his alias was affecting his way of thinking. Neither guilt nor redemption were in his repertoire.

He poured two fingers of smoky Irish whiskey from his contraband stash. The Spencer Tracy affable priest persona was a pain in the ass. He'd thought it an inspired identity, but the saintly act had begun to chafe. His most grating role...but also the most challenging.

He sipped, savored the slow burn sliding down his throat. Definitely the most profitable.

As Father Pat Connelly, a priest knowledgeable about Greek and Roman culture, he'd been hired by the cruise line to educate interested passengers. As Mike O'Connor, a veteran professional smuggler, the reproduction antiquities he'd displayed in the library to illustrate "Father Connelly's" lectures had given him the perfect place to plant genuine ancient artifacts. Hidden in plain sight among the fakes. Once the ship returned to America, fencing the stolen artifacts secreted aboard by him and his partner was their mysterious boss's problem.

He glanced at the bureau drawer where he stored smaller pieces he'd acquired at various ports of call. He periodically rotated them to the library to freshen his lectures. Some were also real rather than reproductions, but nobody else knew that. His own…private investments. If the boss's grand scheme worked, a bonus. If it didn't…his insurance policy.

He swallowed another gulp of whiskey. Damn good thing he'd invested wisely, because it was looking as though he might have to cut and run.

A sharp rap on his door startled him. He opened it to see First Officer Giorgio Tzekas, and swore. "What now?"

Giorgio anxiously slipped inside. The playboy's classic bone structure showed he'd once possessed looks to go with his oozing charm, but too much boozing and sordid nights now etched his face. "Did you see him? Lanky, salt-and-pepper hair, fiftysomething Italian?"

"Bernardo Milo. Yeah, he attended my lecture last night."

"And?" Giorgio's anxiety sharpened. "Did you get the vibe?"

The cop vibe. After fifteen years conning other people, Mike knew when he was being conned. With Milo, he wasn't sure. He didn't know if it was because several things had gone wrong during this operation…or because the scam really had been blown to hell. Mike wasn't big on taking risks this late in the game. He planned to retire in the sunny Caribbean, not rot behind bars in some dank federal pen.

He sipped whiskey, buying time. He trusted his instincts, but he sure as hell didn't trust the cocky bastard in front of him. Every screwup required a sacrificial lamb, and he couldn't think of better roasted mutton than Giorgio Tzekas. The young Greek was an intellectually challenged egomaniac who squandered Daddy's money on easy women and hard-core gambling. Old man Tzekas's friendship with Elias Stamos, the cruise line's owner, was the only reason sonny-boy had a legitimate job. God only knew why their mutual boss in the smuggling ring kept him on. In fact, on one of the first legs of the cruise, the moron had panicked and moved artifacts to potted plants, of all places, where they'd been discovered and spurred speculation and an investigation.

If Mike had his way, Giorgio wasn't going to be his enforced partner much longer. Which meant keeping him obedient and unsuspecting. He shrugged. "Milo seemed real interested in the lecture. He took a buttload of notes, and chatted up the other attendees. He had more artistic know-how than any cop I've ever run into."

"Since he boarded, I've had this weird feeling." Giorgio scratched his chin. "I've never caught him staring, but he just seems like he's around a lot, ya know?"

Milo had sought out Mike to discuss antiquities. The tall, craggy Italian had said he was a contractor who'd restored historical buildings. Art was his hobby and his passion—frescoes mostly. He'd recently lost his son, who'd worked with him, in a car accident and had booked the cruise to recover. The man was intelligent, interesting and seemed lonely rather than threatening. Their conversations had been relaxed and friendly on the surface...but Mike's intuition was twitching. "There's only so much real estate on a ship. We run into the same passengers frequently. Maybe he likes your technique for picking up sluts." He smirked. "Or maybe he just likes *you*."

The distraction worked. The Greek huffed. "I don't bat for that team, and you know it, you bastard."

"I figured you'd do just about anything for money." In fact, Mike knew Giorgio had his own hoard of "private investments." Tzekas had brokered several successful buys for himself and bungled one. Just more rope to hang his idiot self with. Mike inclined his head at the door. "I'm beat. Bye now."

Giorgio hesitated. "Maybe we should tell the boss."

That's all he needed. For Megaera to climb all over his case again. Or worse, get suspicious and decide to micromanage the operation. "Report that you're imagining some guy is looking at you? That would go over like a hooker at mass. I'll keep an eye on him."

Giorgio shuffled his feet again. "Ariana Bennett's mother is still aboard. Claims she's not leaving until her daughter is found. You're the one the boss usually contacts. Have you heard any news?"

"No." Mike rolled his suddenly taut shoulders. Toward the beginning of the cruise, one of his genuine artifacts—an Olympian vase—had been accidentally broken in the library. He'd meticulously pieced it back together and discovered a shard missing. The sharp-eyed librarian had been suspicious of him since day one, and she'd been the only person nearby, the only one who could have taken it. She'd been poking her nose into things that didn't concern her and asking questions, and Mike and Giorgio had reported her to the boss.

Then Ariana Bennett had disappeared.

"She's been missing over a month." Giorgio shifted. "Do you think she's dead?"

"Not my concern." Mike gulped the last of his whiskey. Truth was, he'd been growing antsy. Not about the nosy librarian's welfare...but about his own. If she'd been killed because of his tip-off, it made him an accessory to murder. But he didn't want Giorgio overthinking it. The moron was likely to bolt and leave him holding the bag. "You really had it bad for her, didn't you? Quit whining over the one who got away. There are plenty of babes on this ship to keep you busy."

Giorgio didn't snap at the bait this time. "It *will* be your concern if Ariana is dead and her disappearance is linked to us." The Greek's forehead furrowed. "Murder carries a stiffer penalty than smuggling."

Mike barely resisted the urge to roll his eyes. *Don't strain your brain cells, genius.* "It's too late for an attack of conscience, Tzekas. The boss is a pro. Megaera's plans have worked brilliantly so far, even through the snafus." He clapped a falsely friendly hand on the younger man's shoulder. "Keep the faith."

Mike ushered Giorgio out and refilled his glass. From here on, his eyes and ears were wide-open. If he picked up a hint of trouble, he was a ghost. He would disappear and leave Megaera and her flunky to pay the price.

IMPRISONED IN the swaying belly of a seafaring monster, Ariana Bennett reluctantly floated to consciousness. Had she passed out? Been knocked out? She strained to see, but no light pierced the icy veil of smothering darkness.

No, she had died and gone to hell. Hades was cold and damp and black, and stank of fish and diesel fuel.

She tried to move. Her wrists, bound behind her back, throbbed in tandem with the pulsating heartbeat of twin engines. Her head pounded. Every breath dragged in her parched throat, and her body felt as battered as a discarded piñata.

Like many foolish souls before her, she had challenged the Fates—and lost. She moaned. She would have rather remained in the grip of somnolence. Oblivion was safer.

"Signorina Bennett?" The resonant baritone flavored with a rich Italian accent echoed from the abyss. "You are awake?"

She jerked. She wasn't dead.

But she hadn't escaped the devil.

"Where are you?" His deep voice in the black void seduced her with the promise of warmth. Compelled her to reply.

She compressed her lips. If he didn't know, she wasn't drawing him a map.

"Are you all right?"

That depended on his definition of *all right*. Surviving a mob kidnapping, yacht explosion, failed escape attempt and near drowning probably qualified. If she were a cat, she'd be eight lives short and counting.

"*Ariana?* It's Dante."

A shiver glided up her spine. As if she wouldn't recognize the alluring voice of the man who had held her hostage for almost six weeks.

At the end of August, an antiquities dealer in the Naples market had directed her to a nearby archaeological dig. She'd found

Dante excavating at the site. A fierce, dark Napoletano with a big, hard-muscled body and spine-tingling voice. She'd asked a few questions, and the mob had kidnapped her. She'd been interrogated and almost killed by Dante's partner. Then she'd been drugged and awoken in a strange house. Alone with Dante.

"Answer me, *bella*. I am also a prisoner."

She peered into the oily gloom. That was a new tactic. Fragmented memories of the previous night tumbled into place. Was this an elaborate plan to gain her cooperation? Signor Dante had held her captive for a month before bringing her aboard a yacht. They'd drifted around the Mediterranean nearly two more weeks. Yesterday, a fiery explosion had destroyed the yacht and in the melee, she had been forced to rely on Dante to get her to shore. She'd tried to escape from him, but a few bullets from a guy in a Zodiac and they'd both ended up prisoners.

"We must act. We may not have much time before they return."

They? He actually sounded concerned. If this was a ruse, he'd done a superlative job. If their predicament *was* real, who would cross the mob by attacking him? Unless he wasn't working with the Camorra, Naples's Mafia. Perhaps the Camorra had hunted Dante down and incinerated the yacht. She closed her eyes. Impossible to think with a hammering headache.

Maybe Dante had gone rogue and kidnapped her solo. That would explain why he hadn't hurt her. She was his investment. It also explained why she hadn't been ransomed. Dante labored under the misimpression her family owned valuable antiques, although she'd explained multiple times that they were less fiscally solvent than dot-com investors.

"Trust me," his low tone coaxed.

Right. And he had a cactus farm in Venice for sale. She cautiously shifted on the ice-cold floor, and her abused muscles shrieked. *Were* they both prisoners of the mob?

"Trust me, Ariana," he repeated fervently.

Even before Dante had kidnapped her, she'd felt so alone. So isolated. Her mother disapproved of her job on the ship, and

Ariana hadn't been able to disclose the truth about her mission. Her father's former contacts were leery of her motives. Ariana had made friends among the cruise-line staff, but she couldn't confide in them about her plans to clear her father's name. And she was suspicious of two employees who had expressed a little too much interest in her. The priest was savvy about antiquities and gave lectures to the passengers in the library, but Father Connelly's disposition wasn't exactly saintly. And First Officer Giorgio Tzekas was a player with more lines than the telephone company.

She wanted desperately to trust in something—trust *someone*. Dante had not threatened or hurt her. He'd calmly refuted her fear that he meant her harm, and remained cool and aloof…while implacably refusing to release her.

"I know you are listening, *signorina*. Why won't you answer?"

How did he know? She gnawed at her lower lip. Logic had failed during her five-month journey to restore her father's reputation. She'd gotten nowhere. A woman of order and reason, she had been thrust into an alien universe.

"San Gennaro, *mio bello, aiutami tu!*" Distress tinged his muttered exclamation. "If you wish to live, speak!"

Ariana stifled a gasp. If he were bluffing, a Naples native wouldn't petition their venerated patron saint, San Gennaro. She uncurled and stretched stiff, sore legs. Dante had shown kindness during her captivity. Clean clothing. Books and magazines. Hot cappuccino at breakfast. Of course, he'd locked her in her room when he'd gone to fetch them. But yesterday when they'd been forced to flee the yacht, he had not only saved her life, he had expressed empathy over her fear of deep water and carried her.

"I am bound hand and foot. If you are able, talk to me, *per favore*. We need a plan."

What should she do? Though Dante's large, capable hands could break her in half, he had handled her with carefully tempered strength. He had touched her only when necessary, and with respect. A wise woman would choose him versus the coarse

thugs who had trussed her up and tossed her into the bilge lik
fish bait, even if his interest in her welfare was only because h
thought he could trade her for money. At least he was dedicate
to safeguarding his investment.

Adrift and floundering, she was forced to rely on instinct
Those instincts screamed at her to answer him.

Pain ground her joints as she struggled to sit up. "I—" th
word emerged as a croak, and she cleared her throat "—I can ge
up. Just my hands are tied."

"Grazie a Dio!" He uttered a relieved sigh. "Then you mus
come to me."

Decision made, she refused to second-guess herself. "Easie
said than done. It's as dark in here as the inside of the Trojan horse."

"Beware of Greeks bearing gifts." His wry chuckle was oddl
comforting. "Follow the sound of my voice."

He issued calm commands and she replied as she blindl
navigated the rolling maze. After long, frustrating moments o
stumbling, she bumped against him. He was sitting on a crate
and she maneuvered herself down beside him.

He was so warm. Cold and scared, she couldn't help huddlin
against his hard shoulder.

"You're trembling." He swiveled so they were pressed bod
to body, her cheek resting on his chest. Beneath the smooth cot
ton of his T-shirt, his heart beat strong and steady. The softnes
of his full beard caressed her face as he brushed his cheek ove
her temple. "Are you hurt?"

"No." She retreated from the intimate contact, but staye
close enough so his body heat radiated to her chilled, shiverin
limbs.

"Turn around so we can loosen each other's ropes."

They turned their backs to one another. The mutual explora
tion of his large, callused hands and sinewy arms jolted he
system…reminiscent of the power surge that had once frie
her laptop. She'd read about Stockholm syndrome. Over time
hostages sometimes fell for their captors. But the very firs

moment on the dig site when Dante's eyes had locked with hers, her heart had leaped into her throat and pounded so hard she'd nearly choked.

The intriguing Italian possessed a primal gravitational force. Whenever he was in sight, her gaze was pulled to him and her pulse galloped. Now, weeks later, she'd jettisoned the attempt to convince herself her reaction was fear. Like everything else since her father had died, her involuntary attraction to Signor Dante made no sense. He was so far from her preferred cultured academic, he bordered on Paleolithic.

Not to mention that he was a criminal.

She fumbled with the ropes binding his thick wrists. "Are we prisoners on a ship that belongs to the Camorra?"

"If the Camorra had captured us, we would already be dead." She had enjoyed the fresh aroma of his bay laurel soap lingering in the air after he'd showered, and now, in the icy blackness, his evocative scent conjured a vivid image of sun-warmed herbs growing wild on lush Mediterranean hills. His fingers tugged on her bonds. "I have no idea who is holding us. Or why."

His efforts to free her sharpened the ache in her arms, and she stifled a whimper. "That's reassuring."

"*Perdonami.*" His quiet apology amazed her. She hadn't betrayed her pain...she'd thought. "Don't be afraid, Ariana. I will protect you."

"Why, for the ransom? In any case, we're in no position to put up a fight."

He snorted. "A man's worth is no greater than his ambitions."

Her hands stilled. She had seen keen intelligence in his brown eyes. Who knew her kidnapper was well-read? "Marcus Aurelius, the ancient Roman emperor-philosopher."

"I find him more helpful in such situations than George Clooney."

In spite of the grim situation, she couldn't help but smile. She'd seen rare flashes of *il diavolo's* droll sense of humor before, but they always surprised her. "If you get into situations like this often, you might consider a new line of work."

His broad shoulders moved against hers in a shrug. "Every profession has challenges. How aggressively you conquer them depends on how badly you wish to succeed."

"Exactly how high do your ambitions reach, Signor Dante?"

"Let's hope we are not pushed to find out."

She didn't need sight to know that the expression in his eyes mirrored the fierce resolve in his voice. She had spent almost as much time in the past weeks attempting to decipher him as she had her father's encrypted notes. His bearded face rarely showed emotion. But his eyes gave away far more than he knew. As dark and rich as her favorite caramel espresso, the brown depths reflected a wealth of intriguing moods and emotions.

"Keep working at the ropes, Ariana."

"The knots are too strong."

"As you walked to me, did you feel anything that might sever them? Equipment or tools with sharp edges?"

"No, but I can go back—"

A door slammed open. A glaring halogen lantern blinded her, and she flinched. Two burly men swaggered in, boasting about their good fortune in a combination of broken English, Greek and Russian.

Ariana groped for Dante's hands and clung to him. An uncertain anchor in the storm, he was all she had.

The lowlifes were big and muscular and scruffy. The Greek flipped open a large knife. She gulped, and Dante's fingers tightened reassuringly. She and Dante were suddenly united by the common threat. *The enemy of my enemy is my friend.*

Though Dante was tied hand and foot, he quickly maneuvered her behind him on the crate.

Knife raised, the Greek stepped toward him. Dante pistoned his legs and rammed the man's midsection. The knife clanged to the floor as the Greek flew across the hold.

The Russian swore and slugged Dante in the jaw, and the

impact shoved her into the wall. Dante shook his head, but didn't make a sound.

The Greek regained his feet, staggered forward and snatched up his knife. "You are wanted up top for questioning. Do not cause trouble, Napoletano. Only your mouth needs to be working. Your body can be broken into pieces." His blade sliced the ropes at Dante's ankles. Leaving his arms tied, his captors yanked him from the room.

The engines growled through the hull and the ship pitched. Ariana huddled alone in the icy blackness, stunned and trembling. When she was growing up, her parents had sheltered her. As an adult, she had ensconced herself in civilized academia. Violence confronted her daily, but in distant images from the newspaper or television. If it was too much, she could turn the page. Switch it off. She'd never been a helpless witness to brutality.

She couldn't stop shaking. How could one human being cold-bloodedly abuse another? *Your body can be broken into pieces.* Nausea roiled in her stomach. Were they torturing Dante? She sucked in a quivering breath.

Was she next?

She forced her breathing to slow. Don't panic. *Think.* She'd never been a scrapper. Brains trumped brawn in her world. As a librarian, she held fast to the belief that knowledge was power. Even when Dante had kidnapped her, she had hoped passive resistance would lead to negotiation. Her mother and the cruise line would be searching for her. She had planned to talk her way out, or stall until rescued. She bit her lip. Her usual weapons of logic and reason were useless against savages who brutalized first and asked questions later.

Ariana wriggled off the crate. Why meekly sit and wait? If she was about to be killed, she wouldn't make it easy.

She needed a crash course in fighting dirty.

Squelching worry for Dante, she fumbled through a painfully slow investigation of the dark, swaying chasm. Horrifying images of what the barbarians were doing to him only made her weak and scared. The best way to help him—and herself—was to break free.

She had no idea how long she wandered in blackness before she stumbled over something and fell. Agony screamed through her limbs as she hit the floor. Every movement stabbed red-hot spears into her strained muscles. Panting, she curled into a ball, tempted to surrender.

The thought of Dante stoically enduring torture drove her to struggle to her knees. She cautiously felt behind her. She had tripped over a metal spool of chain. The rough edge might fray her bonds.

Battling the burning ache in her arms and wrists, she scraped her ropes on the spool's edge. If she had been shown a preview before she began her ill-fated journey, would she have continued her crusade?

Absolutely.

Clearing her father's name was worth any discomfort. He didn't deserve what had happened to him. He could no longer speak for himself. She would speak for him. Cramping muscles ceased to matter as righteous determination fueled her efforts. She would shout Derek Bennett's innocence from the rooftops. Make every newspaper that had vilified him print a retraction. She would contact CNN. *Oprah.* She'd even book a slot on *Jerry Springer* if he'd give her a platform.

She didn't get far before the door banged open again, and cold light fractured the blackness. Dante was shoved into the hold, where he collapsed onto the floor. The Greek and Russian sauntered in behind him. Ariana pushed to her feet and stumbled to Dante, knelt at his side. Her heart jolted. His face was bruised, his lips cut, his beard matted with blood. Any doubts she'd harbored about their jailers being in his employ died a cruel death. Nobody would willingly take a brutal beating.

Ignoring Dante, the Russian leaned down, fisted his fingers in her hair and jerked her up. Pain burst over her scalp, and she cried out.

"Do not touch her!" Dante growled as he fought to his feet.

He head-butted the Russian and sent him sprawling. His voice was dark with menace. "Or I will remove *le tue palle* and feed them to you."

Though he was tied and beaten, the fierce Napoletano looked entirely capable of his threat. Ariana unconsciously edged behind him as if he could protect her.

Wishful thinking.

The Russian struggled upright. To Dante's credit, the thugs hesitated before they both charged. Dante fought back with limited mobility, but his attackers landed blow after blow on his defenseless body.

"Stop it!" Ariana yelled. She flung herself between the warring men and received a sharp clip to the jaw. The punch slammed her to her knees.

Panting, Dante dropped beside her. "Stay behind me!"

She blinked away involuntary tears. Nobody had ever hit her before. How did Dante take the pain without uttering a sound?

The Russian knocked Dante flat. Pulse thundering in her ears, she bent over the fallen man. She didn't have much time. "Dante, can you hear me?"

"Ariana." He groaned, turning his head to look up at her. "I have failed you. *Perdonami.*"

"There's nothing to forgive you for," she whispered. "Save your strength and let them take me. There's a metal spool, starboard, fifty paces. It might cut your ropes."

Concerned respect shimmered in his gaze. "Stay strong, Ariana," he murmured. "If you tell them what they want to know, you will become useless to them. *Capisci, bella mia?*"

She gulped. She understood all too well.

The Russian reached for her hair and she scrambled up before he hurt her again. She strove to draw their attention from Dante, motionless on the floor. *Please, don't let him be badly injured.* "Let's get this over with."

The Greek shoved her toward the door. "We find out soon how tough you are."

"Bastardi!" Dante's ragged voice echoed behind her. "If you hurt her, I will kill you. That is a promise."

Dante's valiant defense fueled Ariana's resolve. After the abuse he'd suffered, he still had the fortitude to insult and threaten his assailants. She thrust out her chin, feigning bravado. Much better than bursting into tears.

The men dragged her out the door. Fear iced her blood as they muscled her up two flights of stairs and down a long, dark corridor. The briny ocean smell and sharp slap of the waves told her she was above the waterline.

They yanked her to a halt outside a closed stateroom. The Greek sneered. "You will show respect. You will answer when spoken to. You will not attempt anything. Or—" he sliced his finger across his throat "—no mercy."

His fist rapped on the door, and terror swelled in Ariana's chest. Dante hadn't talked, and neither would she.

No matter what their captors did to her.

Or she and Dante were dead.

CHAPTER TWO

THE GREEK OPENED the door and the Russian shoved Ariana into the murky stateroom. Then the portal slammed shut, sealing her inside alone. Whoever was in here, and whatever was planned for her, the henchmen weren't participating. For now.

Skeletal fingers of moonlight pierced the window shutters and striped the carpet. Ominous silence vibrated from both sides of the door. Trapped in darkness, she could almost taste the thick, black silence.

Maybe the thugs had gone to finish off Dante. Anxiety thrummed inside her. How badly was he wounded? Maybe the men would murder him while she was being "questioned." He might disappear and she would never know what had happened to him.

Why did she care so much?

She swallowed. Because he was her only ally at the moment. Because thoughts of him kept her from screaming with terror over what was about to happen.

Her pulse throbbed in her ears, and she leaned against the wall to support her wobbly knees. An intent gaze crawled over her skin.

Someone was watching her.

She shuddered. As a child, when she had feared monsters lurking in the night, she had burrowed beneath the covers and yelled for her daddy. He had run to the rescue, dispatched the monsters and given her a "magic shield" for protection.

She squelched a threatening sob. There was nowhere to hide. Her father was dead. The shield imaginary.

But the monsters were real.

Ariana inhaled shakily. Don't stand here like a quivering ninny. "H-hello?" Her voice trembled and she cleared her throat and made a sterner inquiry. "Who's there? What do you want?"

"The question is, what do *you* want, Ariana Bennett?"

Ariana jumped at the disembodied inquiry from across the room. Husky, tinged with a cultured Greek accent...and female. Her heart kicked. Not Camorra. Machismo mobsters would never take orders from a female. A Greek female. And the woman had called her by name! "Do I know you?"

"No. But I know you. I'm just not certain what to do with you."

"I don't understand."

"Tell me about your family."

Enlightenment dawned. "There's an epidemic of 'ransom the rich American.'" If she admitted she was poor, she might be killed. But she had nothing to gain by lying. Dante's battered condition proved the mystery woman lacked patience. "Sorry to disappoint you. Most of our money went to defense attorneys for my late father, who got railroaded by the system. The remaining pittance is still frozen, tangled in FBI red tape. Red tape that strangled my father to death. My family has *nothing*. Not even our reputations."

"I see." A pause. "You are angry and mistrustful of the police, and have lost faith in the system's ability to mete out justice. Interesting. Continue."

She had probably said too much already. "Neither the government nor the cruise line will pay ransom. My life isn't worth a thing to anyone with authority." She couldn't keep the bitterness from her tone. "I haven't seen you, and won't divulge information to the police. You might as well release me."

"You could be worth far more than you believe possible, Miss Bennett."

Maybe to white slavers? Ariana shuddered. *Don't give the black widow any ideas.*

Absolute quiet descended, spun into a smothering web. A strategy to rattle her, make her talk first.

Ariana gritted her teeth. While this woman played mental chicken with her, Dante lay below, beaten and bleeding. She cloaked herself in a shield of fury. "You've had me blown up, kidnapped and beaten." She locked her shaky knees. "And now you want to play mind chess."

"Do not let hasty words overstep your abilities. A difficult lesson always follows."

"If you're going to kill me, stop playing games and just *do* it." Her words were a challenge. Fear or submission would only amuse this woman.

At the woman's throaty laughter, Ariana blinked in astonishment. "You're not the pampered, fragile, prima donna I expected."

"After everything that's happened, I'm a far stronger woman than I was five weeks ago."

A manicured hand flitted into view, and moonlight glinted on an ornate gold bracelet. "There is a chair near the window. Sit."

Meekly obey like a trained puppy, or humiliate herself by collapsing? Ariana staggered across the carpet and dropped into an upholstered chair. Moonbeams fractured her vision, shadowing the woman opposite her. No accident. She'd bet this woman calculated every move. The musky fragrance of expensive perfume magnified her captor's aura of power. "Who *are* you?"

"You may call me Megaera."

Ariana started. Megaera was one of the Erinyes, or Furies. Three Greek goddesses of vengeance created by drops of Uranus's blood, they pursued wrongdoers until the sinners were driven mad or died. The "daughters of night" had fiery eyes and dogs' heads wreathed with serpents.

"A goddess of vengeance. Are you seeking revenge…on *me?* How do you think I've wronged you?"

The woman paused briefly before speaking. "You mentioned your father. Now I ask what vengeance *you* are seeking, Ariana?"

Was this about her *dad?* A chill skittered up Ariana's spine, as if death had reached from the grave and stroked her with icy fingers. The hair on the back of her neck rose, and she shivered. *I do not believe in mythical beings.*

What kind of fresh FBI hell was this? An undercover sting? Or was *Megaera* a smuggler priming her to be another unwitting courier of stolen antiquities? Duping Ariana would be more difficult. Her naïveté had been buried alongside her father. "I don't want vengeance," she said cautiously. "Just justice."

"They can be one and the same."

A dangerous philosophy. "There's a line. A point of no return."

"Your family has suffered. What line would you draw? What will you sacrifice to gain 'justice' for Derek Bennett?"

Images haunted Ariana. Her father being led away in handcuffs in front of gaping neighbors. His despair over unreturned phone messages and canceled meetings by his colleagues. The disdain heaped upon the once-proud man, reducing him to a common thief.

She couldn't exorcise the memory of sitting beside his hospital bed, watching his pale face slacken as his spirit faded. The stinging pain as icy raindrops blurred her vision when the casket holding the shell of what had been her father was lowered into the earth.

"I'll do whatever I have to."

"Would you reach into a serpent's nest, though you could be bitten?"

Goose bumps prickled over Ariana's skin. What did this woman want?

A silken rustle of clothing whispered in the darkness. "What is the Napoletano, Dante, to you?"

Ariana tensed. She needed to frame her answer carefully. Was this Megaera looking for an "opportunity" to hurt Dante? The gods and goddesses of legend frequently ensnared mortals with their own thoughtless words.

But the woman who held them captive was human…armed with intelligence and power. And the ruthlessness to wield them. Ariana hesitated. Megaera wanted Ariana to believe she was on her side. Dante seemed as if he were not. Instinct warned her to proceed with caution. "That sounds like a trick question."

"I'll make it easier. Do you wish me to dispose of him?"

An affirmative or a negative could land both her and Dante in serious jeopardy. If Megaera thought Ariana cared for Dante, the woman could use it against them. But Ariana refused to consent to hurting him further.

"Decide quickly. Or I will decide for you."

"Then I…" *Phrase it carefully.* "In future dealings, I want you to treat Dante and me with equal respect."

"An answer worthy of the ancient gods." Satisfaction swam in Megaera's sultry reply. "You risk throwing your lot in with his? Wise. And yet…most unwise."

"I vote for wise."

"It remains to be seen whether your choice reveals mercy— or weakness." The woman's hand rested on the arm of her chair, and moonlight illuminated the golden circlet at her wrist. The antique bracelet adorned with bloodstones sent a shiver of recognition through Ariana. Where had she seen it before?

"Hold fast to your secrets, Ms. Bennett. Do not reveal yourself to anyone." Megaera rose and glided to the door. "And you may be granted a chance to even the score for your father."

The woman left, abandoning Ariana to the gloom.

Her stomach heaved with the ship. What on earth had just happened?

More importantly, what would happen next?

The door crashed open and the Greek swaggered in. Without a word, he yanked her to her feet and marched her toward the yacht's stern. Dread weighted her chest. Was this the end? Would he shove her into the unforgiving sea?

The torturous walk down the rolling deck was the longest of her life.

Clinging to her dignity—all she had left—Ariana refused to cry or beg. She shouldn't have embarked on this ill-fated voyage. Sadie would never recover from losing both her husband and daughter.

At the stern, Ariana braced herself for the final assault. Instead, the thug left. Bewilderment assailed her. Reeling from captivity first in the odiferous hold and then the perfumed stateroom, she inhaled the bracing night air. If these were her last breaths, she would savor them.

Murky gray clouds scuttled across the pallid moon. The ocean churned below, where restless waves prowled to the horizon and tumbled off the earth. Shuddering, Ariana pressed trembling lips together. *Don't you dare start wailing.*

How had she landed on a yacht in the Mediterranean waiting to die? She had never taken risks. Never longed for adventure. She'd been content to experience life through the stories she adored. She had never hungered for ambition. Never burned with passion. Never melded heart to heart with a soul mate.

At what were probably her few remaining moments before death, realization stole over her. She'd only flirted with blurry shadows of the real thing.

She had never truly lived.

It wasn't fair. Wasn't enough.

She wanted *more!*

If she made it through this, she would live her life the way she wanted…on her own terms. No more concessions. No more doubts. When she died, she wanted to leave behind *no* regrets.

She heard a commotion and spun around. Which was more terrifying? Someone creeping up from behind and shoving her into the water…or watching the waves rise up to swallow her?

The thugs struggled into view, wrestling Dante between them. The pair strove to restrain the furious Napoletano. Even tied up, he fought every step…defaming their parentage in admirably profane Italian. Relief crested over her. His injuries hadn't disabled him as badly as she'd feared.

Dante saw her. He stumbled, his tirade broken mid-insult. His gaze swept her body, then locked with hers. His umber eyes mirrored her relief, and her heart jolted. Then he looked away, his features hardening into his usual stony expression.

The Russian opened a watertight door in the stern and motioned them down onto a platform. Her gaze fixated on the waves lapping at her deck shoes. "I'm sorry." She sputtered a frantic apology at Dante.

"Stay calm, Ariana." His low assurance vibrated in her ear. "Get into the boat." He gestured at a speedboat moored to the platform.

Boat? Her limbs quivered as the spike of adrenaline ebbed. She hadn't seen the boat.

The Greek piloted the speedboat and the Russian rode shotgun, with her and Dante trapped in the middle. As if they'd be moronic enough to dive headlong into the ocean with their hands tied behind their backs.

The Greek didn't use the running lights. He either knew where they were going or was taking them farther out to sea to dump their bodies.

Wind whipped her hair as the hull chopped through surf. Shivering, she leaned into Dante. "Will they toss us overboard?" she whispered.

"I doubt it. They would have done it from the yacht and saved the effort."

"You know I can't swim. If you get a chance to escape, go. Save yourself."

He angled his big frame to shield her from the wind. "I am not leaving you. And I will not let anything happen to you."

"You don't lack confidence, Signor Dante. I appreciate the encouragement, but unless you have blue spandex tights and a red cape stashed in your pocket, I don't see how."

It took a few seconds to translate. Then he threw back his head and laughed. His eyes sparkled and his teeth gleamed in his bearded face. Dazed, Ariana blinked at the impact of Dante's unrestrained smile.

The Greek turned and scowled, and Dante lowered his voice. "Don't be so pessimistic, *bella*. Thanks to your cleverness, my ropes are weakened. I only need more time and a sharp object."

"Which you won't find in the middle of the Mediterranean."

"We're headed toward a destination. We wait. And watch."

The Greek suddenly killed the motor.

"Shut up," the Russian snarled. "No more talking."

Ariana anxiously half turned as the beefy man stood, but he merely slid the oars into the oarlocks and reseated himself. His biceps knotted as he rowed.

She glanced up at Dante. Inscrutability shuttered his bruised face, but his forearms grazed hers as he fought his bonds. They had to be nearing their final destination. She fervently hoped he could break free.

Trembling with cold and apprehension, she huddled into the protection afforded by his body, and he moved closer. Though he had often appeared to ignore her over the past six weeks, in reality, he was acutely responsive to her body language. A survival skill when one conducted business with the mob.

Though their whispered conversation had been forbidden, the presence of his reassuring strength helped. The irony wasn't lost on her. Soaking in his heat, she pressed against him, shoulder to firm shoulder, thigh to hard-muscled thigh.

She wasn't convinced they were headed anywhere other than the bottom of the sea. If she succumbed to her rioting fear of how it might feel, how long it might take to drown, she'd start screaming like a banshee.

Think about something else. *Anything.*

She was freezing. Neither she nor Dante were dressed for nighttime on the open water. He had been wearing a long, weathered black Florentinian leather coat over his black T-shirt and black denims, but their captors must have stripped it from him before tying him up. She wore cargo pants with a long-sleeved shirt.

She jerked upright.

Oh. My. God. In the midst of the trauma, she'd forgotten. Was Dante's coat the only thing their captors had confiscated? Muddled by terror, she hadn't thought to check if her iPod and notebook were still in her hip pocket. Ariana twisted in frustration. She couldn't tell. She'd taken the precaution of securing her iPod in a watertight case before accepting the job aboard *Alexandra's Dream* and her notebook was in a sealed plastic bag.

The iPod hid Derek's files, encrypted in ancient Greek, which she had spent months laboriously translating into the notebook. She'd had no idea cruise lines overlapped employee duties and that she'd be required to juggle many nonlibrary-related jobs. Duties aboard the cruise liner had kept her hopping. She'd spent every snippet of free time the past seven months decoding files. Only a long list of names and addresses, so far. Most dead ends. Finally, one had led her to the dealer in Naples. Her first break, thwarted by the Camorra.

When Dante had kidnapped her, she'd lost the use of her shipboard dictionary. Translating the complicated language had slowed to a painful crawl. She groaned. If Megaera's cohorts had stolen her only clues to clearing her father's name, her crusade was doomed.

Dante's lips brushed her hair and his breath feathered into her ear. "Are you seasick?"

Not risking a reply, she shook her head. He had seen her scribbling in the notebook at the house, where she'd claimed to be writing stories to pass the time. Sometimes, she was telling the truth. She'd been writing them most of her life, and they'd been a familiar source of comfort during her captivity. Dante had requested she share them. She had politely declined. Their mistrust was mutual. He had searched her room when she was showering…and when he thought she was asleep. She'd thwarted him by keeping the iPod and notebook on her at all times and in sight when bathing.

"Are you in pain?"

She shook her head again, and his ebony brows lowered. "You're lying."

She hated deception…and she stank at it. "I'm fine."

"Tell me."

Even if she dared confide in him, what could he do? They were both victims of circumstance. Both helpless.

Not comforting.

"How are your bonds?" she whispered.

His mouth hardened. Naturally, he recognized bait and switch. He was a maestro at it. "I'm making progress."

She peeked behind his back, and her throat constricted at the blood coating the rope. "It looks like all you've accomplished is further injuring yourself."

Wounded male pride sharpened his features. *Great.* She'd hurt his feelings. After seven months at sea with a cultural grab bag of employees and passengers, she should be used to macho Mediterranean males.

Dante whispered fiercely, *"Dio provvede."*

God will provide. Odd encouragement from a criminal. "God helps those who help themselves," she whispered back.

"Exactly my point, Ariana. Keep the faith."

She studied his striking profile. The man she'd thought a sullen mobster was a Gordian knot of intriguing contradictions.

The boat's hull scraped land. The Greek leaped into the shallow water and dragged the craft onto a sliver of rocky beach carved out of a high cliff.

Their time had run out.

"Our hosts are not wearing guns," Dante murmured. "Do as they say, and stay behind me, until I tell you otherwise."

Ariana was too anxious to argue. He was the criminal expert.

Sandwiched between their two captors, she and Dante climbed awkwardly out of the boat. Coarse rock scrunched under her deck shoes as she trudged up the beach.

The Greek halted in front of a semicircle of craggy boulders spearing from the sand. "Sit."

Dante uncharacteristically complied. Did he have a plan?

Please have a plan. She followed his lead and sat beside him.

Draped in the cold, black shroud of night, the hostile island appeared uninhabited. A cliff overshadowed the beach, bullying aside the moonlight. Waves pummeled the shore with white-capped fists.

The thugs turned and walked toward the boat, and Ariana reached for Dante's hands. "Are they returning to the yacht and leaving us here to die?"

"Not if I can stop them." He squeezed her fingers, then let go to continue his fight for freedom. "You watch them while I concentrate on escape."

The Greek leaned into the boat and scooped out Dante's leather coat. The Russian snatched it away. The Greek gestured and said something, and then they began to argue in their tangled English.

Ariana understood enough to grasp the conversational gist.

"*Nyet!*" The stocky Russian clutched the coat.

The Greek punctuated his diatribe with a vehement hand gesture. Dante looked up from his urgent task. "*Che?*"

Ariana grimaced. "Abandonment suddenly doesn't look so bad." Dante had said the men weren't armed with guns, but if the Greek still had his knife, he could cut their throats... She bit her lip. And while she was scaring herself with what-ifs, they were losing valuable seconds. "The Greek just said, 'Do as we were told and leave it. *No evidence.*'"

Dante swore vilely in Italian and redoubled his effort. He shifted, felt behind him. "I scraped my knuckles on a jagged rock. With time, I can cut myself loose."

Down the beach, the Greek acerbically reminded the Russian he could buy fifty coats with the price Megaera was paying them. Though the Russian couldn't immediately agree without losing face, the debate cooled.

"Time is in very short supply."

"Then you will have to stall. Distract them."

"*How?* I doubt they'll be interested in my rendition of the Iliad."

His broad shoulders bunched as he vigorously scraped his ropes. He quirked a glossy brow. "There is one thing that interests *all* men, *bella.*"

"You can't be serious."

Admiration flashed briefly in his eyes. "*Sei bellissima,* Ariana."

Amazement curled through her. *Most beautiful.* She shook her head. "Say I get their attention…and then you can't break free." She shuddered. "I *really* don't want to go there."

"My solemn oath, I will not fail you. Once my word is given, I follow through. No matter the cost."

That could be good. Or *very* bad.

It all depended on the man.

"Trust me, Ariana."

Trust him. She rested her forehead on her bent knees.

"We have no recourse," Dante hissed. "If you want to survive, you must do it."

She straightened and saw the Greek and Russian shaking hands. Whether they'd agreed to a fast end for her and Dante or a slow one, she didn't want to know.

Not only were they out of time…they were out of options.

She scooted away from Dante to keep the men from noticing what he was doing while she played seductress.

"Hey…you guys." She forced down her revulsion and attempted a come-hither look. Both men ignored her.

She glanced back at Dante. Muscles corded in his tanned arms and strong neck as he waged his war with his bindings.

Their glances locked, and resolve glinted in his eyes. His wrenching movements had to hurt—a lot—but his set features didn't reveal pain. Her own effort in the hold of the ship had scalded her arms like liquid fire, and it hadn't been nearly as ferocious.

She could fight as hard for their survival. Ariana scrabbled to her feet and attempted an enticing stroll. "You aren't leaving, are you?"

Almost in slow motion, the thugs turned to stare at her.

She tilted her head. "I'm cold. And my arms hurt. If you untie me, I'd be really grateful. We could…um…maybe reach an agreement? Just please don't abandon me here."

Their eyes fired with greedy anticipation. The Greek's lips

curled in a sly grin. Dante's coat slid from the Russian's fingers, and his nostrils flared. A wolf on the scent of prey.

Ariana's pulse lurched into triple time and she bit the inside of her cheek to keep from screaming as the men began to stalk her.

CHAPTER THREE

ARIANA'S HEART THRASHED. Why had she agreed to this terrible idea? With no time to weigh her choices, she'd listened to her intuition...and sided with Dante over dying.

As the men reached her, she backed up several steps. "I'm really uncomfortable. Can you untie me?"

Suspicion creased the Russian's swarthy face. "Why should we?"

"Uh...because if my hands aren't free—" her fingernails dug into her clammy palms "—it will spoil my...fun."

The Greek's slimy smile made her want to throw up. "Not necessary for you to be having fun."

"*Da.*" The Russian nodded. "Only for *us.*"

Oh, suddenly the pigs were in agreement?

"If I'm not having as much *fun,* neither will you." Just talking about it gave her the urge to throw up. The Russian's cruel mouth twisted hungrily, and she forged ahead. "It'll be worth it, I promise."

Before they could dwell on that awful scenario, she threw down the gauntlet. "Are you afraid to untie me? Scared of a *girl?*" She deliberately swept each opponent with a scornful gaze. She needed them tearing at each other's throats again. "Which one of you is a *real* man?"

She may as well have pushed the button marked *predictable.* Both spat denials, and then hurtled into confrontation. The wary Greek was against untying her, while the machismo Russian insisted *he* could handle her.

She shot a covert glance down the beach. Darkness hid Dante's progress, but he was still seated. Not good.

The thugs switched from haggling over whether to untie her to who should have her first. Ariana fought the impulse to flee into the night. Running might buy her three minutes, tops.

Dante, hurry!

The Russian's dubious control snapped, and he shoved her backward onto the sand. Agony speared her bound arms and she screamed.

He crawled on top of her. For nightmare moments, pain and horror paralyzed her. She'd never been in a fight. She was bound. Helpless.

Then adrenaline blasted her system with burning resolve. *Improvise.* She head-butted her assailant.

He jerked back, swiping a palm over his bloody lip. *"Bliad!"*

The Greek gave a snide jab about how well Comrade handled the little girl.

The Russian swore. His huge hand circled her throat, cut off her air. His other hand shoved up her camisole. Bucking beneath his weight, she struggled to breathe as the Greek egged him on.

Dante, where are you?

Her vision grayed around the edges. A desperate burst of strength rammed her knee upward, but she merely grazed the target.

The Russian cursed again and flung out his arm to backhand her.

"Figlio di puttana!" Dante's enraged roar rang out. "Enough!" The Russian was torn off her and went flying across the sand.

She wriggled upright as Dante pivoted and landed a right cross on the Greek's jaw. Her satisfaction at his look of stunned panic amazed her. *Who's laughing now?*

The Russian tackled Dante from behind. Dante battled to his feet, cussing an Italian blue streak and swinging his powerful fists like battering rams.

Fear evaporated Ariana's satisfaction. Dante was beat up and weakened. No matter how determined, he couldn't defeat two thugs.

Exhausted, hurting, she wrestled to her feet and stumbled to the rocks. Feeling behind her, she found the sharp boulder Dante had used. Her stomach tightened. The rock was slick and still slightly warm with his blood.

As the men's combat ripped apart the night, Ariana scraped her ropes on the jagged edge. She didn't have Dante's strength, and her efforts were torturous. She forced herself to hurry, to ignore the sting of her wrists.

Finally, her ropes tore. She staggered to the shoreline where the battling men rolled in the surf. Dante fended off the Russian, sending him sprawling on the wet sand. But before Dante could regain his footing, the Greek pushed him underwater, held him down. A tidal wave of fear slammed into Ariana. He was drowning Dante!

Not while she had any say! She dragged an oar from the speedboat. Splashing into the shallows, she swung. The paddle hit the Greek and knocked him off Dante.

Dante surged out of the water and charged the Russian, who was heading for Ariana. *"Bastardo!"*

The men rolled underwater. Clutching the paddle, she circled the thrashing duo, seeking an opening.

Dante clambered upright, lifting the Russian by the collar, and then froze. He dropped the Russian and leaped at her. Wrapping his arms around her, he swept her beneath the waves.

She lost her hold on the oar. Saltwater flooded her nose and mouth, burned her eyes and stung her cuts. Panicked, she struggled. Why was Dante killing *her?* She was on his side.

As her head swam and her vision darkened, Dante scooped her up and tossed her behind him. "Stay back!"

Gagging, she wheezed in precious oxygen "Are. You. *Insane?"* She swiped her forearm across her eyes…and saw that the Greek had been sneaking up behind her, knife drawn. Her heart staggered. Dante had saved her life.

Moonlight glinted on razored metal as the Greek slashed at Dante, who jumped back. The hissing blade nearly sliced his abs.

"Nyet!" the Russian hollered. "No killing or we do not get our money!"

"I do not give a damn," the Greek snarled. "I will gut them both."

The furious man swiped with the knife, and Dante swayed in a lethal dance to stay between her and the blade. He scowled at the Greek. "She is under my protection. You don't want to do that to *l'amico degli amici*."

The innocuous phrase had a curious effect.

"Megaera said nothing…" The Greek froze and his bristly jaw went slack. "Ah. The explosion…I understand now."

The Russian choked out a dismayed phrase. He shoved Dante, who stumbled into her, submerging them both.

She swallowed another mouthful of brine before they gained their balance. Dante surged out of the water in a combat stance, water streaming off his hard muscles like Poseidon commanding the sea.

She pushed up beside him. The thugs were running toward the speedboat.

"Porca troia!" Dante raced down the sand.

Ariana slogged onto the beach. Thank heaven for such a dedicated protector. No matter what his motives were.

But hours of captivity and two beatings had cost him. The men had too much lead time. Before Dante got halfway there, the boat's motor rumbled to life.

The speedboat rocketed into the night. Dante skidded to a stop. He swung around and frowned, his countenance savage.

They were stranded.

AT SEA ABOARD her rented yacht, Anastasia Catomeris handed more euros to the Greek and Russian than they deserved and then instructed the captain to escort the churlish duo off the vessel. Recommended by a contact as local "professionals," they had reported for duty big on beef, short on brains.

The timely explosion of Dante and Ariana's yacht the night before—possibly mob related—had enabled the hired hands to capture her prey. Tasia's contacts had reported that Dante had been working at a mob dig site near Naples before he absconded with the girl. At first she'd suspected he might be working with the police—or one of her rivals. But her investigation had turned up no evidence of either involvement. He and Ariana must have thought they could escape the Camorra by sailing out of the area. It had taken Tasia time, effort and too much cash to locate the pair. She needed to use caution, because the Camorra would keep searching. The mob hadn't obtained their reputation by operating like a trade workers union. Dante couldn't just quit.

She switched on the gas fireplace in the stateroom and swept off her black veil. She was sick of lurking in the shadows. Always dark. Always hidden. Catching a glimpse of her face in the mirror, she proudly tilted her chin. Megaera, the goddess whose name she had borrowed, might have been hideous, but Tasia was still a stunner. She often passed for half her age—her only worthwhile inheritance from Greek peasants.

She sauntered to the bar and filled a crystal flute with champagne. Her hired oafs had returned from their assignment to deposit her captives on the island bloody, bruised and shaken. They had sullenly admitted to an altercation, but assured her Dante and Ariana were unharmed. The fools had better not be lying, because she needed the hostages alive.

For now.

She had planned and plotted and waited for exactly the right moment. Finally, everything was in place to teach the man who had abandoned her and his infant son the ultimate lesson. She had set Elias Stamos, the owner of Liberty Line, on a collision course with ruin. And what better vehicle for Elias to ride to public humiliation than the ship named after his revered late wife, *Alexandra's Dream*.

Mike O'Connor and Giorgio Tzekas thought they were being paid, and handsomely, to smuggle artifacts to sell in America. The wily O'Connor acquired the pieces, and the not-so-bright but malleable Tzekas used his position as first officer to help get them aboard *Alexandra's Dream* and hide them. However, Tasia had no intention of ferrying the antiquities that far. Once the ship docked in Athens she would plant the final piece with false invoices and then alert the authorities. Elias would be arrested. His sterling reputation as a patron of the Greek arts would crumble, and his patrons would flee. He would deplete his fortune defending himself in court.

If O'Connor and Tzekas played it smart, they'd walk away much richer. If not... She smirked. They couldn't identify her.

Revenge, as rich and satisfying as caviar. Tasia bit into a cracker heaped with the best Beluga. *Mmm.* She could hardly wait to revel in the heady taste of vengeance.

Her "job" as a collection consultant for an Athens museum was the perfect cover. She'd been careful with her spending and had Swiss banked a tidy sum from a long, successful career of smuggling artifacts. But it still wasn't quite enough. After Elias went down, she had one more cache to fence, huge enough to fund the rest of her luxurious life, and then she was done. She would buy her own yacht and sail to the south of France. She would bask in the sun and live in the style for which she had worked her derriere off. And which she deserved after a lifetime of scrimping.

Perhaps she'd even hunt up a new lover. Though her track record was abysmal. Sipping chilled bubbly, Tasia strolled to the chaise beside the crackling fire. What was the saying? Lucky at gambling, unlucky in love.

Wealth never lost its value. Never let her down. Living well was the answer to every problem. The luxury to do whatever you wanted whenever you chose was ultimate power. She didn't need men...except for the obvious. She'd clawed her way up the slippery slope of success without help from *any* man.

Sighing, she settled into the cushions. Elias had been the only man she'd never been able to control. Until Dante. The enigmatic man had refused a bribe and stoically taken a beating without a betraying word. Too bad, because the savage Napoletano could be a very worthwhile...investment. *That* man would never cower at her feet. And she enjoyed an edge of danger, in and out of the bedroom.

Tasia licked a salty morsel of caviar from her lower lip. She'd spared his life because she appreciated beautiful things— and didn't destroy them without good reason. And because her contact at Interpol couldn't confirm exactly whose side Dante was on. If she made him disappear, there would be consequences. She needed to know what she might lose before making a decision. Her contact was running a background check on him, and his fate would wait until Tasia received more information.

Ariana, on the other hand… She frowned. Seeing her had stirred softer feelings than Tasia had expected. She was her father's girl, smart and courageous. Ariana's intelligence, knowledge of antiques and bitterness toward the police could be useful. As could her mission to redeem Derek's reputation. Tasia drained her glass. Ariana's mother had joined *Alexandra's Dream* to search for her daughter, and Sadie and Elias had grown close. Ah, the gratification Tasia would gain from recruiting Ms. Bennett and hurting Elias even more. Double the revenge. He would learn the sting of betrayal, firsthand.

Would Ariana cooperate? Tasia abandoned the empty plate and flute on a table and draped a cashmere throw over her legs. As much as she would enjoy working with Derek's daughter, Tasia couldn't afford to let sentiment impede her goals. The girl's future also remained undecided.

For now, the pair would remain trapped on the island…until Tasia decided to fetch them.

She stared into the hungry red flames and her lips curled in a slow smile. Or *not*.

THIGH-DEEP in the cold surf, Dante flung a universal parting gesture at the fleeing speedboat. Muttering, he splashed back to the woman shivering on the beach. Like him, she was soaked to the skin, bruised and scraped. He'd failed her for the second time in twenty-four hours. Rage made him shake. "Are you all right, Ariana?"

"Yes." She unsteadily brushed aside a wet tendril of chestnut hair. "Heckle and Jeckle tore out of here like you'd sprouted horns. What's so scary about being 'a friend of the friends'?"

After almost six weeks, he had yet to discern if she was a bereaved daughter seeking the truth about her father, or a wily operator attempting to run her own game. In either scenario, if she knew who his friends *really* were, she would jeopardize his goals. Possibly his life. He scooped up his fallen coat.

"Ah. It's a 'don't mess with the mob' thing, right?"

He'd known from the moment she'd asked her first question at the dig site that she was not only beautiful, but extremely intelligent. Which made her extremely dangerous. *"Sì."*

She planted her hands on her hips. Her eyes—as blue and unpredictable as the Mediterranean Sea—sparked. "Well, why didn't you yell it *sooner?"*

He threw back his head and laughter rolled out of him. His studious librarian had far more *audacità* than he'd imagined. And the worse things got, the stronger she became. Forced into close proximity with her bright, alluring heat, his imagination had been working overtime.

Her full lips pursed, and his body tightened. Amusement fled. Allowing her to divert him could get them both killed. He still hadn't decided if Signorina Bennett was hiding something far more hazardous than a fiery spirit. "A man does not throw the phrase around lightly—and not unless he can back it up."

"But you can." As mutual mistrust engulfed their newfound camaraderie, unease chased away her smile. A chilly gust plastered her sodden clothing to her body, and she trembled violently.

His adrenaline rush ebbed and ice crept into his bloodstream. Where were his brains? Mentally castigating himself, Dante caught her by the hand. He knew where. And if he wanted to keep Ariana and himself alive, he'd damn well better retrieve them.

Towing Ariana up the strand, he pulled her into the semicircle of boulders forming a windbreak. He tossed down his coat.

Then he turned her to face him, grabbed her sodden shirt by the plackets and stripped it off her.

When he tugged up the hem of her camisole, she shrieked and her knee slammed into his groin. Searing nausea twisted his guts, sent him reeling.

"What the *hell?*"

"I think that's *my* line." She stumbled backward. "Just because we're lost on an island in the middle of nowhere doesn't mean we're going to go native."

Dante groaned and eased upright. He didn't retch, so he straightened and stared at the enraged woman. Had stress unhinged her? *"Non capisco."*

"I flirted with those goons because it was a life-or-death emergency." She inhaled shakily. "I am *not* a party favor."

His jaw dropped. "San Gennaro, *mio bello!* We've been together nearly six weeks. You should know better." Dante resisted the urge to inventory vital, perhaps irreparably damaged, anatomy. He'd rather take a fist in the face any day. "You are not a woman who engages in casual relationships."

She rubbed her hands along her arms. "And you know that, *how?*"

"Just as you have been safe with me, I have been safe with you." At least partially. While his attraction had been instantaneous, it was bearable. Resistible. Despite her vibrant coloring and the glint of impertinence in her gaze, she had shielded herself inside a bunker of aloof poise. She seemed coolly unaware of her latent passion…while his senses spun every time he got near her. If her guilelessness was an act designed to intrigue him, it had worked.

He'd never seen her come fully alive. Until fate had forced them into life-or-death peril. And the new determination in her sparkling eyes, the newly resolved set to her full lips intrigued him more than ever. He shrugged. "You have not attempted to use your sensuality to manipulate me."

"My…" She opened her mouth, then closed it and shook her head. "Then what was with the fast track to seduction?"

"I was trying to save you from hypothermia. Believe me, *cara,* if I seduced you, you would know it." He dropped his voice to a husky purr. "And it would not be forced. Or fast."

Her eyes widened. "Uh…you suddenly started ripping off my clothes—" she cleared her throat "—so I'll be *warmer?*"

"Wet fabric loses all ability to insulate. The wind makes it worse, like being inside a refrigerator." He gestured impatiently. While they debated, her lips had paled and her graceful limbs shook uncontrollably. "You are shivering because your body is working too hard to get warm. Exhaustion will soon set in, and combined with hypothermia, will kill you."

"You're shivering, too."

He peeled off his wet T-shirt and draped it over a boulder. "I am also removing my clothing."

Bemused, he watched her astonished glance slide over him, then skitter everywhere but his bare chest. Sudden warmth infused his chilled skin.

"But if we're…naked—" she swallowed audibly "—we'll still freeze to death."

"My coat is dry. We'll share it…and our body heat." He tugged off his boots. "Be sensible, *bella.* Every moment you delay, you grow colder."

When she hesitated, he scowled. "I don't want to have to take your clothes from you. But I will."

Her wary gaze assessed him far too long. He moved toward her. "Do not force me to choose."

She flung up a trembling hand. "You win." She bit her lip. "But I don't care if I turn into a human snow cone…I am *not* taking off my underwear."

Dante chuckled. "I doubt a few scraps of damp silk will cause you harm."

She wrinkled her nose. "There's a highly effective technique called communication. Next time, before you grab…ask."

"A lesson I'm not inclined to forget." And if he was, the ache in his groin would remind him.

"Sorry. I was a bit on edge after…" She shivered again, and her eyes darkened.

Dante battled the desire to enfold her in his arms. He had to remain detached…for safety *and* sanity. "I understand." He'd committed a multitude of sins in the line of duty, but sending Ariana into harm's way ranked at the top. He'd burned with helpless rage while the bastards had mauled her. Desperately struggled to break free and prayed he would reach her in time. "*Perdonami.* It killed me to put you through that."

"I knew what I was risking. I don't outsource responsibility for my decisions." She circled her finger. "Turn around so I can undress."

He half turned to offer her the illusion of privacy. Being naked was as natural as breathing to him, but since she was self-conscious, he left his briefs on after removing his pants.

Their clothes should be dry by morning, draped in the wind outside the rocky semicircle. He donned his leather trench coat before sitting in the sand.

Propped against a boulder, he looked up at Ariana. Heated desire steamrollered over him. *San Gennaro!* A few scraps of damp silk may not cause her harm, but they might be his undoing.

Adorned in a strapless apricot satin bra and matching panties, she stole his breath. He'd kidnapped her wearing only the clothes on her back and he had bought her new ones. He'd chosen the lingerie, tormented by the knowledge of how lovingly it would cup her generous curves.

The moonlight burnished copper highlights in her hair and bathed her creamy skin in luminescence. Still and perfect, she stood before him a glowing alabaster sculpture—Venus rising from the sea.

When it came to the intriguing Ariana Bennett, his body by-passed his brain. It made him crazy in more ways than one, but there wasn't a damn thing he could do about it. His arms opened for her. "Come here, Ariana."

"I suppose it's better than hypothermia," she muttered.

Put firmly in his place, he laughed. "The sentiment every man awaits from a woman's lips."

"You weren't supposed to hear that." Stiff and reluctant, she lowered herself to his lap.

He tucked her against his chest and wrapped his coat around her. She not only looked like a marble statue, she felt as cold and unyielding. He rubbed his hands over her back to generate heat. "Think warm thoughts."

Her slender limbs trembled and her teeth chattered. "This takes the prize for the most…friendly first date I've ever had."

"It's survival," he reminded himself as much as her. "It's nothing personal."

Her breathing rapid, she was trembling too hard, betraying her unease with their intimacy. "From where I'm sitting, it feels… ah…enormously personal."

Their mutual misgivings didn't quench the simmering attraction. He swore softly. The troops had bounced back from medical furlough to active duty. "I *am* a man." With a gorgeous, nearly naked woman cuddled in his arms.

"As if your manliness was ever in doubt."

"Relax, Ariana. I would never take advantage of a woman in distress."

"What are we going to do, Dante? We could die."

She was striving to be brave, and the quiver of fear in her voice tore at his heart. "I am not so easy to kill. And I won't let you die, *mia cara.*" He knew some of her stiffness was due to the fact that she was hurting, but to her credit, she didn't complain. He had no weapons, no food, no water. The only thing he could do was keep her warm and prevent her from going into shock.

He sought a diversion. For her *and* himself. "Tell me a story."

She started. *"What?"*

"You have an affinity for stories, yes? I have never had time for such things. It will take our minds off our discomfort, pass the hours until morning."

"Hmm…okay. I'll tell you one of my favorites." She inhaled.

"Once upon a time, on a Greek island far, far away, a mortal princess named Psyche—which means soul—grew famous for her beauty. Have you heard this one?"

"No."

"All right. Well, Psyche was kind and generous, and everyone adored her and claimed she was more exquisite than Aphrodite, the goddess of love. Even on her best day, Aphrodite was temperamental, and she grew enraged. She ordered her son Eros, the god of love, to shoot Psyche with a magical arrow and make her fall in love with a revolting monster. But Eros tumbled headlong in love with the princess and couldn't force himself to carry out his duty."

She finally relaxed in his embrace, and Dante smiled. "I am all ears."

Ariana chuckled. "While it's not nice to fool Mother Nature, it's deadly to mess with Aphrodite. She cursed Psyche with a spell so no man would find her appealing. Psyche's worried parents trekked to the Oracle at Delphi, who proclaimed that the princess was destined to belong to an entity who flew through the night like a huge winged serpent. A being so powerful that even Zeus, the king of the gods, could not withstand him.

"Psyche was smart enough to understand she'd annoyed the goddess and courageous enough to protect her family. She accepted the future the Fates had decreed. Her grieving family accompanied her to the top of the mountain where the beast would find her. Psyche couldn't stop her tears as she hugged her parents and sisters goodbye.

"Alone, she braced herself to die, but instead, a gentle wind lifted her up and rocked her to sleep. She awoke inside a palace. A kind male voice proclaimed her mistress of the mansion. After she'd bathed, gowns and jewels appeared, along with a sumptuous banquet."

"*Va bene*. I am beginning to see why you like this story."

She returned his smile and his pulse skipped a beat. "That night, when darkness enveloped the castle, the man spoke again, and said he was her new husband. Psyche couldn't picture the compelling voice belonging to a hideous beast. His words were loving and sweet, and he treated her tenderly.

"Unbeknownst to Psyche, Eros had secretly taken her for his bride. Because he feared Aphrodite's wrath on his beloved, he couldn't reveal his identity.

"Psyche grew to deeply love her undercover husband. He promised her everything she wanted, except seeing his face. He warned her if that happened, he would be forced to leave. She assured him his appearance didn't matter, she loved his heart. She pleaded for him to come to her in the daylight, but he sadly refused. He said the day she saw his true form, their happiness would die."

Dante shifted, and his abused muscles protested. Suddenly, he wasn't liking this story so much. When Ariana hesitated, he rubbed her back. "Go on."

"One night, Psyche reminisced about her family. Because Eros was a god, he knew a visit would rain down doom, but surrendered to the aching loneliness in his bride's voice.

"When Psyche's sisters arrived and saw the spoils, they jealously taunted her with the rumor that gullible Psyche was married to a dragon who planned to devour her. They urged her to peek at him while he slept. Psyche resisted, but finally curiosity prevailed, pushed by peer pressure. Was her husband her true love…or an evil monster? After he fell asleep beside her, Psyche lit a lamp. Instead of a deformed beast she saw the glorious beauty of the god of love…and realized he'd been protecting her from the mother-in-law from Hades.

"Overcome by shame, contrition seared her heart. In her shock, her hands trembled and she spilled hot oil onto her lover's shoulder. Eros startled awake and realized what she had done. He cried out in sorrow, *'Where there is no trust, there can be no love.'* He fled, and the palace crumbled into dust, leaving Psyche alone and miserable."

Ariana's voice softened, and she curled into him. "When Aphrodite learned her son had disobeyed her, she imprisoned him in a high tower. But Psyche refused to give up her one true love. Aphrodite wanted Psyche to suffer. She gave Psyche two impossible tasks with lethal consequences. Psyche was aided in the first by a colony of ants and in the second by the river naiads. What neither Psyche nor Aphrodite realized was that Eros was watching over Psyche from his prison and sending her help.

"When Psyche succeeded, Aphrodite decided to send her son's bride to hell…literally. Aphrodite commanded her to go to the Queen of the Underworld and capture her beauty in a box. She was warned not to open it.

"A forlorn Psyche thought Eros had abandoned her, and resigned herself to the fact that no human could find their way back from the dark Underworld. But as she descended into Hades, a voice whispered the escape route in her ear. It was Eros, disguising his identity on the secret telepathic channel."

Dante's lips quirked as he enjoyed Ariana's original narration, and he was relieved that she seemed warmer than before.

"Once Psyche returned to the sunlight, she vowed to resume her fight. But time in hell had made her a disheveled mess. If she wanted her man back, she had to look gorgeous. Psyche opened the box to borrow a smidgen of the Underworld Queen's beauty. But the spells of gods are too powerful for mortals and knocked her out.

"Lucky for her, Eros escaped. He found his wife unconscious in the forest and woke her with a forgiving kiss. He went over Aphrodite's head to the gods on Mount Olympus. The star-crossed lovers' devotion touched them, and Zeus summoned Aphrodite and put his foot down. Eros had proved his love for Psyche, and Psyche had proved her dedication, patience and obedience.

"There was only one solution. Psyche was brought to Olympus and Zeus offered her the cup of immortality. She drank the ambrosial nectar and was transformed into the goddess of fidelity. Eros swept Psyche into his arms, and the lovers were united, heart and soul, for all eternity."

Ariana finished her tale and went silent. After a few moments, her soft, warm cheek rested on Dante's chest.

He listened as her breathing grew deep and even. The night closed around him, and the tenderness tugging at his heart turned to sharp claws of terror.

Like Eros, he'd been sent on a covert mission to bring down a woman…and found himself confronted by a dilemma he'd never expected. Assaulted by feelings he didn't dare investigate.

During Ariana's captivity, her lovely face had creased with concentration as she had listened to her iPod and scribbled in her notebook. She wasn't merely writing stories. He'd tried to confiscate both items, but she'd thwarted him.

He frowned. Did she still have them, or had they been lost during the explosion? Ariana murmured and snuggled closer. The fact that she'd lowered her shields and fallen asleep in his lap did something strange to his insides.

Where there is no trust, there can be no love.

The cold, hard truth. His stomach knotted. Deception was his job. He lied and stole and strove to earn people's trust…so he could betray them. He was damn good at it.

One way or another, he would obtain the information he needed. He glanced down at Ariana and his throat constricted.

How much of his soul would it cost him to use that information against the woman sleeping trustfully in his arms?

CHAPTER FOUR

DANTE ENDURED THE NIGHT in a restless vigil that enabled him to leap to awareness. His eyelids slitted open as an anemic sunrise crawled above the horizon.

Gunmetal clouds glowered overhead. Wind-lashed waves reflected a leaden sky. A vile mood gnawed at his temper, and his body ached with pain...and arousal.

In contrast to the foul elements, the sweet morsel sleeping in his lap was warm and soft and tantalizing. And off-limits.

He scowled. It was going to be a terrific day.

He'd been livid when Ariana's meddling at the dig site had caused his boss to yank him out of the smuggling ring to protect her. He'd lost eighteen months of planning and groundwork. Lost his position inside the Camorra.

Dante clenched his jaw. He'd used the resentment to sustain distance between them. But after six weeks babysitting Ariana, he'd lost his perspective. Last night when she was vulnerable, he should have targeted the opportunity to interrogate her again. Instead, he'd encouraged her to indulge in fairy tales.

He'd lost his damn mind.

He shifted away from the boulder digging into his spine, and Ariana stirred. Her long lashes fluttered up, and he fell into her deep, blue gaze. He hadn't been afraid when the Greek was holding him underwater, but now fear uncoiled inside him.

He was in over his head.

Drowning.

Ariana's wary glance assessed him. She'd have to be oblivious not to notice his reaction. Signorina Bennett had plenty of smarts.

"Hi." Her husky contralto sounded sleepy. "I don't think this is exactly what the cruise line intended when they offered me a job with travel and excitement."

He surfaced, clinging to a life preserver of irritation. Liking her would only make double-crossing her more painful. He fought the urge to smile, managed a frown. "If we're going to survive, we cannot loll around all day."

"Drat, there goes my plan to stake out a beach blanket and sip lemonade." She wrinkled her nose. "Are you always Prince Charming in the mornings?"

"There's a reason the story you related last night is called a myth. Devoted princes, love eternal and happily ever after don't exist."

"But every woman pines for a high-maintenance guy who demands she sacrifice herself." Ariana snorted. "I don't know why Psyche thought a man was worth that much trouble, *or* pain."

He narrowed his eyes. "And Eros was foolish to sacrifice his duty and honor."

"Well, now that we've solved the imaginary problems of mythical beings, we can concentrate on escape." She sat up, and he didn't miss her wince of pain. "Priority one—where's the ladies' room?"

Like him, she was cut and bruised and must be hungry, thirsty and sore. Some women would complain, or cry. He couldn't help but admire her fortitude and determination. "Twelve meters down, second boulder on the left."

"See?" The sensual brush of her silky limbs ignited a fire in his belly. "You *can* smile without cracking your face. That wasn't so hard, was it?"

Obviously, Ariana had chosen to ignore his blatant arousal. *Hard* didn't begin to cover it.

"Dante, would you mind indulging me again?"

His pulse leaped, and his intent gaze held hers captive. Mia

cara, *I would indulge you as many times as you could handle…
and more.*

Her pupils dilated and her breath hitched in a small sound
that made his heart stumble. "Um…please close your eyes so I
can dress?"

Dante ground his back teeth in frustration. "Believe me, *bella,*
you do not possess anything I have not seen before."

"No doubt, but I'm not in the habit of providing a free peep
show. And there aren't enough euros in the western hemisphere."
She waved. "Now close those big brown eyes."

Cold reality chilled his ardor. She was right.

Involvement with her could cost him *everything.*

He had a job to do. He couldn't afford to pay her price. Both
of them would pay dearly—with their lives—if he botched it.

He hadn't survived years in a cutthroat occupation by being
gullible enough to shut his eyes or turn his back on anyone. But
he ducked his head when she slid off his lap—as much for himself as for her.

He finished dressing first and shot a glance sideways. Though
she blocked the furtive movements, he watched her unearth a
plastic-wrapped parcel from beneath a rock and cram it in her
hip pocket. She still had her secrets.

And so did he.

Dante averted his gaze as she rose and stepped toward him.
"I'm ready." He pivoted, and she gingerly rubbed her back.
"Camping on the beach sounds so romantic in stories. I don't
know about you, but sleeping on sand redefines *abrasion.* When
I get back, we can explore."

As he watched her slowly meander down the beach, a lightning bolt of desire seared him and he swore. Ariana was either
remarkably naive, or the most cunning opponent he'd ever
crossed blades with. And he'd parried with plenty of players.

Either way, he was in trouble.

He had to stay alert. Censor every word and action, so he
didn't end up speared on his own rapier.

Then again, perhaps that was his destiny.

But he'd prefer not to die today. Dante stalked in the opposite direction to complete morning necessities, and then strode to the foamy surf. He stepped over the abandoned oar and crouched to wash his hands. Hoping to invigorate his brain, he splashed his face with cold seawater.

"Dante!" Ariana yelled.

Adrenaline rocketed through his system. He snatched the oar and surged to his feet. Heart pounding, he spun, ready for battle.

Stumbling toward him, she pointed at the bluff. "Look!"

Dante tilted his head. At the top of the mountain, weak sunlight flickered on glass. The energy pumping through him ratcheted up a notch. "There appears to be a house at the crest of the bluff." Set back from the hillside, the cottage was a speck in the craggy landscape.

She grabbed his hand. "Let's go!"

"Un momento." Dante shocked Ariana by towing her up the rocky shoals and into the lee of the cliff.

Her temper ignited and she rounded on him. "What is your problem?"

"You are my problem." Dante glowered at her. "Like it or not, you are mine to protect. And I will do what I must to keep you alive."

Ariana inhaled a slow breath. He meant well. Dante *had* saved her life…several times. And taken several beatings. "I appreciate that. But I asked you to stop yanking me around like a sock puppet."

"I am not accustomed to decision by committee. In my world, hesitation is lethal." Dante scrubbed a hand over his beard. "We were not left here at random. We don't know who resides in that house. Who is watching us. Whether they will help us or try to kill us."

Her hopes plummeted. Absolutely right. She was in his territory, and he held the key to survival. "Valid point." If Dante thought he felt odd making decisions by committee, he had no idea how off balance she felt at reacting with her emotions.

The life-or-death events she'd faced the past few weeks, and especially the past few days, had outed a primitive facet of herself. A wildness that scared her, but once loosed wouldn't be caged. "Now what?"

Dante's biceps flexed as he raised his knee and snapped the bottom off the oar. His swift, graceful demonstration of masculine power left her gaping. No one of her acquaintance could do anything as impressive.

Dante handed her the staff and inclined his head at the twisted, vertical path scored into the bluff. "Now we climb."

The rugged goat track was barely wide enough for them to trudge side by side. Steely clouds crowded the sky, and as they left the beach, wind gusts buffeted them. He insisted she wear his coat, though two of her could fit inside. It smelled deliciously of supple leather…and Dante.

She struggled to keep up his challenging pace. Dried scrub and rocks jutted from the terrain and gnarled cypress trees clung to the hillside. Her sore muscles protested every step, and the walking stick helped. During her years of asthma attacks, she had endured not feeling well, but even then, whining wasn't in her nature. Dante had said she was his problem, and her pride refused to give him more reasons to resent her. She would *not* be a burden. She raised her chin and soldiered on.

Talking would have deflected her misery as they toiled up the rocky incline, but Dante's monosyllabic replies discouraged her numerous attempts at conversation. The only sounds were the surf's rhythmic crash from below and squawking seagulls.

A rabbit darted from the undergrowth. Ariana jumped and barely dodged a plant bristling with barbed spikes. Like the man beside her, the landscape was wild and dangerous—and if you didn't understand how to navigate it—lethal.

Ariana frowned. "It's your fault that I'm your problem. I didn't ask you to kidnap me." Dante arched a silent brow, and her mind circled in the same frustrating pattern since she'd awoken in a strange house alone with him. Who was the cryptic

Napoletano, and what did he want? He couldn't be a cop. She'd witnessed the FBI's ruthless tactics to solve a case, but law enforcement had no more interest in her. The police wouldn't hold her hostage for weeks. And they would have sent backup after the yacht explosion.

Was he a mobster? Maybe. If Dante *had* worked for the Camorra, they'd revoked his membership; the Greek had attributed the bomb that had nearly killed them to the mob.

As they climbed higher, the briny smell of the sea blended with the pungent tang of evergreens. The theory that Dante had kidnapped her fit best, although he'd given no indication of a response to a ransom demand. Still, his overprotective streak could be motivated by reluctance to face murder charges should anything happen to her.

But spending the night held on his lap had altered her outlook. If she was merchandise, why did he treat her so tenderly? Whenever she'd been afraid, he'd comforted her. He'd repeatedly put his body between her and harm.

"Ransom isn't forthcoming, I've made that clear. Wouldn't it be easier *and* safer for you to return me?"

He scowled.

The grade steepened, and her breath sawed in her throat. To her left, the bluff dropped in a sharp precipice. In spite of her resolve, she began to lag. Each time she stumbled, he caught her. Every time she slipped, his palm settled on her back for support. But he continued to rebuff conversational overtures.

A huge bird of prey startled from a treetop and soared over the Mediterranean. "Was that an eagle or a vulture?" He grunted. Whatever, it was still a big, scary hunter.

"Who do you think is waiting for us at the summit?"

He shrugged, and she sighed. She was chilled, exhausted and sore. Her body thrummed with pain. Even her hair follicles hurt. Sticky and grimy, she was forty-eight hours overdue for a shower, and she would wrestle a mountain lion bare-handed for a coffee and a Milky Way Midnight.

An unpleasant thought struck her. "Dante? I remember reading that mountain lions are indigenous to parts of Greece."

"*Sì*. As are wolves, bears and wild boar."

She gulped. "*Now* you get chatty."

He slanted her an enigmatic look. "I don't recall you being this relentlessly talkative in the mornings."

"I'm only doing it to torture you." They'd spent over a month of mornings together. But he'd revealed more of himself during the past forty-eight hours than the previous forty days. His solicitousness didn't match his gruff demeanor, and the dichotomy intrigued her. She pondered the puzzle as she forced one foot in front of the other. "Besides, the last several days have taught me a few things. I'm happy to be alive and ambulatory."

Perhaps their near brush with death had forced out attributes he normally concealed, as well.

Sudden insight staggered Ariana, and Dante's sure hand shot out to steady her. They had more in common than she'd dreamed possible. She wasn't the only one who substituted anger for unsettling emotions. He also disguised his vulnerable, softer feelings, as she had done since her father died. And Dante spoke abruptly, but treated her in a solicitous way.

Actions did not lie.

Hurt over her father's needless death had provoked anger in her. And the events of the past six weeks would have crushed a lesser woman. She'd had no one to depend on but herself, and had grown strong with the will to survive at all costs. Facing a string of life-threatening, frightening situations had infused her with resolve and courage she didn't know she possessed. What was Dante's reason for erecting a defensive wall?

She normally avoided the strong, silent type. Way too conflicted. Then again, her relationship with Geoff had been open and easy. She'd thought it a positive sign that they'd never quarreled. The breeze snagged her hair and stirred up dust devils on the path. Chilled, she moved closer to Dante's heat. Maybe the awareness that sparked between them wasn't merely biology.

Was it possible Dante was specifically attracted to *her*…and that upset him? She surreptitiously studied his imposing profile.

What else was he masking beneath his impassive facade?

She'd always been afraid of deep water, but now she longed to dive in. She yearned to know what made Dante tick on a primitive level she didn't have the nerve to question. Or the strength to deny.

Besides, she had nothing else to occupy her thoughts. Since the only thing that had drawn Dante out so far was humor, she tried a teasing tack. "So…Signor Testosterone, you're obviously in tip-top shape. What do you do for exercise other than boss me around, catch bullets between your teeth and leap to conclusions?"

His lips twitched, and then a reluctant grin curved his sensual mouth. "You are not about to give up, are you?" His smile changed his face. In a blink, he transformed from forbiddingly handsome to Roman sex god. Her pulse fluttered. A victorious thrill twined around her heart whenever she succeeded in coaxing Dante's incredible smile. "I like all types of physical activity." His smooth, deep voice was unaffected by exertion. "I enjoy challenging myself to peak performance."

I'll bet. Her heartbeat sped from a jog to a gallop. "Um… anything special?"

"Boxing, archery and football."

His big body rippled with muscles, his lightning reflexes possessed the grace of a predator. Boxing and archery explained his power and coordination. And if he played brutally competitive, grueling European soccer, no wonder he had stamina.

She squelched wayward speculation about Dante's stamina. Who did he compete with? "You must have been in heaven when Italy won the World Cup again. It's at least the fourth time in a row, right?"

"Sì," he replied with a proud grin.

"I do some bicycling."

"I have noticed you are…fit." Dante arched a dark, glossy

brow, and her stomach flipped. He surprised her by asking, "On or off-road?"

"On. But I like touring and racing."

"Anch'io."

"Really?" His admission astonished her. He was hardly a typical cyclist. "What type of bike do you have?"

His answer launched them into a discussion of brand names and pedal cycle configurations.

Almost to the top, they trudged around a hairpin corner. Several trees stood sentinel over a clump of rocks surrounded by scraggly bushes. More fatigued with each upward step, she tossed her pride. She would crumple if she didn't get a breather. "I'm exhausted. I could use a break."

"We're nearly to the house."

"You might have the fortitude of a bull, but cut me some slack. This isn't the Bataan Death March."

"It is a bad place for an ambush." He glanced at her face, then warily around the small clearing. *"Va bene.* Five minutes."

She dropped next to a boulder. Dante sat opposite her, where he observed the track from both directions. Realization hit. His prolonged silences and seeming lack of attention during their uphill slog were because he was in guard-dog mode, watching and listening for danger.

She set down the staff and stretched to relieve her stiffness. "These branches have ripe olives hanging on them!"

"Probably why they are called olive trees," he said wryly.

"Smart aleck." She reached to pluck the purplish black globes. "Did you know Greek mythology claims that Athena, goddess of wisdom and peace, struck her magic spear into the Earth, and it turned into an olive tree? The spot was then named Athens, in honor of her. Ancient Greek courts sentenced people to death if they destroyed an olive tree." Her stomach grumbled. "I'm *starving.*"

A smile tugged at Dante's lips. "You're a veritable font of information."

Her mouth watered with anticipation as she bit into the first juicy olive. Bitterness stung her tongue and her eyes streamed. She turned away and spat out the hard, sour pulp. "That tastes disgusting!"

Dante's smile blossomed into an impish grin. "Did you know although olives ripen in mid-October, they must undergo a pickling process before they're palatable?"

She shuddered. "You might have mentioned that before I ate one."

"Sometimes, practical knowledge is more valuable than academic." Mischief danced in his warm caramel eyes. "I know how you despise taking orders."

She rapid-fired olive missiles at him, which he laughingly dodged. She shuddered again. "You're lucky the throat spasms didn't trigger an asthma attack."

His laughter died and his expression grew thunderous. "You should have told me you suffer from asthma!"

"Not for years. I was teasing you, sorry."

"How long since your last episode?"

"They tapered off as I grew up. It's why I had a sheltered childhood."

Compassion glinted in his gaze. "That must have been difficult. Is that why you never learned to swim?"

"I didn't do a lot of things. But Mom wore herself out to ensure I was comfortable. And Dad would come home after a long day at work and sit down on the floor and play board games with me. When I didn't feel well, he read me stories. On good days, he took me to the museum with him and let me examine antiquities while he related their history. That's how I became fascinated with ancient myths."

"He sounds like a good father."

"He *was!*" And she still missed him every day. "No matter what anybody thinks, he was a decent man." She dumped the remaining olives into the dirt. If she had to, she would spend the rest of her life proving it. "Dad was the one who taught me to ride a bike, when I was fifteen. I was humiliated by not being like other kids. He took me to the museum's parking lot after hours where nobody would see my bumbling. For hours, Dad ran behind my bike holding me up and encouraging me to keep trying."

"You loved him very much."

"And he loved me." Her chest tightened, and she cleared her throat. "What were your parents like?"

Pain flitted across his face. "I didn't have parents." His glance shifted, and he stood. "We need to go."

Ariana's muscles resisted as she clambered to her feet and reached for the staff. Her heart ached more than her body. Dante didn't have parents. Had no one ever loved him? Was that why he held himself sternly aloof?

"Ariana!" Dante's voice dropped. She picked up the stick, and he lunged, grabbing the front of her shirt. As he spun her around, he tripped over the staff. He shoved her away and sprawled at the base of the rock formation.

Sputtering, she sat up. "What—"

Propped on one elbow, he went as still as a graven image. "Do not move."

A chill crawled up her spine. "W-why?"

"Do *exactly* as I tell you, and you will be fine."

She darted a frantic glance around the clearing. "Is it a spider? A huge, hairy Greek spider?" A shiver rippled over her. The last time she'd spotted a spider in her apartment, she'd run outside until Geoff had gamely squashed it. "I've seen their webs in olive groves." Why hadn't she remembered *before* plopping her rump down under an olive tree? "Is it on me?"

"Nothing is on you. Hold still."

Panic raised her voice an octave. "Please tell me there's not a scorpion."

"No. Stay still."

Leaves rustled in the bushes beside Dante, and then parted in the wake of a thick triangular head, cold yellow eyes and brown and white scales. A scream swelled inside her, and she gulped it down. "Oh, my God," she whispered. "A snake!"

"It's fine," Dante murmured. His unwavering gaze caught hers. "Do not panic…and do not move."

Her stomach pitched. Triangular pitted head meant a viper. Poisonous. She'd read that pit vipers were attracted to body heat, and some species were very combative. Out here in the wilderness, a bite would kill Dante.

"Easy, Ariana," Dante coaxed, his tone soothing. "Look at me, not the snake." How could he be so calm? "Remain motionless and he'll leave."

The monster was nearly twice the circumference of her forearm and almost four feet long. Its forked tongue flicked, and the hair on the back of her neck prickled. "He's not leaving," she whispered. "He's crawling toward you!"

"No matter what happens, *do not move.*"

The hostile viper hissed, flashing curved fangs in warning. "You want me to sit and watch you get bitten?"

"*Sì.* Stay out of his way."

She battled the urge to scream and run away. Dante was helpless. There was no cavalry. *She* had to save him. Slowly, carefully, Ariana eased her arms from Dante's bulky coat, then slid the staff toward her.

Dante scowled. "What are you doing, *cara?*"

"Saving you."

"No!" he gritted. "Do not!"

She ignored him, ignored roiling terror and concentrated on the snake. Her hands were shaking, and she sucked in a breath. She only had one shot. She couldn't miss, or Dante would die. "He's slithering toward your right arm. On three, roll left."

Before he could protest, she counted. "One. Two. *Three.*"

Ariana thrust the staff beneath the viper's sinuous length at the same instant Dante rolled away swearing. She flipped the hissing reptile across the path.

It coiled and struck at her. She screamed and slammed it with the staff. Stunned, the snake hesitated before attacking again. She hit it once more, and then Dante was beside her. He shoved her aside and snatched the stick.

Ariana couldn't look away, couldn't stop screaming as he dispatched the reptile.

Dante knocked the gigantic, limp body over the side of the bluff, dropped the staff and then tugged her into his embrace. "Shh. Everything is all right."

Trembling uncontrollably, she choked back more screams. "Is it dead?"

He hugged her. "It is not prudent to leave a lethal predator alive to attack again."

"Excellent," she whispered. "Excuse me." Ice cold and dizzy, her vision graying at the edges, she tottered to the boulders. Her quivering legs gave out, and she dropped to the rocks and hung her head between her knees.

"Easy, *mia cara.* It's all over." Dante's warm, supple fingers kneaded her neck. "Take a breath."

She struggled to comply, to gain control. Air slowly inflated her tortured lungs, vanquished the dizziness.

"That's the way…breathe. Slow and easy." He eased her up and enfolded her in his arms.

Even with his support, she shook so hard, she could barely stand. "Was that monster an adder?"

"Adders are shy." He rubbed her back in slow circles. "It was a Levant viper. Extremely aggressive. And lethal."

Nausea churned in her stomach. "B-because I was weak, needed to rest, it almost k-killed y-you."

"No, *cara.* The snake would have attacked when we walked past, and we would have stood no chance." He stroked her hair. "You were very brave. You saved my life." His embrace tightened. "At great risk to your own."

Her fingers fisted in his shirt and she clung to him as despair assailed her. "I might have killed us both, anyway."

His wide palm cradled the back of her head. *"Non capisco."*

Ariana squeezed her eyelids closed. She would *not* cry and embarrass herself further. "After my bloodcurdling screams, whoever is waiting for us in that house knows without a doubt we've arrived."

CHAPTER FIVE

CAPTAIN NICK PAPPAS stood on the bridge of *Alexandra's Dream* and stared out at the glittering Mediterranean. He would never tire of the challenge of guiding the massive ship through unpredictable waters. The comfort and safety of over a thousand passengers and hundreds of employees was in his hands.

One particular employee's welfare nagged at him, as it had for the past five weeks. What had become of the intelligent, personable librarian?

Gideon Dayan, his lean, sandy-haired security officer arrived, and Nick listened to Gideon's daily report before asking, "Any word on Miss Bennett?"

"No. Her mother is worried sick, and rightly so. And the private investigator hired by Elias Stamos hasn't turned up any viable leads, except that she was last seen talking to an Italian worker on the dig site at Paestum." Gideon's brow furrowed. "Some of the local authorities have suggested she might have willingly run off with him."

Nick gave Dayan a sharp look. Nothing got past the former Mossad officer. "What's your opinion?"

"She seemed too levelheaded to ditch her job without notice and take off with a man she'd just met." Dayan shook his head. "I think the authorities can't find her, and are trying to cover their asses."

"That surprises you?" He hadn't thought Miss Bennett seemed like a woman who would indulge in a reckless relationship, either.

"Not one iota, sir."

"Although…sometimes a man and a woman ambushed by an undeniable attraction are capable of…impulsive actions." As Nick knew well from the reblossoming of his romance with Helena Stamos.

"I'm well aware of that, sir." Gideon's lips twitched as he fought a brief battle with a smile.

Nick flicked his glance to the horizon. The crew knew about Nick's new love, just as Nick knew that Gideon had recently taken personal risks when he fell in love with Meilin Wang, who was now living in Paris, and whom Gideon would join shortly.

He glanced back at his security officer. Not allowing yourself to love, even when there was risk, would mean dying a little more inside each day.

"With all due respect, sir—" Dayan hesitated "—I…wish there was more we could have done other than notifying the authorities and having Interpol put out a missing-person alert."

"We did all we could." Nick frowned. He didn't trust the various foreign police agencies to place the welfare of one "missing" American woman at high priority. And the FBI couldn't get involved until there was evidence of foul play. "We have a thousand other lives in our hands. Notify me immediately, night or day, should any information come through. Dismissed, Officer Dayan."

"Yes, sir."

Gideon departed, and Nick resumed staring at the water. He'd hated leaving Ariana. Each individual on his ship was *his* responsibility. Ariana Bennett was his responsibility.

He rubbed his temples with his fingertips. He couldn't shake the wrenching feeling he'd let her down. Where was she…and was she all right?

STANDING BY THE SIDE of the trail, Dante continued to rub Ariana's back with comforting strokes. "After that ruckus, whoever is in the house may believe we were attacked by roving wolves and are dead."

"I *hope* you're kidding." She slanted him a cautious glance. "I've seen enough Greek wildlife."

"Relax, Ariana. The only wolf in these woods is Italiano." His grin gave her knees a whole different reason to quiver.

She leaned against him, absorbed the steady thump of his heartbeat. Dante was big and strong and capable, and she didn't care who he was or what he did for a living. She did not want to let go of him. After confronting the reptile from hell, she deserved an indulgence. "I couldn't stop screaming."

"Women and snakes are mortal enemies from the beginning of time, yes?"

An unsteady smile sneaked out. "He was hunting *you*." Shuddering, she studied the clearing. Dante had maneuvered them behind the olive tree. She gazed uneasily at the leafy branches. "Do you suppose he had friends?"

"No. The species is hostile and aggressive. They're known to strike without provocation, and cannibalize one another."

"How could you remain immobile, waiting, knowing that *thing* was coming after you?" Dante had let the monster stalk him to protect her. And earned her gratitude and respect. His sacrifices on her behalf almost balanced the scales for kidnapping her. While his incentive might be in question, there was no doubt he'd served his penance.

Dante's broad shoulder lifted in a fatalistic shrug. "There are moments when one must commit wholly to a course of action. I have learned that sometimes, evasion may save your life, but damn your soul."

His declaration enveloped Ariana in tenderness. Though she suspected he was not only a kidnapper but also a thief, he possessed commendable dedication and chivalry. And he walked his talk...all the way. "That's a pretty gutsy philosophy."

"Perhaps." He brushed a lock of hair back from her temple. "But you understand. It is the same reason you risked your life to defend me."

Pulse pounding, she stared into his unwavering brown gaze.

She'd never known anyone like him. The mysterious man incited a tornado of contradictory feelings. Dante embodied all the male C-traits she abstained from: contrary, confusing and complicated. She inhaled another slow breath. "Sorry I blasted off like that. It was involuntary."

"Those who await us have already been alerted to our presence." His deep voice sounded unconcerned. "Perhaps not the exact timing, but they know we are here. Megaera is not a woman who acts without forethought."

"Yes, if someone wanted to ambush us, last night when we were exhausted would have been the time." Her fear had dissipated beneath Dante's soothing back rub. His rhythmic strokes down her spine loosened her muscles and flushed her skin with a languid glow. Soon she'd be nothing but a melted puddle at his feet. "Megaera was one of the Furies. I doubt it's the mystery woman's real name."

"No?" Dante's droll look of mock surprise coaxed a chuckle from her. "And here I believed it was because she was an unfortunate-looking *bambina*."

She smiled, enjoying their camaraderie. "Sorry. My brain stores trivia like squirrels hoard nuts, and it pops out at odd times."

"When Megaera questioned you on the boat, I am glad you were not hurt." His conversational tone didn't change, but cuddled against him, she couldn't miss his subtle tension. "What did she offer you, *cara?*"

Megaera's final words taunted her. *Hold fast to your secrets, Ms. Bennett. And you may be granted a chance to even the score for your father.* Had it been a veiled warning not to trust Dante? A threat?

Ariana bit her lip. Who did she trust least, Megaera or Dante?

Dante's tender touch and warm concern had lulled her into letting down her guard, feeling safe in his embrace. While his scowling intimidation had never compelled her to talk, his charm and humor arrowed past her defenses. She was liable to spill any information he wanted. She listened as Dante's heartbeat kicked up a notch. Maybe that's exactly what he was after. "Did she offer *you* something?"

An oh-so-brief hesitation. "Money. You?"

"She didn't offer me money." She gazed up at him. "Obviously, you didn't accept. Why?"

All traces of softness disappeared from his bearded face. "I prefer to work alone."

"You weren't picky about your coworkers at the dig site. And you were so desperate for money you kidnapped me. But you turned Megaera down?"

The significance of Megaera's warning hit home. Razor-sharp suspicion sliced her and she stiffened. *Was* money the reason Dante had kidnapped her? Or something else entirely? "Did you know my father? Does this have something to do with him?"

"I did not know your father."

Suddenly dizzy, she jerked away from him. "Tell me the truth!"

"Calm down, Ariana. I swear to you, I did not know Derek Bennett." Dante's sensual mouth firmed into a hard line. "Let's go. Every moment we delay gives the inhabitants of the house more time to prepare."

Ariana's gaze dropped to the dead brown grass. She had denied that Megaera had tried to bribe her with money, but not that the woman had made her an offer. Dante had denied knowing Derek Bennett, but not that his agenda excluded her father. They had both sidestepped the truth.

And both recognized the dual deception.

Was Dante a smuggler? That would explain his presence at the dig site. Had he kidnapped her because he believed she knew something that would bring him personal gain? Pain lanced her heart as icy uncertainty choked the fragile roots of their newborn intimacy.

Dante picked up his fallen coat and draped it around her. Cold and bereft and lonelier than she'd felt since her dad had died, Ariana blinked away tears and turned toward the path.

Neither spoke for the remainder of the short journey.

They trudged around an upward bend in the trail, and Dante

drew Ariana into a high stand of laurel bushes. "Stay here while I investigate."

"Wait!" She grabbed his forearm, warm steel beneath her fingertips. "Not an inspired idea." Misgivings and other, scarily softer feelings for him aside, Dante was all she had. "If anything happens to you, I'll never survive on my own."

His eyes narrowed. "I'll be back.'"

"While your self-assurance is inspiring, I want to go with you. We work well as a team, and an extra body can't hurt."

"A very enchanting body, indeed." He cupped her cheek, inciting a storm of turmoil inside her. "But I cannot be distracted by defending you, *mia cara.*"

She sighed. Arguing with Dante was as frustrating as boxing with a shadow. And as productive. "At least take the staff. It's better than barging in bare-handed."

"I have no intention of 'barging' anywhere. No one will see me unless I wish it." His dark, intense gaze holding hers captive, he leaned closer and feathered his thumb along her cheekbone. "And I will not leave you defenseless."

Her breathing sped up. Was he using seduction to befuddle her? He was willing to walk into a dicey situation unarmed, but in the battle between the sexes, he was loaded with lethal weaponry.

She thrust the staff at him. "You need this more. I'm hiding in the bushes. You're about to confront unknown people with unknown motives."

He shook his head. "I can handle myself."

"You testosterone jockeys are all alike." She barely resisted the urge to stamp her foot. "You think you're invincible."

A glossy brow arched again. "Better to live one day as a lion than a hundred as a sheep."

"Nobody thinks sheep's heads are trophies."

"I plan on keeping my head firmly attached." His amazing grin flashed. "Besides, I have incentive to return, yes?"

What did *that* mean?

Between that thought and the next, he slipped away. Ariana

peered through foliage, saw nothing. The big guy moved with the silent grace of smoke.

Her nerves jittered. Who would he face inside the house?

Though her limbs ached from abuse and exhaustion, she was too anxious to sit. Her ears strained for sounds of conflict, but only picked up the sea's distant rumble and the wind scratching at the bay leaves.

Ariana slid her chilled arms inside Dante's coat and hugged the leather garment around her. In ancient Greek, bay laurel was called *daphne,* after the nymph Daphne, whose mother turned her into a laurel bush to escape Apollo's brash advances. Apollo then developed the habit of wearing bay twigs in memory of his missing love.

For Ariana, the laurel's fresh, earthy scent was a poignant reminder of Dante. She'd never again smell it without thinking of him. She peeked out, searched for him. Saw only sullen gray clouds and wild, windswept landscape.

Alone in this primitive land, it was easy to believe ancient legends might have been true. That gods and goddesses had trod the craggy terrain, searching for truth, redemption and love—the same intangible treasure sought by centuries of mortals.

She took another nervous survey of the area, then fished her iPod from her pants pocket and checked the clock. The glowering sky made it seem much later than one in the afternoon. She would give Dante thirty more minutes.

Then the lamb was going in after the lion.

She fidgeted. What if Dante had walked into a trap? What if there had been a fight, and he'd lost? What if he were beaten, tied and helpless?

She swallowed panic. What if he were dead?

Ariana could not deny the fact that while she didn't fully trust him, or understand his motives, she cared about his welfare. A difficult dichotomy to reconcile. One that couldn't fit neatly into a database or be explained by any reference book. Her crazy, disparate feelings couldn't be alphabetized or cataloged. She was adrift, and floundering so far out of her comfort zone, she was in another universe.

How much time had crept past? As she reached for her pocket again, a large hand gripped the back of her neck. Yelping, she spun, swung the staff.

Dante caught it in midair. "*Attenti.* It's me."

She pressed her palm over her racing heart. "I hope you know CPR."

A slow smile curved his full lips. "I am proficient in mouth-to-mouth."

No doubt. Her worried gaze spun from his thick tousled hair to the toes of his large boots. He didn't appear to have additional injuries, and she whooshed out a breath. "Cute. Too bad innuendoes don't cure heart failure." She lowered the staff. "Don't keep me in suspense. What about the house?"

"I have, as you say, good news and bad news."

"Why am I not surprised? I could really use some good news about now."

"The house is unoccupied."

"Okay." She heaved a relieved sigh. "And the bad?"

"The island appears to be deserted."

She started. They'd been abandoned? Great, other than scaly or furry critters, they had no enemies to battle. And not-so-great. How would they survive? Who would rescue them? She gulped. And what was she going to do stranded alone on an island with Dante? "How can you tell?"

"The top of the bluff affords a panoramic view. I saw nothing but woods and sea." He bent to retrieve the ax he'd dropped to block her blow with the staff.

Uneasiness assailed her. Did he expect to run into trouble? "If there's nobody here, what's the ax for?"

He shrugged. "Insurance."

"At least we'll have shelter while we plan our next move."

"Even better, there is food." He offered her his hand along with a roguish wink. "I'm certain I spied a jar of olives in the pantry."

Ariana considered the enigmatic man for a span of heart-beats, then placed her hand in his. "I prefer them in martinis."

His huge hand enveloped her smaller one in strength and warmth while they walked up the trail. All right. She would give the charismatic Napoletano her hand, her cooperation, even an odd, bewildering friendship forged by extreme circumstances. But she would guard her secrets, protect her heart.

She would not allow him her trust.

With that issue settled, some of her tension drained, making her shoulders sag. Stress and exhaustion had taken a toll.

They trudged around the final bend. She was prepared for a haunted house, but instead saw a small stone cottage. The lone dwelling was adorned with sturdy wooden shutters and a front door painted the cerulean blue indigenous to Greece. Surrounded by cypress trees, native foliage and banks of scarlet and orange chrysanthemums, the house exuded an aura of rustic charm. She glanced at Dante. "Sure it's empty?"

"It appears to have been vacated for some time."

Grapevines entwined a wooden portico and spread an emerald canopy over the door. Fragrant burgundy grapes dangled from the branches. Her stomach growled at the fruity scent, and she twisted off a handful. She paused and smiled at Dante. "Know anything about the evils of wild grapes?"

He returned her smile as he rotated the iron knob and swung open the front door. "Unlike olives, the perils of grapes become apparent only *after* they are fermented."

Chuckling, she held them up. "Here. You have to be as starved as I am."

"I am used to doing without. I will eat after we are settled and safe."

She eyed his tall frame. He didn't look malnourished. Perhaps he meant in the past. The thought of him lacking food as a child weighed heavily as she stepped across the threshold and leaned the staff against the doorjamb.

Dante strode to a huge flagstone fireplace in the far wall and set down the ax. While he squatted to stack kindling and logs, she devoured grapes and glanced around.

The interior was cold and dim, with arched doorways, flagstone floors and rough-hewn ceiling beams. Dark wood trim contrasted rough, whitewashed plaster walls. The furniture was an eclectic mix of antiques, including an authentic gramophone. The rustic paintings and plastic-draped furniture cushions reflected a warm combination of dark blues, golds and reds. "Do you suppose this is a rural vacation cottage?"

"Perhaps."

"If we can't get off the island, maybe all we have to do is survive until the owner shows up."

"Vacation season is over. It could be next summer before anyone 'shows up.'" He frowned. "Megaera purposely stranded us here. Rescue is unlikely. We must find our own way off." He started to say more, but a log shifted and he turned back to the fireplace.

Her gaze traveled across the room. A rectangular table with four chairs separated the sitting area from a small kitchen. With a squeak of delight, Ariana rushed to the sink and pulled the handle. Crystal water gushed out of the faucet, and she thrust her hands beneath the chilly stream. "Indoor plumbing!"

"There is a well. You will be happy to hear that I also discovered a propane water tank, which I lit earlier. And the kitchen range operates on propane."

She rummaged in a cabinet for drinking glasses and rinsed two. She gulped two full glasses, then filled the other tumbler and carried it to Dante. "A hot bath? I've died and gone to heaven."

"*Grazie.*" He drained his glass and handed it to her.

"Do you want another?"

"Not at the moment."

She had to admire his self-discipline. She set the glasses on a table next to a walnut sofa bench. To the left of the fireplace, an open arched doorway revealed a bedroom. A second doorway was square with a closed door. "That's the bathroom?"

"*Sì*." He struck a match from the box on the hearth and held it beneath the kindling. A plume of smoke furled upward and yellow flames crackled.

She headed toward the door. "You checked it out?"

He nodded. "It is clear of inhabitants."

She lurched to a halt. "Would you please inspect it for spiders?"

Dante gave her a crooked grin as he rose. "My courageous *signorina* who took on two hired killers and a deadly Levant viper armed with only an oar is afraid of *bugs?*"

"Counting Heckle and Jeckle, I've tangled with my quota of hairy creeps this week."

"The war is far from over, *cara*." One corner of his mouth curved in a rueful smile. "And to my detriment, I would lay odds on your victory." Leaving her to ponder another obscure statement, he strode into the bathroom.

She frowned. He was the most puzzling, fascinating man.

Before long, he returned. "You may bathe without companions. Hairy or otherwise."

"Terrific. Did you happen to see any clothes around?"

"No, but I noticed towels in the washroom cupboard." He indicated an empty iron box on the hearth. "While you are bathing, I'll get more wood."

The bathroom sported the same rustic whitewash and dark wood, and patterned tiles in jeweled colors. She cranked open the faucets in the deep, claw-foot bathtub. Megaera didn't seem like the roughing-it type, and if she stayed at the cottage, she'd have basic supplies. While the tub filled, Ariana opened the cupboard beside the sink, happy to find bath towels and travel sizes of soap and shampoo.

She peeled away her sandy, salt-stiffened clothes and undergarments. No way was she putting the disgusting things back on until they were washed. A search of the single bedroom had turned up one set of sheets and two cotton blankets. Autumn nights were chilly, and she didn't want to drag around the only bed linens. Towels would have to do.

Rhythmic thumps from outside made her stand on tiptoe to peek out the high window. Dante was in the courtyard behind the cottage. Stripped to the waist, he was chopping wood. He turned to select a log from the pile, and bronzed muscles rippled in his back. He swiveled forward and positioned the log on a chopping block. Long legs spread wide, he raised the ax with corded arms. His biceps flexed, then he swung the blade and sliced the log in half with one powerful blow.

Perspiration glistened on his sculpted torso, and a droplet of sweat meandered through the dark hair on his wide chest. It trickled over his hard abs and shimmered down the fine trail of hair that delineated his flat stomach before disappearing into the waistband of his jeans.

He selected another log, and every cell in her body ignited as he repeated the primal male dance. Her belly tightened and she clutched her towel. How could she possibly be attracted to such a dangerous man?

Dante leaned his ax against the block and picked up a glass of water. Tipping back his head, he gulped. Liquid spilled down the strong column of his throat, and he rubbed it into his tawny skin.

Ariana moaned. How could she *not?*

Behind her, bathwater cascaded over the tub and splashed onto the floor. She dropped the towel and sprinted to shut off the faucet and pull the plug to drain the overflow.

Tingling everywhere as though Dante had touched her, she stepped into the steamy pool and leaned back, immersing herself to the neck in languorous heat. She sighed with longing and closed her eyes. Rhythmic thuds from outside inspired sensual visions of shirtless Dante, hard and hot and handsome. He would need the tub next.

And she would love to join him.

DANTE PICKED UP THE AX and then glanced at the cottage. Ariana was inside, bathing. Naked. Warm. Wet. Her feminine curves creamy with fragrant lather. He pictured himself stepping into the tub with her and pulling her into his lap. Running his hands over her soap-slicked skin, cupping her full breasts in his palms.

His body hardened. Swearing, he viciously halved a log. That runaway train was on a crash course to damnation and ruin.

He'd let greed swallow his honor once…and ended up in jail. Where he'd discovered what was truly important. Integrity. Dedication. Freedom—physical *and* emotional. Over the years, he'd learned to make do, go without.

To live with all kinds of hunger.

He cleaved another log. He'd seen what had happened to his cohorts who surrendered to the glittering lure of temptation. Some were in prison. Many were dead.

He refused to cross that line.

Dante shut down his feelings, channeled energy into chopping. He stopped only when his exhausted muscles protested. He swiped a forearm across his sweaty brow and barked out a wry laugh. He'd whacked enough wood to heat the cottage for half the winter.

"Dante?"

His gaze jerked up to see Ariana standing at the back door, flushed and damp, with only a towel wrapped around her lush figure. His body tightened, killing his mirth. That she'd managed to sneak up on him unaware was one more rusty nail hammered into his coffin. "What?" he growled. "Is there a gnat in the kitchen?"

Her eyes widened, then she planted her hands on her hips, disturbing him with the possibility of towel slippage. "Don't bite my head off. I thought you might like to know the bathroom is free."

She spun and stomped into the cottage, leaving him with the enticing image of a waterfall of chestnut hair tumbling over her bare shoulders and the curve of damp towel cupping her bottom. Need slammed into him with the force of a wrecking ball.

Gripping the ax handle so hard his knuckles hurt, he ruthlessly squelched desire. He had to find a way to escape the island long before the firewood ran out. They barely had enough food to survive a week.

Dante kicked a log from his path and stalked toward the house. And his resistance to temptation was in even shorter supply.

the trick is, the more time you spend here, the relaxing his thumb will find ahead. The key is full strength food over me seven.

Dante knelt beside the bed, then rolled over, a fan line against coolness to someone... as the covering they softly

CHAPTER SIX

HOT AND ITCHY, and not just from physical exertion, Dante strode inside and thrust the ax into Ariana's hands. "Here."

She gaped at him. "You want me to chop wood while you bathe?"

He snorted. "We have enough to last months. The ax is for self-defense."

"If you say so." Her startled glance assessed his set face, glided over his sweaty bare chest and then shot south, where the troops were at full attention. She gulped. "Um...defense against whom?"

"I believe the island is deserted, but am not one hundred per cent certain. I won't take chances with your safety."

"I'm not sure I could..." She looked at the blade and grimaced.

He spoke with the ominous conviction of experience. "You'd be amazed what you can do when the need arises."

"True." Her delicate chestnut brows tilted. "I never imagined I could set foot on a cruise ship. Or that I possessed the courage to challenge two thugs and a poisonous reptile."

Her passionate nature had also supercharged his imagination. Dante rolled his tight shoulders. He knew better. "You have done an exceptional job. Your courage is admirable."

Delight lit her eyes. "Thanks. You're not lacking in the bravado department yourself."

Dante inclined his head at the door, disconcertingly pleased. He was normally immune to what others thought of him. In his line of work, he had to be. "I have improvised a barricade bar. However, if anyone breaks through, strike first."

"I'll try my best." She gingerly set the ax down and leaned the handle against the wall. "But I'm not exactly proficient with sharp implements."

He grinned. "With that reassuring knowledge, I will sleep more soundly tonight."

"Don't get any ideas. A girl can always change her mind."

He already had ideas. And seeing her rosy from her bath, knowing she was naked beneath the towel inspired more. All bad.

He stacked wood beside the fireplace, attempting to ignore the way her sapphire gaze lingered on his torso when she thought he wasn't looking.

As he headed for his bath, Ariana walked into the stone pantry off the kitchen. "Toss your clothes outside the door," she called. "I'll scrub them in the kitchen sink when I do mine."

"I've been doing my own laundry since I could reach the washtub."

"You chopped the wood." She sounded miffed. "It makes sense to divvy up the chores."

Inside the washroom, Dante stripped off his filthy garments, then piled them outside the door. Letting Ariana tend to his clothes felt uncomfortably intimate. He was accustomed to taking care of himself. Trusted only himself. Attachments led to weakness. The sharks he swam with tracked the scent of weakness like blood in the water. To exploit. To destroy. He was self-sufficient not only by nature, but circumstance. His survival depended on it.

He rummaged through the cupboard. Not that he had a choice. His work was hell on relationships. He'd never dated anyone who wanted to invest in a man who was out of contact for indefinite lengths of time, often had to leave without notice, and was constantly a single wrong word away from being killed.

On the rare occasions when he was able to disclose the truth about what he did for a living, women ran out on him faster than a felon eluding bail. He got lonely at times, especially since he had no family. But he'd never met a woman worth giving up everything for.

Dante hardly recognized himself in the mirror. His shaggy hair could use a trim, and his face was a mess of cuts and bruises, his mustache and beard encrusted with sand and blood. Megaera's hired thugs had expressed dismay over the yacht explosion. They hadn't caused it, which left one possibility. The Camorra had discovered that Dante hadn't fulfilled his promise to murder Ariana.

His fingers tightened on the sink. He and Ariana were now on more than one hit list.

Cleaning up would make him less recognizable to *all* their pursuers…whoever they were. He studied the deadly old-fashioned straight razor in his hand, then the bar soap on the sink. He gave a fatalistic shrug.

Simply one more risky improvisation in the line of duty.

A long soak in hot water eased his soreness. Clean, and with a towel slung around his hips, he swung open the bathroom door…and jerked to a halt.

Kerosene lamps illuminated the glowing room, and candles sparkled beneath dust-free glass globes on a chandelier over the table. Ariana had removed the protective plastic sheets, and pillows cushioned the furniture arranged in a cozy semicircle around the fireplace.

Her scrubbed clothing hung beside his on chairs near the crackling fire. She'd even cleaned his boots. Through the bedroom doorway, he saw the neatly made bed.

Ariana stood at the stove with her back to him, still clad only in a towel, humming *"O soave fanciulla"* from *La Bohème* and stirring a savory canned soup. His stomach cramped with hunger pangs that had nothing to do with food.

Growing up, he and Zia Ines were mired in the grinding struggle against poverty, too exhausted to indulge in niceties. Now he was too busy to bother and never around anyway. He didn't know how to make a house into a home. The world he existed in was ugly and savage. Brutality was rewarded and life tenuous.

The welcoming sanctuary ignited a yearning inside him he hadn't known existed. The peace enveloping the simple cottage pierced his heart with longing. He'd spent time with other women, been in many houses, but had never felt as though he belonged. Never *ached* to belong. His soul had been starving for beauty and warmth…and suddenly Ariana had created a banquet that dangled tantalizingly within reach.

Dante clenched his jaw. He'd learned the hard way it was futile—and dangerous—to pine for things he could not have. He would never trade the surety of serenity for the satisfaction of action. Never exchange permanent peace for the adrenaline rush of living on the edge. A wife and children would never replace his "blood brothers."

It was a choice he could not make.

He thrust his fingers through his damp hair. Why was he even thinking about it? His fate had been sealed at age twelve, and he'd never looked back. Even in the never-going-to-happen scenario that he *did* want a real family, his occupation would only endanger them.

After two decades, he was way too deep inside to ever get out.

Ariana turned. "Hi. I found a can of lentil soup—" She gasped. Staring at him, she froze. The wooden spoon in her hand clattered to the floor

"I thought a towel was the fashion of the day."

"It's not that…well, it is…but—" She gulped. "Your *face!*"

"*Sì.* I am sporting souvenirs of our battles. And I lost a fight with a straight razor."

"Your beard is gone. Before…I didn't know…" She inhaled shakily. "Holy Zeus!"

"Cuts and bruises." He shrugged. "It is not so terrible."

"No," she breathed. "Hence the whammy." She bent to retrieve the spoon. "Ah…you're still bleeding a little."

He touched his fingers to his chin. "Nothing fatal."

"I'll get the first-aid kit." She bolted from the room. Perhaps she was uneasy because the blood was an unpleasant reminder of the previous day's battles.

"Are you all right?" he called.

"Yes. I'm just collecting my wits...um...the kit."

"Don't fuss. I'll survive."

"The last thing we need is for you to get an infection." She walked back in and pulled out a chair at the table, which she'd set for dinner with white stoneware and a copper gardening pitcher brimming with red, orange and yellow chrysanthemums. "Sit. Now."

Grinning, he complied. "An offer no gentleman can refuse."

She opened a first-aid kit on the table, then placed her soft palm against his forehead.

"Che cosa?"

"Are you feverish? You're having delusions of being a gentleman." She nudged his knees with hers, and he spread his thighs so she could step between them to reach his face.

Her leg slid against his bare thigh and desire detonated inside him. He gritted his teeth against the white-hot explosion of need. "I am many things, *bella*. A gentleman is not among them."

"Maybe not by Webster's definition." She poured peroxide onto a cotton ball and then leaned forward, inadvertently giving him an alluring view. "But you're smart and brave and you've saved my life more than once. At great cost."

Dante swallowed and closed his eyes. She had no idea what this was costing him.

The wet cotton ball dabbed his cheek. Her hair trailed over his shoulder in a silken caress. The satiny mound of her breast grazed his upper arm, and every muscle in his body tensed against the yearning to reach for her.

Sweat beaded on his upper lip. Years of discipline had taught him iron-clad self-control. He lived by a strict code of conduct devised to ensure that he stayed alive. He'd been wooed with beautiful women, priceless artifacts, money beyond his wildest dreams. And never veered from his purpose. Never questioned his ethics.

Until now.

Ariana's fingertips brushed his forehead and he opened his eyes. Her mouth was a mere breath from his. "Am I hurting you?"

"No." His hands fisted. How much was he expected to endure? Her sensual torture was tougher to withstand than a beating.

"The soup should be done soon. You must be famished."

"Ravenous." His glance tangled with hers and he jolted, stunned to see his own desire reflected in her uncertain gaze. Mesmerized by the glowing blue depths, he flinched at the sting of antiseptic on his chin.

"Sorry." She leaned closer, pursed her lips and blew on the cut. Her breath feathered over his mouth, intoxicating him with the scent of sun-ripened fruit and warm woman. "Does that make it better?"

"No," he rasped. "But this will." Her eyes flared in startled surprise as he tugged her into his lap, wrapped his arms around her and captured her mouth with his.

Ariana went completely still. Not resistance, but not response, either. He hesitated for a heartbeat. Then she uttered a quiet moan, her fingers tunneled into his hair and she kissed him with desperate demand.

Rational thought shut down and he became lost in sensation. Reveling in the heady taste of her acceptance, he forgot everything and found refuge in the lush haven of her mouth. Her flowery scent dizzied his senses as he slid his tongue into the welcoming warmth.

Coming home.

Until this moment, he hadn't truly known what he was missing. And from this moment on, he would never be able to forget.

A groan vibrated in his throat, and he deepened the connection, drinking her in. Ariana's generosity quenched his loneliness. Her indomitable spirit silenced the demons of suspicion and doubt. She flooded his soul with light, with hope, filling the empty place deep inside where he hid the scars of cynicism and mistrust.

She danced to his rhythm as naturally as if they'd been longtime lovers. Giving. Taking. Breaths mingled in silent sighs. He'd intended to linger, but passion flamed inside him, and Ariana's speeding pulse urged his to join her in the race toward pleasure.

He cradled her head in one hand, supported her body with the other and leaned her back, leaned into their kiss. Groaning, he savored the taste of her. Her fingertips stroked his nape, caressed his naked spine, and goose bumps shivered along his skin. Her palms slid over his shoulders, down his chest, as if learning the shape of him.

He ached to touch her in return. This wasn't just desire. It was far more than lust. Need blazed through his veins in a fierce, primal drumbeat. He never wanted to let her go.

Dante scooped her up and shoved the flowers and dishes aside. He laid her down on the table and nibbled along her jaw to the tender spot beneath her ear. She gasped, and her nails bit lightly into his back, the slight pain heightening his pleasure. She was shaking. So was he.

He'd been starving many times in his life, but had never known such driving hunger. Consuming need. He tasted the curve of her shoulder, the delicate hollow of her throat. His fingers dipped into the valley between her breasts and tugged open the towel. "I am going to devour every inch of you, Ariana."

"Yes. Please." Her breathing rapid, she arched against him, and the spicy perfume of crushed chrysanthemums mingled with her unique feminine scent. Her pebbled nipples grazed his chest and her heartbeat galloped against his.

He skimmed his hands down her lush curves, teased her silky curls, and she moaned at his touch. She felt so right, so perfect. He was burning up. The only way he could satisfy his scalding need was by sinking deeply inside her.

He had to have her…had to make her his. He cupped her breast and bent his head to suckle the hard nipple.

"Dante!" Ariana gasped and yanked his hair hard, jerking him from the haze of pleasure. "Stop!"

Dante froze. *Stop?* He blinked in frustrated disbelief. *Now?* He struggled to draw a shaky breath that stung his lungs. Gritted his teeth. San Gennaro, *mio bello,* give me the strength.

Coughing, she shoved at his chest. "The soup is on fire!"

He dazedly looked up and his blurred gaze focused on the stove, where flames and smoke roiled from the pan. Snarling a phrase he hoped she didn't understand, he lunged and yanked the pot from the burner.

As the hot handle singed his palm, he swore again, dropped it into the sink and ran the water over it. Blackened gunk sizzled and acrid smoke thickened the air.

Coughing, his eyes streaming from the noxious cloud, he turned away from the too-enticing sight of Ariana as her trembling hands fumbled with her towel. He stared furiously at the water pouring from the faucet. What in the name of all that was holy had gotten into him?

Water overflowed the pan, and he wrenched the faucet off. The whole damn cottage would have burned down around him.

Worse, the Camorra could have waltzed right in…and caught him with his pants down.

"Dante?" Ariana's tentative touch on his shoulder made him jump. "Did you get burned?"

"No." He snapped out the lie. He'd never been so badly burned… and he didn't mean his hand. His emotions were as charred and smoking as the ruined mess in the sink. He was no randy schoolboy, but he'd never before been slammed senseless by passion.

Now that he'd reveled in the shared explosion of erotic energy between them, ached with the hunger, there was no going back. No way to salvage the wreck. Wrenching emptiness cut through him.

He could never again trust himself to touch her.

And the loss stained him with regret.

"Are you mad at me?" Her voice sounded as shaken as he felt.

Fury churned inside him. Not at her, at himself. He knew better than to get so carried away. "No."

"Then why won't you face me?" Her unsteady whisper stabbed him in the heart. "Are you offended by... I didn't purposely—"

He turned and looked at her. Huge mistake. She faltered and bit her lower lip, plump and pink from his kisses. Her skin was flushed from the friction of his, her hair tousled by his hands.

The hungry lion of desire pacing within him roared and bared its claws. Surely she wasn't that naive. The towel precariously riding his hips left nothing to imagination. He ruefully shook his head. "Do I appear offended by you, *mia cara?*"

Her glance flickered down his body and she blushed. "It was just first aid." She gulped. "I had no idea. I didn't think—"

He hadn't been thinking, either, not with his brain. Dante shrugged in a casual manner he was far from feeling. "There are two of us at fault."

And, he'd learned in his dealings, two sides to every person. His gaze lingered on Ariana's quivering body...on her slender neck and bare shoulders. She didn't have her iPod and notebook with her. He was hit by a sizzling flashback of how soft and inviting her body had felt beneath his, and his breathing hitched. He was sure of that. Instead of rolling around naked with her on the kitchen table, he should have just eaten and then searched the premises for evidence of Megaera's identity. Then again, it was another no-brainer. He snorted. As if any red-blooded male would choose soup over sex.

She twitched the hem of her towel. "I'm sorry. Honestly, Dante, I wouldn't lead you on. I'm not the type who starts something like this and then doesn't follow through. Not that I start it and *do* go through with it." She inhaled a choppy breath. "I mean...I'm not a prude, but I'm also not in the habit of..." Her expression dazed, she wrapped her arms around herself. "I don't know what happened."

"No need to apologize, *bella.*" He studied her appalled face. Even now, he wanted to pull her into his embrace and kiss away her hurt and bewilderment. "Our reaction is quite normal considering all we've been through. It has been documented before. People are genetically wired to preserve the species."

"A response to danger?" She looked doubtful. "Some sort of biological imperative?"

"Sì," he lied. The attraction between them was far more than mere biology. I won't lose control again." Both a promise and a warning. Was Ariana Bennett as ingenuous as she appeared? Or was she a calculating opponent using sex to distract him? If she had seduced him to divert him from obtaining information from her, she'd succeeded.

Skepticism snuffed out the banked embers, and he went cold. He'd learned the hard way to trust no one. If she had been an assassin, he'd be dead. As his friend Silvio's lively grandfather had often warned him, wine, tobacco and women reduce a man to ashes. He stared at the travesty in the sink.

Ariana's dubious gaze followed his. "So much for dinner. I never could cook well. I always seem to get distracted."

The dejected slump to her shoulders roused his primal, protective urges, *Dio* help him. *"A tutto c'è rimedio, fuorché alla morte."*

"There's a cure for everything except death?" Her crooked smile banished his chills, wreathed him in renewed warmth. "Well, the patient looks terminal."

He nodded with mock gravity. "More like cremated."

Her wobbly giggle brightened her countenance and shot an arrow of triumph through his heart.

He trained his gaze on the shard-strewn flagstones. He'd better tread carefully. Dishes might not be the only things that got shattered if he forgot his role again. "If you handle the ah…destruction, I will tend to the meal."

"Deal. But first, I'm going to get a fresh towel."

When she scuttled into the bathroom, he conducted a fast sweep of the main area, but didn't find her iPod and notebook.

Ariana returned before he could widen the hunt. Tendrils of

newly damp hair told him she'd splashed her face with cold water. As for himself…there were not enough icebergs in the Arctic Ocean to bring down his temperature.

While she wielded a broom, he scanned the stone pantry that performed double duty as a primitive cooler. No hiding places among the meager supplies. He opened another can of lentil soup. While she reset the table, he measured flour, sugar, salt, water and olive oil into a bowl.

He and Ariana strained to act casual, as if they weren't skimpily clad in squares of terry cloth. As if the lure of hot, naked kisses didn't hum tautly between them. As if the temptation of forbidden pleasure wasn't a siren call to recklessness.

Both failed miserably.

He was hyperaware of her bare limbs. Of the long, graceful line of her neck. Of the expanse of exposed creamy skin.

Especially now that he knew how sweet her warm mouth tasted. How her satin skin quivered beneath his caresses.

Ariana's awkward movements revealed she suffered similar torture. She made a quick trip to the courtyard, and then stepped through the back door carrying another bundle of flowers. She peered around him. "What are you making?"

"Bread. Somewhat like focaccia. But flat, because we have no yeast, and smaller, to cook faster."

"Dinner buns." She was careful not to touch him, but her intriguing scent tantalized his senses.

"They are cheap and filling." He'd never again smell chrysanthemums without becoming violently aroused. His arms stiffened as he fought to keep his hands in the bowl. "Without yeast, I hope they do not taste like rocks."

A smile tinged her voice. "Then you don't want me making them. Dad used to choke down my awful creations and pretend to love them, bless him."

The perfect opening. He had to gain her trust in order to get the information he sought. Establishing rapport required careful finesse, like the dough beneath his fingers. A heavy hand would toughen the bread…and the mark. "The way you talk about him, I feel as if I knew him."

"Everyone liked him," she said softly. "Which made it even more terrible when people turned away from him after he was arrested on smuggling charges. Thanks to the relentless FBI." She swallowed hard. "You've already heard it before. So, how did a tough guy learn to make bread?"

"Tough guys are made, not born." He rinsed his hands and wiped them on a kitchen towel, then swiveled to stir the soup. Proving himself was easier with men. Violence often bought him membership into the inner circle. Women required emotional intimacy before giving trust. He would share with Ariana in order to coax her to share with him. The method was cold, calculating…and effective. He'd done it dozens of times.

"Do tell."

He invented lies for a living. But lying to Ariana was different. He'd never before felt the sick weight of reproach in his stomach. Smelled the stench of fraud in his nostrils. Tasted the sting of treachery on his tongue.

Do your damn job. The sooner he got it over with, the sooner he'd be free of Ariana. Free of temptation. He'd learn to deal with the guilt.

Dante turned to meet Ariana's compassionate gaze, and his heart stumbled.

Or perhaps both of them would be forever scarred by his betrayal.

CHAPTER SEVEN

GUILT. THE unexpected marauder clouded Dante's judgement. The last time he had felt shame was years ago, when prison bars had slammed shut behind him and he knew Zia Ines would learn his sins.

He glanced at Ariana's expectant face, then at their clothing cozily draped before the fireplace. After their near-disastrous collision, maybe he should wear his pants, wet or not.

Instead, he jerked a pan toward him. If his self-control was that flimsy, he could shoot himself and save the Camorra the effort. "Zia Ines taught me to cook when I was a boy. She said if I wanted to eat well, I should learn to cook."

"I like a progressive woman. Your aunt Ines raised you?"

"My mother's aunt. She was too old for the burden of a child, yet she took me in." He scooped dough into the pan. "I often wondered if Zia resented the load thrust upon her. But she never showed it. She cleaned houses to make a living, and was exhausted at night. Starting when I was six, I did most of the chores."

"That's young for such responsibility. Was it only the two of you?"

"*Sì.* She was a stern disciplinarian, but kind and generous. And she had a great wit. We were very close." He had fabricated a standard background that withstood the sharpest scrutiny. Yet, for the first time with anyone, he spoke the truth. He didn't want to lie to Ariana any more than he had to.

It didn't make him feel less of a bastard.

"She sounds delightful. She's…gone?"

"Five years this August." Zia Ines had clung to life several days past his birthday, then succumbed to pneumonia.

"You're alone now."

Her gentle concern heightened his urge to enfold her in his arms, and he shoved the bread into the oven. *"Sì."*

"I'm sorry." She reached out, then seemed to think better. After refilling the copper pitcher with water, she carried it and the flowers to the table.

"Do not pity me, Ariana. I have the life I chose." He turned to face her. Watched her carefully. Her response could be a key to her secrets. "Can you say the same?"

The pitcher clunked onto the table. Ariana stood with one hand frozen on the handle and the other clutching rainbow chrysanthemums. Candlelight kissed her skin with melted gold and haloed her chestnut locks. An exquisite painting he'd once brokered of Flora, goddess of flowers and fertility sprang to mind. Flora was reputed to have amassed a fortune as a courtesan, which she bequeathed to Rome.

Dante gripped the stone countertop. He would keep his vow not to lose control. But, San Gennaro, if Flora was half as fascinating as Ariana, he understood why men had fallen at her feet.

Ariana dropped the bouquet into the pitcher. "Forty-eight hours ago, I had never thought twice about how I've lived."

"You were happy?"

"Content." She studiously arranged flowers. "At least I thought…before I stood on the stern of Megaera's yacht, terrified I was about to drown."

He'd stared into Death's eyes before, with no regrets. Weeks ago, he would have changed nothing about his life. Why the sudden dissatisfaction? Why the knife thrust of loss?

Dante looked out the window, where blue-black clouds scudded above the tumultuous sea. Being as skittish as a spring lamb unsettled him. Unsuspecting lambs got slaughtered. He returned his glance to Ariana. "And now?"

"I realize I've sublimated my wants, abandoned my goals for

others' expectations. My parents, my professors, my boss." A hesitation as she crushed a wilted leaf in her palm. "Geoff."

Dante had a thick dossier on Ariana with details about Geoffrey Turner that even she probably didn't know. But he feigned ignorance to draw her out. One more falsehood. "Geoff?"

"A professor I was…fond of. We broke up after Dad was framed." Grief shadowed her graceful profile. "Another regret."

A spur of jealousy caught Dante off guard. Like guilt, envy was an anvil he'd jettisoned. Troubled by her pain and his concern, he cranked off the flame beneath the soup pot with a resentful twist of his wrist. "What *do* you want, Ariana?"

"To clear my father's name."

Dante's heart thudded against his ribs. Because of him, she might not succeed. He carried the bubbling soup to the table. He didn't want to be the next person in line to let her down. To hurt her. To be another of her regrets. "For him?" He set the pot down. "Or you?"

She swiveled to face him. "You know how to drill to the heart of a matter." Her considering gaze assessed him. "There's a whole lot more to you than you let on."

Uh-oh. She was in no way short on brains. He'd best be careful not to tip his hand. Feigning casualness, he ladled steaming soup into her bowl. "There is also more of you I have not seen."

She slanted him a rueful glance accompanied by a crooked smile. "You've pretty much seen it all."

Yes, he'd seen her body. But he wanted to know what was in her heart.

Before he could serve her more soup, she gestured. "That's plenty."

"Your stomach is as empty as mine, *bella*. Do not deny it."

"I filled up on grapes. I don't want much."

Bittersweet emotions constricted his chest. Ariana was attempting to take care of him. She was willing to go without so he could have more. He had tried not to let Zia Ines do that, and he wasn't about to allow Ariana. His mother had made the ultimate sacrifice for him. Watching the women in his life make sacrifices on his behalf went against everything he stood for. Another reason he hadn't cultivated any ties. "We will share equally."

She planted her palms on the tabletop, and her towel dipped slightly, exposing tantalizing curves. "You're bigger, and expended more physical energy. You need more food."

"We both need to stay strong." He resolutely moved his gaze to her face. *In every way.*

Her mouth firmed. "I won't eat the rest."

Dante smothered a smile. He was used to getting his way with women. When he'd first kidnapped Ariana, fear had kept her compliant, and the fact that she now felt comfortable enough to rebel thrilled him. Butting heads with her challenged him on every level. He dished the same scanty amount into his bowl as he'd put in hers. "Neither will I."

She called his bluff. "It will go uneaten, then."

She wanted to engage in a battle of wills, eh? At the same time he'd discovered the opposite sex, he'd discovered he'd been born with an inherent knack with the ladies. He had more effective weapons of persuasion in his arsenal. Casting her a sultry, heavy-lidded glance, he curled his lips into the slow grin that made women go glassy-eyed. "Surely you don't want to deny yourself something so…satisfying."

The color in her cheeks deepened. "I'm not that hungry."

"My mistake." He lowered his voice to a husky purr. "I was under the impression you couldn't wait to sink your teeth into my buns."

She rolled her eyes, but he watched her closely and noted the exact moment when she decided two could play this game. "Is that right?" Hips swaying, she sauntered around the table until she reached him. She stepped so close that he could count each long, sable eyelash as she raised her chin and captured his gaze. "I don't, as a rule, crave leftovers."

Her heady fragrance enveloped him, beckoned him to touch, to taste, and he swallowed with a mouth gone bone dry. "Like fine wine, certain things become better with age and experience."

She walked her fingers up his bare chest, and blood roared in his ears, making it tough to hear. "Like Italian cured ham?"

He was so intently focused on the sensual brush of her fingertips, the wash of light illuminating her features, the sparkle in her eyes, that her question barely registered. "Perhaps."

Her caress feathered over his collarbone, and time slowed as he drowned in her sapphire gaze. Her tongue peeked out and moistened her lips. "Dante," she cooed.

Recent memories of how soft and warm and sweet her lips had tasted punched a kick of heat into his belly. He forced his reply through the thickness in his throat. *"Sì?"*

"About your buns…"

His question emerged in a gravelly voice. *"Che cosa, bella mia?"*

She smiled impishly. "They're smoking."

He followed her merry glance to where a gray cloud streamed from the oven door. He blinked free of his daze. Swearing, he strode to the stove and yanked out the smoking pan. Fortunately, he rescued the bread before it was scorched beyond repair.

Why did his mind, body and heart careen out of control whenever Ariana got close? Could he get any more addled?

She laughed. "Don't think you can bat those big brown eyes and lob Italian charm bombs at me. I have your number, now."

"And it is 1-1-2, Europe's emergency disaster code." A reluctant grin sneaked out. He'd been right. The little saucebox was playing him. As a pro, or an amateur? He piled the hot bread on a plate.

She swished past him into the pantry and emerged with a jar of homegrown honey. "No butter, but look what I found." Her full lips tilted in a diabolical smile. "Nectar of the gods. Aphrodite used to anoint herself with it and invite her lovers to lick it off her body."

His erection twitched beneath the towel and he cursed. Apparently, Ariana possessed preemptive feminine nukes. Damn her, now that she'd had a taste of the power she held over him, she knew exactly how to torture him.

Signorina Bennett had no idea how precariously he was balanced on the razor's edge. Or what a dangerous game she was playing.

He followed her to the dining area, diligently not watching the sensual sway of her bottom.

Verbal sparring matches were Dante's stock-in-trade. His shield and sword. It wasn't often anyone bested him. He was missing something obvious. Something important. He should be able to see it…yet he was night-blind. Destiny was creeping up on him. Feral and unpredictable, it stirred behind him, stared at him, its hot breath prickling the back of his neck. Every time he tried to pin the feeling down, it shifted, eluded his grasp. Like trying to capture starlight in the palm of his hand.

Fear uncoiled in his belly. He never peered too closely at the future. Why was he suddenly questioning everything he stood for? Everything he was? Everything he thought he'd wanted?

Dante was careful not to slam down the plate before stalking past her. "You may use the sink. I'll wash up in the other room."

He shut the bathroom door and performed another quick search for her iPod and notebook. The bedroom was the last place to look. Since the arched entryway was doorless, he couldn't search with Ariana around.

He washed his hands and then headed back to the table. When he slid out her chair, she glanced up and thanked him. The simple gesture warmed him from the inside out.

His instincts prickled. He might be in worse trouble than he'd thought. Suddenly, his entire way of life was on the firing line.

Disconcerted, he strode to the opposite chair, and bowed his head to offer a silent blessing. While he was at it, he threw in a plea for clarity, and the strength to resist temptation.

He raised his head to meet Ariana's puzzled stare. Noting the tender expression in her eyes, the baffled crease of her brows, he gestured. "You are uncomfortable blessing the food?"

"Not at all." Her gaze dropped and she fiddled with her spoon. "I just don't understand how you can believe so strongly in a higher power and…" She exhaled. "Never mind."

"You wonder if I am concerned about divine judgment." His mouth twisted in a wry smile. "For my sins."

"I don't mean to sound holier-than-thou or anything. I'm far from perfect. Everybody is…but…"

But not everyone lied. Stole. Killed. Was it still a sin if it was done in the name of survival? Or justice? He flipped his napkin into his lap. "One way or another, no matter what he believes, someday every man has to answer for his actions."

"You're not worried karma will bite you?"

Did his motive atone for his methods? He hoped so. Though in his hour of greatest shame, Zia Ines had told him that his good intentions had set him on the path to ruin. He paused to spoon up soup. He refused to regret his choices. Second-guessing himself would get him dead. "I will accept responsibility, pay the consequences of my choices."

With a start, he realized she'd deftly led him off the conversational path into a thicket of distraction. Purposefully? He drizzled honey on a chunk of warm bread and devoured it before speaking. "What about you?"

"I'm willing to do the same."

Did she understand how dire the consequences would be if she continued in her quest? "You derailed my earlier question quite skillfully."

"You're implying I led you on to hijack the conversation?" She huffed. "I told you, I don't play that game. If I don't want to talk about something, I say so. *You* fired the starting gun in the seduction Olympics. I merely gave you a run for your money."

And had run away with the gold. With the long-standing habit of someone who had often been without food, he ate quickly. "You're doing it again. Are you unwilling to say whether you are crusading for your father, or yourself?"

Her eyes narrowed to cobalt lasers. "It's for both Dad *and* me. Why does it matter?"

"Because, *bella,* you cannot compensate for your father's actions. Realizing that will save you great pain."

She paused with her water glass in midair. "You believe he's guilty!" Her hand began to shake. "What do you know?"

"Now you're the one leaping to conclusions. I haven't passed judgment on your father." Though he harbored suspicions. And his gut instincts were usually on target. "I am attempting to keep you from being hurt."

"Ironic from the man who kidnapped me." Watching him intently over the rim, she sipped water, lowered the glass. "Why *are* you holding me hostage, Dante?"

"We've traveled this ground." He couldn't disclose his reasons without putting her, himself and others in peril. "When you have served your purpose, you'll be freed unharmed."

"*What* purpose? It doesn't seem to be personal. And it can't be financial." She bit her lip. "I'm of no value to you."

His throat tightened. "You are wrong." She held immense value for him. More than she realized. "But it's better if you don't know."

"Better for whom?"

"For *you*, Ariana. I have taken care of you so far. Trust me."

Her stare scalded him. "Why should I, when you're hiding things from me? Lying to me. I abhor liars."

He swallowed a mouthful of bread that ached all the way down. When she found out the truth, she would hate him. "Have you never lied, then?"

"Of course I have, to protect someone's feelings, but it's not the same."

"Is it not?"

"Are you saying you kidnapped me to protect me? From who? From what?" She slammed her palm on the table. "Who *are* you? Tell me!"

He shook his head. "It would only endanger you."

"I know you won't hurt me. What's stopping me from walking out the door?"

"Not a thing. Except that we're marooned in the wilds of Greece and it's cold, growing dark, and you're barefoot and wearing only a towel." He shrugged, contributing nonchalance to the lie. He would get physical to stop her, but counted on her common sense to do the job. "And assuming you wish to forgo the safety of the cottage and trade my company for spiders and snakes."

He heard her teeth grinding from across the table. "I don't understand you. I don't understand any of this."

He covered her hand with his. "Be patient a while longer."

"How long? I miss my job." Her chin quivered, and the little hitch in her voice made him feel like a beast. "I miss my mom."

Compassion squeezed his heart. He despised having to hurt her in order to protect her. "I know, *mia cara.* I am sorry."

"Then let me go."

"I cannot."

Moisture welled in her eyes, and she tugged her hand from his grasp and shoved her half-eaten soup aside. "I'm done." She pushed to her feet and strode into the kitchen.

Dante followed. She stood enveloped in shadows looking out the window at the rapidly darkening courtyard. "Ariana." He rested his hands on her slender shoulders from behind. "When this is over, I will help you clear your father's name."

A tremor quaked through her, but she didn't turn around. "Why? I can't pay you."

"You have paid enough. It is important to you…and therefore to me." Chagrined at how violently her body was trembling, he stroked her nape with his thumbs. "Will you share with me what information you have?"

He held his breath as long, heart-shaking moments ticked past. The pulse in her neck galloped beneath his fingertips, betraying the internal battle raging within her. "I—" she gulped "—I don't have any."

Unlike him, she was lousy at deception. He sighed. "So much for trust."

She shrugged off his hands. "Just leave me alone."

He walked back to the table and gathered dishes. His ability to read people kept him alive. Ariana's distress—and innocence—seemed genuine. After what had happened to her father, she'd already been hurt more than anyone deserved. He carried the dishes to the kitchen and stacked them in the sink. Nevertheless, she was still lying to him. Though he had his own selfish motives, he ached to win her trust and help her.

Weighted by sorrow, he poured detergent, ran hot water. How could he earn Ariana's trust when his every word, every action was masked by a cloak of lies?

Focus on your goal. The end *would* justify the means. Even though Ariana would despise him when it was over. He swiped a soapy cloth over the table. If only he could so easily scrub his conscience.

He snuffed out the candles in the candelabra. When he returned to the kitchen, Ariana stood at the sink washing dishes. He glanced at her impassive face. "Are you all right?"

Fixated on her task, she nodded. "Emotional tantrums are pointless. I understand you're set on your mystery mission." She looked up, determination glinting in her eyes. "And you'd better understand that I won't give up mine. Not for you, not for any reason."

Admiration winged through him. Beneath her soft, sweet exterior lurked a backbone of tungsten. A wellspring of loyalty.

He slipped into the bedroom while she washed dishes. The bureau was empty, as was the closet. Nothing beneath the mattress. He knelt and lifted the rug on one side of the bed, then the other. His clever *signorina* hadn't stashed her things anywhere inside that he could find. Time to widen the hunt.

He jumped when Ariana suddenly spoke behind him. "Dante, I— What are you doing?"

Simultaneously speared by guilt and anger, he stiffened and muttered a curse. Caught in the act for the second time in two hours. If he didn't shape up, he'd be in the morgue. "I saw a spider."

She squeaked and leaped backward. "Don't let it get away!"

He smacked his palm on the flagstones, feeling like a jerk for scaring her. "It won't."

She cringed. "Are you sure it's dead?"

"Proprio morto." Just as he would be if his libido continued to short-circuit his brain. He surged to his feet. "You need something, yes?"

"Um…" Her glance traveled over his bare chest in that disconcerting way that made his body tighten. "I thought I saw movement in the courtyard and heard odd noises."

Adrenaline rocketed through his veins. "Why didn't you say so?" He sprinted for the rear entrance, snagging the ax from beside the fireplace on the way.

Ariana followed. "Probably just the wind."

He pushed her against the wall next to the back door. "Stay inside, away from the windows."

Her eyes widened. "What if you need help?"

He scowled. "Help me by keeping out of the line of fire." He eased the door open. "Bar the door behind me."

Dante spun out low and to the right. He crouched behind the huge clay flowerpots beside the back door until he heard the bar drop into place. Ax ready, he scanned the courtyard, then the trees beyond.

Air rushed out of his lungs and he lowered the ax. "Ariana, come out."

The door creaked open. "What is it?"

"Galline."

She wrinkled her nose. "Chickens?"

"They are roosting in the trees." He waved. "And there is a goat, also."

The goat lifted his head from where it was munching on scrub bushes and bleated, and Ariana smiled. "Great! Eggs! And we can milk the goat."

"You may try." He grinned. "But I think that will only annoy him."

"Him?" She did a double take. "How—never mind."

He cast another look around. "It is rapidly growing dark."

She shuddered. "And colder."

"Fully exploring the grounds will have to wait for tomorrow, when our clothes are dry." He followed her inside and engaged the bar.

"It feels like there's a storm brewing." Shivering, she made a beeline for the fireplace.

His senses warned him that something was brewing. "I am sure of it."

He lingered in the kitchen as he watched her embrace the shimmering heat. Her hair tumbled over her shoulders in glossy chestnut waves, and firelight bloomed like roses on her skin. She stretched out her palms to the flames, her profile serene.

Dante sighed. It was going to be a *long* night.

She glanced up, caught him staring. Their gazes collided, and awareness arced between them. Then she shifted her attention to the ax. "Did you wash your hands?" At his puzzled frown, she inclined her head toward the bedroom. "Spider entrails."

"Va bene." He strode to the sink and washed his hands. Ariana had experienced a rough couple of days. She'd been scared and hurt, and he'd upset her over dinner. For this evening, he would forgo his attempt to extract information.

Foolish? Perhaps. He returned to her side at the fireplace and pitched in more logs. It didn't mean he was going soft. He frowned. No chance of that with the lovely Signorina Bennett in the vicinity.

His instincts had never failed him. And they screamed that if he pushed too hard, alienated her, she would never confide in him. If necessary, he could, and would, lean on her for answers.

Dante stalked to the bookshelves next to the gramophone.

Now he was even lying to himself.

He reached for a leather case. "Do you play backgammon?"

"Yes, is there a board?" He turned, brandished the case, and she smiled. "This will be fun."

Not nearly as enjoyable as sweeping her off her feet, carrying her to the bed and loving her until dawn.

They sat at either end of the wooden settee in front of the fire and placed the board in the middle. The cushions Ariana had piled onto the furniture made the seat surprisingly comfortable.

She handed him his ass on game one, mostly because he was bewitched by the smoothness of her skin, the sensual curve of her lips, her sweet fragrance.

He concentrated during game two, but she still won.

She shot him a dubious glance as she moved her last checker off the board. "You're not mad?"

"Over a game?" He snorted.

"I get the feeling you're a man who doesn't like to lose."

"True, in most cases. But backgammon is a game of both skill and luck." He shrugged. "If the dice favor you and your strategy is stronger, you deserve to win."

With a wicked smile that blazed to his bone marrow, she buffed her fingernails on her shoulder. "So you won't mind when I beat the pants off you *again*."

He smiled in return. "I am not wearing pants."

Her glance drifted over his bare torso. "Like you have to remind me."

"Apparently not." When she flushed, he grinned. "And we will see who loses this time."

They battled back and forth through the evening, stopping the play only long enough for a makeshift supper of bread, cured smoked pork and applesauce.

Ariana triumphed again, one game ahead. She pumped her fists in the air. "Ha! Got you!"

Who knew his librarian had such a competitive streak? Amused and aroused by her merciless rivalry, he stretched and checked his watch. "It is growing late."

"Beautiful watch. I'm glad rolling around in the sea didn't ruin it."

"It is waterproof. A gift from Zia Ines on my last birthday before she died. It is the only thing I have left of her. My only family. She had it engraved on the back." The instant the words left his mouth, he regretted them. Why had he spilled his guts?

Her voice was gentle. "May I see?"

He unfastened the watch and handed it to her.

"Time and tide wait for no man." She rubbed her thumb over the inscription as she translated the Italian phrase. "Was she trying to tell you something?"

His mouth twisted wryly. "She thought I was frittering away my life. She was tired of waiting for 'grandchildren.'"

"It's not too late for you to settle down and have a family."

"Women who are seeking husbands do not desire a man such as me." At the curious glint in her eyes, he hastily added, "Not that I desire commitment."

"Do you like children? Don't you want any of your own?"

He hesitated before answering honestly. "If it were possible, I would like *tanti bambini*."

Speculation creased her face. "Isn't it?"

"It is possible." He shrugged. "Given my line of work, not probable. Or safe."

"You could quit."

"I cannot," he said tightly.

"Why not?"

"Too much is at stake."

Her discomfiting stare bored into him. "Money doesn't solve everything."

"No, but it is one hell of a motivator." Money. Power. Passion. The three top motives for murder.

"Earlier tonight, you asked me a question." Holding his gaze, she offered him back the watch. "I'll ask you the same question. What do you want, Dante?"

He'd reached his limit. His hand closed possessively over hers. "I want you to come to bed with me."

CHAPTER EIGHT

PLEASURE SPARKLED through Ariana's veins like heady wine as the weight of Dante's muscular body pressed her into the mattress.

Even as her arms embraced his broad shoulders, she tensed in confusion. *Wait.* How had the situation so quickly escalated? Hadn't she made it clear she didn't want to go this far?

Or had she only thought it?

She wasn't sure of anything where the charismatic Napoletano was concerned.

"Do not fear me, *mia cara.*" He cradled her face in his hands. "I won't hurt you."

"I'm not scared of you." She gazed into glittering espresso eyes fringed with thick black lashes. His beautiful, eloquent eyes glowed with intelligence, compassion and desire...for her.

"Then why do you hesitate?"

Before she'd met him, her emotions had been as pale and smooth as the white candles perched stiffly in the candelier over the table where they'd eaten. Nothing inherently wrong with them. But they remained pristine, unaware of their true purpose, unsuspecting of their capacity for transformation...until someone touched a match to the wick and they flared to light.

Dante's kisses set her aflame. His heat melted her reserve. Their shared passion burned brightly, illuminating the emptiness inside her. She threaded her fingers through his silky hair. "I'm afraid of what you do to me," she whispered.

She thought she had experienced love, passion, pain...but those were shadows compared to her newly intense feelings.

Her world had been muted until Dante. The difference between watching *Madame Butterfly* on a small black and white screen and then from the front row of an opera house. Suddenly her life had burst into a soaring aria, dazzling colors. And she had no control. No way to tone down the volume or brilliance.

No way to prevent being lost and alone when the performance was over and the stage went dark.

The emptiness would echo colder and lonelier when Dante left her. She would return to existing, not living. A mere observer in the drama of life.

Yet she trembled in fear at taking the next step.

Dante's mouth brushed hers with enticingly sweet kisses. "What have I done to you?"

No matter how much her brain protested, her heart insisted she was safe in his embrace. Protected. The tender expression on his face when he had declared her valuable to him had diluted her doubt, wrapped her in awe. "Nothing is black or white anymore. I see everything differently now. Feel different."

He playfully nipped her lower lip. "And that is bad?"

"Yes. *No.*" She sighed in delight as his finely bristled cheek grazed her jaw. "I don't know."

He nuzzled her neck, and his warm whisper tingled into her ear. "I love the way you smell. The way you taste."

She shivered and her nipples pebbled. "I can't think when you do that."

"Do not think." The husky cadence of his voice rumbled in an intimate caress as his hand drifted down to gently cup her breast. "Listen to your heart, Ariana. Simply feel."

"Mmm." She arched against him. "Feels nice."

His mouth roamed her collarbone, his hot breath teased her taut nipple. "Tell me what you want, *tesoro.*"

"*Dante.*" Her eyelids fluttered shut on a moan as she surrendered. "Touch me. Kiss me. Make love to me."

He went absolutely still above her. His heartbeat pounded furiously against hers. "Ariana." Her name was a ragged exhalation.

She opened her eyes and saw his stunned brown gaze inches from hers. "I've shocked you."

"Ariana," Dante repeated. "You were speaking in your sleep."

"What?" She blinked and the room swam into focus. The lamp he'd left burning at her request imbued the plaster walls with a soft orange glow. Her bewildered gaze darted back to Dante. He was beside her in bed, not on top of her.

Horror assailed her and she gulped. *Oh, my God.* What had she done? What had she said?

Dark with passion and deeper, scarier emotions, his glance ensnared hers. "You dreamed of me." The arousal hardening the chiseled planes of his face told her she'd revealed way too much.

She tugged the covers up to her neck. "I am so sorry." With him naked beside her in the double bed, she had intimate knowledge his face wasn't all that was hard. He had matter-of-factly shunned the discomfort of sleeping wrapped in a towel, but she couldn't. After their backgammon game, he'd pointed out that sharing the bed was simply another matter of survival. The floor was rough and cold, and they had two blankets. Sleeping together was practical for comfort and warmth.

She had made him promise the arrangement would be platonic. "I don't blame you for being angry."

"I'm not angry." He rolled to his back, presenting a finely sculpted masculine profile seen gracing statues in the museums of Florence. She'd thought he was gorgeous before he shaved. The impact of unveiling his defined cheekbones and the lush curves of his sensual mouth was shattering. How was a woman supposed to resist a flesh-and-blood Roman god?

He sighed. "However, I *am* only human. There is a limit to my restraint."

"I know. I'm sorry. I can't help what I dream." He had primed her imagination by kissing her before dinner. Hot. Consuming. Devouring. Dante's clever mouth had revved her engine from zero to eighty in seconds.

If the soup hadn't burned, she would have ended up giving him a lot more than her friendship.

"Go back to sleep, Ariana."

As if that would happen. It had been tough enough the first time. She'd squinched her eyes shut when he'd undressed and climbed into bed beside her. She'd lain rigid for hours, afraid to move in fear she'd accidentally touch him, tormented by imagining how magnificent he would look naked. She'd heard every gust creaking the branches, each pop and crackle of the fire and the steady rhythm of Dante's every breath. "Go ahead. I'm going to get up."

"Don't be foolish." The blankets rustled, and his warm thigh grazed hers before he pulled his leg back. "It is three-thirty. The fire has gone out, and it's dark and cold. I gave my word I wouldn't touch you, and I'll keep it. You need to rest, or you will be ill."

"It's not you I'm worried about." She scooted to the edge of the mattress. "I'm not normally like this. Not sensual."

"That makes no sense." His low voice was husky with sleep.

"It seems contradictory after what happened between us, but I don't take intimacy lightly. There has to be a heart connection. And trust." It had happened only twice in her life. And neither experience had been as powerful as just *kissing* Dante.

She'd never experienced *anything* like the bond she felt with him. Maybe the forbidden danger gilded the attraction. She wouldn't be the first woman to fall for a bad boy.

"'There can be no love without trust.'" He sounded as confused as she felt. "I thought you didn't believe real life can be like the fairy tales."

"I don't. Not often, anyway. But sex isn't merely physical for me. There has to be emotional closeness, sharing. It's like giving a part of myself away, forever. If it were just for fun, it wouldn't really be worth the bother."

In the thick silence, she felt the intensity of his gaze. "You do not find lovemaking pleasurable?"

"Oh, it's fine." She didn't dare look at him. Didn't want to be tempted to disprove her theory by discovering that making love to him was an all-consuming experience. "But honestly, a warm hunk of double-fudge cake is every bit as enjoyable as a warm hunk."

"Hmm. I am thinking perhaps you need a better baker."

She thought of his kiss. "I think we'd better end this conversation."

"You trusted me enough to get into this bed with me. And I will not betray that particular trust." He sighed again. "Sleep in peace, Ariana."

That particular trust? What an odd turn of phrase. Sometimes she got the distinct impression Dante spoke in secret code. And not due to the language differences.

She stared at lamplight trembling on the ceiling. Lying quietly by Dante's side was torture. Yet the heat of his body, the sound of his even breathing was comforting. She had thought easy-going, educated professor Geoffrey Turner was the perfect man. She couldn't imagine him coping with the current circumstances.

Somehow, she had to endure sleeping beside Dante until they were rescued. What would happen if she dreamed about him again? Her resistance to him was weakening by the moment.

What would happen if *he* lost control?

Her worries chased themselves around like monkeys on crack. Finally, exhaustion hazed into a reluctant, fitful doze.

ARIANA DRIFTED AWAKE in an empty bed. It was early and over-cast. The fire's lively snap lured her to awareness, and a familiar, rich aroma teased her nostrils. She drowsily sniffed. "Do I smell *coffee?*"

"Ah, Sleeping Beauty awakens," Dante called. "I found coffee beans in the pantry."

Practically drooling, she clambered out of bed and hitched up her awry towel before staggering into the kitchen.

Clumsy with grogginess and haste, she tripped over Dante, who was leaning against the counter. His left hand was wrapped around a white stoneware mug, and he held the cup out as he caught her with his right hand. His arm slid around her waist to keep her from falling and he hauled her against his bare torso without spilling a drop.

"*Buon giorno,* Ariana. Where's the fire?" Laughter rumbled in his chest, right above where her nose was pressed to the expanse of bronzed muscle dusted with dark hair.

You're the fire and unfortunately, I'm the moth. "Good morning," she croaked. He smelled more mouthwatering than the coffee, like soap and warm, vital man. He must have bathed already, and again had a towel riding his lean hips. She jerked her gaze away from the danger zone. Thick, inky waves spilled over his forehead, and dark stubble defined the stubborn line of his jaw and framed his full lips. Wherever she looked, she got an eyeful of irresistible, primal male.

She gulped. "You can let go of me now."

He slid his arm from around her, then reached out to stroke her cheek. "You look...tousled. *Sei bellissima.*" The sleep-warmed timbre of his voice, the flare of heat in his eyes said he would have liked to have been the one who'd rumpled her.

If he didn't stop talking to her in that erotic voice and watching her as if he wanted to devour her, she was going to combust.

She stepped away and shakily poured a cup of coffee. In spite of herself, she inventoried him from gorgeous head to beguiling bare toes. "Why didn't you get dressed?" Embarrassment burned her face. "Aren't you...chilly?"

His dark-as-sin eyes were anything but cold. "The fire died after we went to bed and our clothes are still damp."

"Splendid." More torturous time together in practically nothing. "The drawbacks of hand-washing clothes. If it's not raining, we could hang them outside in the wind."

"It's not raining yet. Our underclothes are dry. So are our shoes, thanks to your clever idea of stuffing old newspapers inside to absorb moisture."

"Survival tricks from living through Philly's winters." As she savored the steaming coffee, she stared at Dante's lean abdomen, her gaze followed the enticing treasure trail of dusky hair leading from his navel down beneath his towel. If their underwear was dry, had he donned his black briefs, or was he still naked?

He cleared his throat. Caught ogling, she jumped and her flush burned hotter. "Um…what's for breakfast?" she asked.

His grin broadened, white and wicked in his stubbled pirate's face. "What are you hungry for?"

Nothing I can risk having. "Well, room service at the Waldorf is out."

He handed her a bowl of eggs. "Can you scramble these without incinerating the kitchen while I make bread?"

"Very funny." As long as he didn't kiss her again, she'd be fine.

He disappeared into the pantry and she stacked eggs on the counter, filled the bowl with water and then piled them back into the bowl.

Dante returned and paused to peer over her shoulder. "I know you said you are not much of a cook, but really, *cara…*"

She wrinkled her nose. "I'm absentminded, but I do have decent practical knowledge. Since these didn't come packed in a carton with a handy 'use by' date, the bad ones will float to the top." She pointed. "See?"

"Much better than finding out by smell." He playfully tugged a lock of her hair. "If I forget myself and start to sing, you will have rotten eggs to pelt me with.

His good humor warmed her as she placed the bad eggs in a separate bowl. "Someone woke up on the right side of the bed."

"I awoke with you in my bed." Surprised, she glanced at him and his roguish grin sizzled warmth to steam. "And we are still alive. In my job, I never know which day will be my last."

The cold slap of reality subdued her, and she returned to her task. "Why do you risk your life?"

She felt him tense. "Because I must."

"Are you in some sort of trouble? Do you owe money?" She cracked shells with more force than necessary. "No matter what it is, there's another way out. Goals can change. People can change. I'll help you."

"You said you have no money."

"But I have contacts. You're intelligent and capable. I can get you a legitimate job."

"You pity me? Wish to 'rehabilitate' me?" His hands settled on her shoulders, and she fumbled with an egg. He sounded puzzled. "Am I the next candidate for your crusade?"

"No." She accidentally crushed the egg, splintering the shell. "You're smart and kind…and determined and fearless enough to do *anything.* In many ways, I admire you."

Heart aching, she wiped her hands and turned to face him. She stared into his beautiful, astonished eyes, and the thought of the light being permanently extinguished from them tore her apart. "I don't want anything to happen to you."

His measuring gaze assessed her for long moments, and then he shrugged. "I will live the number of days I've been given, and no more." He picked up the bowl of rotten eggs and set them outside the back door. "I will bury these later."

"Dante." Blinking back tears, she bit her lip. "You're not a bad person. I see so much good in you. I don't know what's happened to you, but it's not too late to go in a different direction."

Tenderness wreathed his smile, and more encouraging, hope. "I don't intend to toss my life away."

"Just because you don't have family anymore doesn't mean your life isn't precious to—to…other people."

Watching her intently, he cupped her cheek in his hand. "What is it worth, I wonder?" Leashed hunger glinted in his dark gaze, and Ariana's heart leaped with anticipation as he lowered his head.

As soft as a sigh, his lips gently caressed hers. "You have a generous heart, *tesoro mio,*" he whispered. When she would have dropped everything and flung herself into his arms, he gently set her back from him. "Perhaps we will speak of this again."

He pivoted and began mixing the dough. "Now we must focus on survival."

Ariana forced her unsteady fingers to pick eggshells from

broken yolks. She worried about his fate after they escaped the island. She had family, friends, a job. What would happen to him?

She inhaled quivering breaths. He'd called her his treasure. And the reverent way he'd looked at her made her want to believe he saw her as worth more than money. That he would eventually talk options because he believed his life *was* worth starting over. Hope and happiness began to weave a tapestry of faith inside her.

She was getting through to him.

Perhaps she could influence him to change his mind and change his direction. Survive not just today or tomorrow, but live a long, healthy life.

Over breakfast, Dante outlined his plans to scout the area and build a signal fire. After they ate, he rose and went to the fire to check his boots. Humming, Ariana rinsed and stacked dishes in the sink.

"'Ode to Joy.' An interesting choice to wash dishes by." Dante appeared carrying a tan blanket. He was wearing dark wool socks, boots and the leather coat with his towel.

Her song broke off, and she choked back mirth. "If you want interesting, let's discuss that ensemble."

"It is cold out." He smirked. "If you laugh, I will be forced to shoot you."

"Neat trick without a gun, tough guy." Her laughter fought to escape, and she turned away. "I can't help it. You look like biker Tarzan."

"I'll be warm." Big, gentle hands draped the blanket around her. "And so will you." He brandished safety pins. "I found a sewing kit in the linen closet." He tucked the folds around her and pinned the blanket. Her head knew his touch wasn't meant to arouse, but her body received a sensual message.

When he finished, she was trembling. She pulled away and went to the fireplace to retrieve her deck shoes.

Outside, brisk wind buffeted steely clouds, and foamy gray waves crashed against the bluff's base. Chickens pecked in the courtyard. The birds hadn't ventured far today because the storm must be near. Ariana was careful not to betray where she'd hidden her iPod and notebook. She'd retrieve them when Dante was occupied.

She clutched the kerosene lamp he'd given her. The glass globe protected the flame. "What's the lamp for?"

He leaned the ax beside doors set into the ground next to the foundation. "We are going into the cellar, and I need my hands free." He pulled the handle, and rusty hinges shrieked in protest.

She peered at the stone staircase descending into blackness. "Cue the mask-wearing, chain-saw-wielding lunatic."

Dante hefted the ax over his shoulder and flashed her a lethal grin. "One cannot operate a chain saw without arms."

"*Grazie.* Lovely mental image." But she was comforted all the same. Dante wouldn't let anyone hurt her.

Holding the lamp aloft, she reluctantly trailed him down the stairs. The spooky stone enclosure was cool but dry.

Like a tomb.

A labyrinth of ghostly cobwebs entangled the ceiling beams, and she shivered. Power-tool-toting maniacs only existed in movies. Rodents and giant spiders, though…

She froze on the bottom step. "Um…an ax doesn't deter rats and spiders."

Dante turned. Lamplight glowed in his eyes as he offered her an encouraging smile. "I was down here when I checked out the cottage yesterday. It is pestilence free." He extended his left hand. "Come, *mia cara.* Let's see what riches we can discover."

Ariana refused to behave like a baby in front of him. As she walked toward him, a specter leaped from the shadows, and she yelped.

"Easy, Ariana," Dante soothed. "It is merely a mirror image."

She pressed a hand to her hammering heart. A large, cracked mirror leaned against the wall. The frame matched the bedroom bureau. She studied her disheveled reflection in dismay. How could Dante wake up on a deserted island looking as scrumptious as Eros, while she rivaled Medusa?

"Ariana?" Dante smiled. "Look, a taste of civilization."

She crossed the room and held up the lamp to examine wine bottles nestled inside a wooden rack. "All premium labels."

"*Va bene.*" Smiling, Dante set several bottles on a bench. He rifled nearby boxes. "Canning jars, useless. Playing cards, books, gramophone records...entertainment." He put that box beside the wine and then opened another. "Ah, clothing."

Ariana added extra kerosene, bottled water and matches to their stash. Dante parked the lamp at the foot of the staircase. He hefted the big box onto his shoulder, picked up the ax and ascended the stairs. Ariana followed with the lighter box of clothing.

They carried their burdens into the house. Ariana set hers on the table and dug into the box. "Someone has champagne taste." She lifted out several black ladies' suits. "Ooooh. Gianfranco Ferré. And a Fendi handbag!" She sighed. "This purse probably cost three grand!"

Dante leaned over her shoulder in that masculine way, making her feel both unsettled and protected. His superheated energy sent awareness prickling over her skin, and her nipples tightened.

She couldn't move away because she was trapped between his big body and the table. At least that's what she told herself.

Dante snorted. "Is there anything useful...other than over-priced orgasmic handbags?"

She elbowed him in the ribs. "So I'm a girl."

"*Sì.*" His smoky baritone tickled her ear, making her tremble. She would know his warm leather and spicy bay scent blind-folded. "I have noticed."

Ariana sucked in a steadying breath. "Here." She extracted a pair of women's black wool skinny leggings and two V-neck cashmere pullovers, one black one, one ivory.

"They are not my size."

She laughed. "There's more. Be patient."

"Patience is not one of my stronger virtues."

She unearthed a man's black-and-gray tweed sport coat, the same color as the glowering clouds outside, two pair of black dress slacks and a burgundy cashmere mock turtleneck sweater.

Dubious, she eyed the coat. "Far too narrow in the shoulders." Then she examined the pants. "The waist measurement might adjust, but the length is too short."

"Better than a towel. I'll let you have the washroom." He scooped up the sweater and slacks and strode into the bedroom.

She retrieved her underwear from in front of the fire and went into the bathroom. She put on the apricot satin strapless bra and matching panties. During her captivity, Dante had bought her underwear along with other clothes. The man's taste in undies was exquisite. Gossamer wisps of creamy satin and hand-embroidered lace in mouthwatering pastels. She didn't even want to contemplate how he'd known her perfect size.

The wool pants were *really* tight. She had to lie on the floor to zip them. She was a curvy woman with actual hips, unlike the current crop of emaciated actresses and models.

Ariana got up, struggled into the cream sweater, and then looked in the mirror. Holy cannoli. The clingy garment made her breasts jut out. But as Dante had stated, any clothes were better than a towel.

She took a minute to brush her wild mane of hair. Warmer, but feeling awfully exposed in the formfitting clothing, she emerged from the bathroom.

Dante fed several logs into the fire and then stood. Her breath snagged in her lungs. The silky cashmere hugged his broad shoulders and wide chest, delineating every muscle. The dark, rich red shade of aged claret perfectly complemented his olive complexion and black hair and teased golden highlights from his deep brown eyes. Her mouth watered with a sudden, fierce craving for wine and chocolates.

Her gaze drifted lower. His borrowed slacks were sized for a short, stout guy. They gaped at the waist, and the hem stopped at midcalf. She clapped a hand over her mouth. Dante didn't strike her as the type of man who appreciated being laughed at.

He looked down at himself, and then surprised her by laughing himself. "I look like a dimwitted schoolboy."

"If you were a girl, those pants would be called capris. Maybe you could start a new fashion trend."

His glance cruised over her. "You are a trendsetter, as well."

Flushing, she wrapped her arms around herself. "This outfit is cut for a sleeker figure."

Heated appreciation fired in his eyes. "I prefer a woman who doesn't resemble a signpost. I like your curves, Ariana."

How could he incite her hormones into a riot simply by looking at her?

After discovering the designer jackets wouldn't button over her breasts, Ariana donned the man's sport coat. She rolled up the sleeves as she and Dante went outside again.

The breeze smelled damp with imminent rain. Dante rescued the lamp from the cellar and shut the doors. Chickens squawked and flapped as she and Dante crossed the courtyard to explore the stone shed.

The door and shutters were the same cerulean blue as the cottage door. Dante passed her the lamp and preceded her inside. Shrouded silence hung in the gloom, and a horrible stench assaulted her nostrils. Eyes watering, she raised her arm to cover her nose with her sleeve. "Ugh, what died in here?"

"It didn't smell this way before." Dante's face was grim as he rounded a tool-littered workbench. He thrust out his hand to keep her back. "Put down the lamp and wait outside."

"Dante?" She caught sight of the tarp-draped object on the floor, and dread swelled in her throat. "What is *that?*"

CHAPTER NINE

DANTE BLOCKED Ariana's view. "Go."

"I'm…" She swallowed nausea. "If that's something…bad, I'm not leaving you to deal with it alone."

"You are not used to such things." He herded her toward the door. She dug in her heels, forced him to stop. "And you *are?*"

"Ariana." He gripped her shoulders, turned her around and propelled her onto the stoop. "Outside, *per favore.*"

He slammed the door, shutting her out. She leaned against the wall, flinching at the ghastly scraping noises. Denial tangled inside her. She didn't want to hear the calm confidence in Dante's voice. Didn't want to watch him nonchalantly handle what she suspected might be a corpse.

She pressed icy fingertips to her temples. Get a grip. Dante had proven he was a man who knew how to deal with a crisis.

The door opened, and the appalling stench oozed out. She pinched her nose and spun away as Dante's head appeared in the doorway. "I am bringing it outside. Do not look."

She cringed. "Then it *is* something dead?"

"*Sì.*" Amusement tinted his voice.

"What's so darned funny?"

"It's not as sinister as we suspected."

"What do you mean?" She glanced around to see him carrying a shovel heaped with the decaying remains of a huge rat. Gagging, she whirled back to face the shed.

"I told you not to look. Curiosity killed the cat, yes?"

"Apparently, nosiness isn't healthy for rats, either."

The shovel chopped into the ground, and she walked to the edge of the bluff while he buried the body. Ariana studied the leaden horizon and turbulent sea. "This isn't the cove where they first stranded us, right?"

"No, we hiked up from the other direction. Why?"

"Because there's crude steps cut into the rocks leading down to the beach."

"*Va bene.*" He appeared at her side. "That will make it easier to launch the boat."

"Boat?" Elation and regret churned inside her as she followed him into the shed. She wanted off the island. Yet that meant her interval with Dante was over. And she wasn't crazy about the idea of sailing into the unknown. Physically *or* emotionally.

She passed nets and fishing equipment hanging from pegs. "Where is it?"

He pulled the draped tarp aside with a flourish. "Here."

"That's not a boat." Spirits sinking, she stared at the tiny, dilapidated wooden vessel. "That's a sieve with oars."

"I will repair it."

She shot him an appalled glance. "Surely you don't expect us to sail the open sea in that death trap?"

"We barely have enough food to last a week." He shook his head. "Which is better, starvation or a chance at rescue?"

Sophie's choice. She looked out the window at the wild Mediterranean, then back at the rot-ridden rowboat and gulped. "We can fish. And there's bound to be wild greens, berries, mushrooms in the woods. Maybe even game."

Dante's sensual mouth firmed in the stubborn line she'd come to know well. "I am not a puppet to sit and wait for Megaera to fetch us." With a finger under her chin, he raised her gaze to his. "I will keep you safe. After all this time, everything we have been through, do you still mistrust me, Ariana?"

"No." Not with her physical safety. And the more time she spent with him, the more her trust grew.

"First things first." He sliced rope on the ax blade to tie into a makeshift belt for his pants. "If we can signal a passing ship, we will not need the boat."

She would pray for a passing ship. Hard. "Would you cut me one of those?" She measured with her hands. "About so big."

Another thing she appreciated about Dante—as a man of action, he didn't ask useless questions. She corralled her hair and used the rope to tie it into a high ponytail.

Disappointment grazed his sculpted features. "Your hair is truly your glory. I like it loose."

Her stomach did a happy little jig. "You may not think it's quite as attractive whooshing up in flames over a signal fire."

His palm settled at the small of her back as he escorted her out of the shed. "I never wish to cause you hurt."

Deeper, darker meaning lurked beneath the simple statement. She frowned. There he went, speaking in secret code again.

As she collected wood for the signal fires, he returned to the shed. She walked past the window and saw him stealthily searching the small enclosure, and realization clobbered her between the eyes.

Her steps faltered. There hadn't been a spider in the bedroom. Dante had been casing the cottage for her notebook and iPod. He'd been focused since the beginning on getting his hands on the useless-so-far information. Why? Wavering, she bit her lip. Maybe he *could* help her clear her father's name. She studied his strong, somber profile as he exited the cottage.

No. She trusted the cryptic man with her life, but wasn't quite ready to entrust him with the only thing left of her father…his reputation.

As he came back outside, Dante shrugged off his leather coat and shoved up the sweater sleeves, revealing brawny forearms. Following his instructions, Ariana helped him stack wooden pyres into triangular distress signals.

He arranged logs. "I'll get green branches, while you select gramophone records. The burning shellac will create black smoke, visible during daylight."

She took his coat inside and chose a few chipped records.

Dante set kerosene and matches beside the back door for easy access. If…no…*when* they saw a ship, they could run out and ignite the fires.

"Dante, we should bring up the mirror. A mirror flash can be seen for fifty miles." At his astonished expression, she shrugged. "I read it somewhere."

After he wrestled the mirror up the cellar stairs, he dragged the boat from the shed. Daylight exposed splintered boards and gaping holes. Fear slithered up her spine. The unreliable craft looked like a floating coffin.

Dante carried out planks and constructed a makeshift saw-horse from logs and boards. He grasped the hem of his sweater and peeled it over his head before he began to slice wood with the edge of the ax.

She sighed. "As much as I hate to contribute to the making of *Titanic, The Sequel,* we could bleed sap from the stand of pines and coat the hull."

His lightning grin flashed. "A watertight seal. Brilliant." He shot her a look of male appreciation. "I suppose you have read how this is done?"

"Nice to be proficient at something, even if it is trivia."

"You sell yourself short." His warm murmur sparked along her nerve endings. "You excel at more than trivia, *cara.*"

Whoa. She left him carving wooden spigots to find containers. Then she collected the spigots and hammer and strode to the pine grove surrounding the cottage.

"Do not stray out of my sight," Dante called.

The independent woman balked at his caveman attitude, but part of her was touched. And, okay, she got a little thrill from his protectiveness.

He worked doggedly on repairing the boat, trying to outpace the coming storm. Ariana returned to the cottage for food. Frowning, she perused the pantry's contents. Dante was right, their food supply was dangerously low. She brewed coffee, then dished up smoked fish and sandwiched chunks of aged goat cheese between leftover bread. Grapes served as "dessert."

She carried lunch outside, where Dante wolfed down the weird meal without complaint and swigged coffee while working.

He concentrated on the boat while she explored overgrown yellowing vegetation. At some time in the past, someone had planted a garden, and a few vegetables and herbs had self-propagated. She bent to glean what she could. The ocean thundered in the distance and the breeze sharpened as oily clouds loomed closer. The wind cut through the sport coat and sweater. Unlike Dante, she wasn't toiling hard enough to stay warm. Shivering, she rubbed her hands together.

He looked up from hammering and frowned. "Ariana, you should go indoors before you catch a chill."

She shook her head, amazed that he was still aware of her even when his attention was elsewhere. "I need to help you."

"I would like some water, *per favore*. Then you should stay inside."

He disappeared into the shed without waiting for her to protest, and she retrieved her iPod and notebook from a flowerpot of chrysanthemums on the back patio. A perfect hiding spot. Tough guy would never think to poke around in flowers.

Ariana took her things indoors, fetched Dante his water, and then returned to the cottage. She hung up his coat and hers. After stoking the fire, she lit lanterns and settled at the table with her iPod, paper and pencil.

Time passed quietly as she zeroed in on complex translations. A/K kept popping up. She chewed the end of her pencil. Athens? Her father had been in Athens two weeks before he was arrested. Why the *K* then? A key regarding artifacts bought or sold there?

This was tough without her dictionary. She rubbed her forehead. Maybe initials. But whose? They didn't fit with dealer names and addresses she'd decoded.

"Ariana." Dante's voice was deathly quiet.

She guiltily looked up to see him standing in the doorway. His body was taut, his face bleached. Mind whirling with questions, she rose halfway.

Then she saw the blood.

His right hand was clutching his left forearm, and blood streamed from between his fingers and dripped onto the flagstones. "I need your assistance."

"Dante!" Shock and panic erupted inside her. She surged to her feet and her chair clattered to the floor as she rushed to his side. "What happened?"

"The ax slipped."

"Sit down." She steered him to the nearest seat. He wasn't as steady as he wanted her to believe, staggering when she guided him into the chair. She sprinted to the kitchen, grabbed dish towels, raced back. "Keep the pressure on." Blood seeped through his fingers, through the towels.

She ran to the settee and gathered pillows. His breaths were choppy as she helped him raise his arm onto the pillows. "Prop your arm above the level of your heart."

He was breathing too hard, too fast. His face was white, his skin clammy. Signs of shock. "Do you feel faint?" She piled on more towels. "Sick to your stomach?"

"No."

"Hang in there." She dragged another chair close and propped up his feet, ran to the bedroom for a blanket to drape around his bare torso. "You're going to be all right."

"I know."

Her heartbeat stumbled. Was he *too* composed? Another sign of shock?

She gently held her fingers to the pulse point at his neck. Faster than normal, but strong and even. "The bleeding is slowing. Do I need to help apply pressure?"

"No." He pushed down harder on the towels, grimaced. "Ariana, you have to stitch it."

She blinked. "S-stitch it?" she repeated faintly.

"The cut went deep. A bandage will not stop the bleeding. It must be stitched.

"Oh, no." She backed up.

"Ariana." His voice was still lethally calm. "Do you wish me to bleed to death?"

Cold disbelief chilled her. "What kind of crazy question is that?"

"Get the sewing kit," he said patiently.

Even as her mind shrieked in denial, she stumbled to the bathroom and collected the sewing kit, peroxide and first-aid kit.

She shoved her notebook and iPod to the floor and dumped the supplies on the table. There was a small package of ibuprofen inside the first-aid kit. Dante inclined his head toward the kitchen. "The wine, *per favore.*"

"I have peroxide to sterilize the wound."

He barked out a ragged laugh. "The wine is going on the inside."

Ariana stood in the kitchen and stared dazedly at the bottles. Red or white with painkillers? She shook her head. She was losing it.

She snatched up a bottle of red and brought it to Dante. Her trembling hands fumbled with the corkscrew. "The cork won't come out."

Dante took the bottle and smashed the neck against the table, breaking the top off. "Problem solved."

"What about glass splinters?"

"*If* any got into the bottle, they will sink to the bottom."

"Save me from tough guys," she muttered. She poured a full wineglass and fed him four ibuprofen tablets. He was a big man, and considering he was about to suffer amateur surgery hour, he'd need the extra boost.

He drained the wine and she poured him a second glass, then a third. He inclined his head. "Do it."

Stiff with fright, she gingerly raised the wad of towels to reveal a gaping slice. She gasped. "That must hurt something awful."

He laughed again. "I recommend you don't take up nursing."

"Believe me, not in the plan." She swallowed the sickness welling in her throat and attempted to thread the needle.

Dante squared his shoulders. "Pretend you're hemming a skirt."

"Probably not the best time to inform you that between cooking and sewing, I nearly flunked Home Ec." She swallowed again. "I sewed a blouse with one sleeve inside out."

His lips twitched. "Just don't attach my arm inside out."

Ariana sterilized the needle in the lamp flame. Dante eased his arm from the pillows to the table. She uncovered the wound again, uncapped the peroxide. "I'm afraid this is going to sting like liquid fire."

"It must be done."

She tipped the bottle, and the antiseptic sizzled in the cut. Dante went rigid, silently clenched his jaw.

Her chest tightened as she picked up the needle and bent over his arm. She froze, hands shaking violently. The thought of stabbing the needle into his torn flesh iced her blood. "I don't think I can."

"I will be all right, Ariana. I'm not afraid of pain."

"I am." Clammy fear slicked her palms. Her stomach jittered. "But I'd rather be in pain than hurt you."

"Look at me, *tesoro mio*." His gaze embraced hers. The faith in his eyes, the confidence on his face arrowed into her heart. "You will do fine. I have complete trust in you." Eyes locked on hers, he smiled. The world trembled, shifted on its axis. In that heart-shaking instant, she knew she would—she *could*—do anything for him.

Tears threatened to burst free. "How wrong is this? The patient is comforting the nurse." She picked up the glass of wine and slugged it back. No time to indulge in fear. No time to fall apart. Dante needed her, and she would come through for him.

"Okay." She steeled herself. "Ready?"

Dante nodded, and she forced her fingers to steady, forced herself to thrust the needle cleanly into his arm.

He jerked, hissed in air through gritted teeth. When she faltered, he briefly placed his uninjured hand over hers. "Continue. Do it quickly."

Just get it over with. Don't mess around with tentative jabs and hurt him even more. She blanked her mind and made herself sew stitch after stitch.

Dante sat silently. As she continued her dreadful task, sweat glistened on his skin. Perspiration beaded his forehead and upper lip. His good hand gripped the edge of the table until his knuckles turned white, but he held himself as steady as stone. She couldn't imagine the amount of self-discipline it took to sit immobile while she tortured him.

Finally, she cut the thread and dropped the needle. She poured peroxide over his arm again, then slathered the cut with antibiotic ointment and bandaged it.

"Done." She looked at Dante's grim, pale face and taut jaw.

He released a slow breath, and the tension drained from his body. "Not so terrible."

"Sure, compared to root canal without Novocain."

He smiled at her and poured the last of the wine into the glass. "You did an excellent job."

"Glad you think so. Do you want to sit by the fire?" She hovered while he moved to the settee, but he seemed steady on his feet.

He sipped the ruby wine and color returned to his face. She touched his warm, bristled cheek. "You okay?"

"*Sì.*" He patted the cushions. "Sit with me."

"In a minute. I…need a minute."

Ariana stumbled into the bathroom, where she leaned against the closed door and fought a shaking, sweating battle with nausea. Her knees went weak, and she slid down to sit on the cold tiles. She pressed her forehead to her knees. *Don't give in.*

But suppressed fear and pain hit her with a wave of dizziness. Her willpower couldn't squelch the sickness, and she finally crawled to the commode and surrendered.

After long, beastly moments of misery, she felt Dante's warm hand stroke her back. "Easy, *tesoro.*"

She moaned. "Oh, *no.* What are you doing up?"

"Just breathe." He went to the sink. Water gurgled from the

faucet, and then a cold wet washcloth settled on her nape. "Relax, it is all over. Take deep breaths."

"I'm fine." She carefully stood. While she'd been wallowing in weakness, he'd dressed himself in his own clothes. She wiped her face with the washcloth. "Please go away."

He took the cloth and handed her a toothbrush piled with toothpaste. "That is not happening."

"You have to be sore." Perilously close to tears again, she turned her back and brushed her teeth, then soothed her parched throat with cool, minty mouthwash. The only thing holding her together was determination not to further disgrace herself. "*Please,* sit down."

"You took care of me." He pulled her into his embrace. "Now let me take care of you."

Waves of cold shame slapped her. He'd sat stoic while she'd sewn him up, and *she* was tossing her cookies. She trembled, fighting to regain control. "It wasn't the blood or stitching that got to me." The words caught on a half sob. "I hated hurting you."

"I know." He smoothed a gentle hand over her hair. "But sometimes, you have to do what is best for a person in the long run, even if it hurts them."

She looked up at his face. She didn't know who Dante was. And yet, on a deep, primitive level, she knew the real man inside. He was intelligent, kind and held firmly to his own code of honor. Understanding staggered her.

She cared about him. Far more deeply than she'd cared for anyone, ever.

How, why…her intense feelings made no sense. But she had no say. No choice. No matter how hard she fought it, it was meant to be.

She slid her arms around his neck. She had played by the rules all her life. Played it safe. She'd still gotten hurt. Still ended up empty and alone.

Ariana stood on tiptoe and touched her mouth to his. She

tasted wine and dark, heady desire. For the first time ever, she tossed aside logic. Didn't care about reason.

Some things were worth the pain.

CHAPTER TEN

As ARIANA SANK into the warm haven of Dante's mouth, his fingers tangled in her hair and he took the kiss deeper. He groaned low in his throat, a fierce, male growl of pleasure and pain.

Breathless, she eased back from his taut body. "Sorry, did I jar your arm?"

"My arm is not the part of me causing discomfort." His breathing was as frayed as hers. With a wry smile, he cupped her face in unsteady hands. "This is wrong."

She frowned in confusion. "Why?"

"You have just experienced a difficult ordeal."

"Me? You were the one holding solid as a rock under my shaky needle."

"You are upset, your actions driven by emotion."

Darned straight, but she was shell-shocked from the emotional bombshell of how much she truly cared for him. "Rational thought is vastly overrated. Been there, done that, have nothing to show for it but regrets."

Enigmatic shadows concealed the emotion in his dark eyes. "Further regret is what I wish to prevent."

"More doublespeak." She rested her hand on his chest, where his heartbeat hammered beneath her palm. She wasn't the only one experiencing tumultuous feelings. "Let's quit dancing around and put it out there."

His mouth curved in a crooked grin. "My desire for you is no secret." He raised her hand to his lips. "Come, sit by the fire with me. In one hour, if you ask again, I will not refuse."

For once, she ached to indulge her impulses, and *he* was cautious? Her glance wandered over Dante's tight shirt, and then lower to the straining fly of his jeans. Heat blossomed in her belly.

His chest rose and fell with rapid breaths. "Keep looking at me like that at your own risk, *cara*."

Consequences. Every action brought repercussions. Every choice would cost her. And him.

Though he disguised his pain, he was favoring his left arm. A clutch of remorse tightened her chest. Since when had she grown so inconsiderate as to put her wants ahead of Dante's welfare?

She edged past him, through the doorway. His hand on her back vibrated with the same tension arcing along her nerve endings.

She perched on the settee beside him, but couldn't keep still. Her fingers drummed, her foot tapped. Awareness of Dante sang in her heart, a libretto both joyful and sad. Would the ending to their saga be happy? Or tragic? Perhaps better not to know.

Ariana glanced out the window, startled to see darkness crowding the pane. "What time is it?"

His husky chuckles loosened the constriction inside her, flooded her with warmth. "It has not been an hour yet."

"Wise guy." She wrinkled her nose. "It seems early to be so dark."

He glanced at his watch. "It's a quarter past seven."

"Are you hungry?"

"I could eat."

She headed for the kitchen, relieved to have a task. Without the stress of Dante injured and bleeding, she was able to uncork a bottle of white wine. Ariana poured a glass to soothe her stomach and nerves and went out to refill Dante's.

He was leaning back on the sofa, eyes closed. Good, he should rest.

She tried not to dwell on what would have happened if he hadn't hit the brakes when she'd propositioned him. She didn't merely desire a hot affair. She craved an emotional connection with Dante. Needed to know what made him tick. How he thought. What he felt.

He was still guarded around her. Wasn't yet ready to share the mysteries hidden inside his heart.

Ariana sighed. Maybe not ever.

She completed the grisly chore of mopping up his blood, and then retrieved her notebook and iPod from beneath the table. Dante wasn't the only one not talking. Though she'd come to a stunning realization about her feelings for him, she still clung to her secrets. Harbored uncertainty.

Their clothing was finally dry, and she brought her cargo pants and shirt into the bathroom. Tucking her notebook and iPod safely into her hip pocket was small solace.

She tiptoed past Dante, into the kitchen. She chopped a salad of wild greens from the garden. Boiled eggs, olives and crumbled cheese went on top. A dressing of olive oil and vinegar accented with herbs made her feel quite accomplished.

Dante's sinfully long eyelashes drifted up as she approached with the plates. "You changed clothes."

"Stop looking disappointed. I like being able to breathe." She inclined her head. "Dinner is served."

He smiled. "Looks delicious."

"Thanks for not complaining about my culinary skills."

"When you have gone without, you do not complain about food."

"Have you often been hungry, Dante?"

"*Sì.*" He slowly straightened. "When I was young."

"After losing your parents, that must have been traumatic." She sat beside him, passed his plate. "Would it help to talk about it?"

He propped his bandaged arm stiffly on his thigh as he accepted his food. "I have never seen the point in rehashing the past."

"Keeping your emotions bottled up isn't healthy." She touched his hand before releasing his plate. "I'm a good listener."

He simply ate doggedly, as if he wasn't hungry but knew he needed sustenance.

She picked at her salad and watched him wrestle with the decision. Knew when the tension eased from his broad shoulders and he set his empty plate aside that he'd made his peace.

He inhaled. "Zia Ines worked like a dog, and we were barely making it when she got sick. She bartered away her few family heirlooms, but the antique dealer cheated her. We were left destitute." Dante lowered his glance to his injured arm. "She needed food. Medicine. I was twelve. And desperate."

Her throat stung with empathy, making eating impossible. "That's when you first got involved with criminal activity."

"*Sì*. I hustled a job gutting fish at the market, but it did not pay much. And I could not attend school." He hesitated, then shrugged. "I wanted something better. Wanted more than to spend every waking hour of my life eking out a miserable existence. I started as a pickpocket. Then the Camorra offered me a great deal of money to run a few errands."

No. She gripped her plate. "You work for the Camorra?"

"Not anymore." He stared into the fire. "I don't condone the way they operate, nor do I like it. However, at times, I am forced to deal with them."

"I see. You're independent now." A trickle of relief diluted her anxiety. "Thank you for being honest with me."

"Do not thank me—" His breathing was jagged. "You aren't shocked to hear these things?"

"After what happened to my father, I don't trust the cops any more than I do the criminals."

He slowly turned his head and looked at her. The grief in his eyes staggered her. "There is much more than you know. Things I cannot say."

"I realize that." She abandoned her plate. "I've never suffered hunger or deprivation. I have no right to judge." She covered his uninjured hand with hers. "You had to survive."

Wonder washed sorrow from his face. "You don't condemn me."

"You're a good man, Dante." She squeezed his fingers. "I haven't been poor, but I understand what it's like to have your back to the wall. I know about feeling desperate to help your loved ones."

"Because of your father."

"Yes." Taut lines around his mouth told her he was repressing both physical and emotional suffering. Dante understood her drive to clear her father's name because he, too, had been hurt. Her heart ached for both the hungry boy he had been and the man enduring quiet pain. "I'm sorry you and your aunt had such a rough time."

"*Destino.* It is the way of life. Things do not change by wishing them to be different."

Apprehension niggled. "I get the impression that what you're not saying is more important than your words."

"You are perceptive." His watchful eyes studied her, much as he might appraise a painting or a sculpture to assess authenticity. "When you are unsure—and the doubts will come, *bella*—listen to your heart. It speaks the truth." He turned his hand palm to palm with hers and held on tightly. "Look with your soul-sight. *Intuito.* What do you call it…intuition. It will lead you to do what is right. Promise me."

He was trembling, and cold fear rolled over her. "Dante, what are you planning?"

"Promise, Ariana." His low voice vibrated with intensity.

"All right, I promise."

"*Grazie.* You are a woman of your word." His thumb stroked her hand. "Now I ask you to be honest with me."

Apprehension surged back. "I'll try my best."

"How far will you go to protect your father's name?"

She stared at their linked fingers. His hand was so large, hers fit completely into his palm. She knew from experience his hands were capable of shattering tenderness. And shattering violence. Could she say the same about hers? "Megaera asked me that question."

"And your reply?"

Her glance jerked upward to the fierce intent on his face. "Are you asking if I'd break the law?"

A muscle ticked in his jaw. "Would you?"

She couldn't be sure. And that scared her more than any darkness she'd confronted in him. At least he was honest about his choices. "Would you judge me?"

"The wrong side of the law is not a life I would choose for anyone." Compassion glinted in his gaze. "I would not judge you, *mia cara*. I would bleed for you."

Her heart turned over. "I wouldn't ask you to. Don't want you to. It's my choice."

She carried plates to the kitchen. The wind slapped the cottage, whispered dark warnings. Impending doom chilled her with foreboding, and she hurried back to huddle near the flames. She turned to study Dante. "How are you feeling?"

His eyes were weary, his mouth drawn. "I am fine."

"You're beat. And hurting. You should go to bed." When his sharp glance snagged hers, she smiled ruefully. "Alone."

"So, you have made your decision." He got up and walked into the bathroom. After she heard him climb into bed, she brought him two more ibuprofen with a glass of water. He thanked her, and she felt his gaze linger on her as she left.

She washed dishes and cleaned the kitchen. Then she curled on the settee in front of the fireplace where she could see Dante sleeping in the next room in case he needed her.

Ariana decoded files for several hours, growing increasingly troubled. The Greek culture minister's name popped up. Derek had done business with him for years…but the phone number and address weren't the official ones. She also found confusing discrepancies in inventory and sales.

Misgivings assailed her. What if she was wrong? What if her investigation proved her father guilty? No one would know. She wouldn't have to turn him in. Her fingers crumpled the page. *No*. He was *innocent*. Her glance shot to the slumbering Dante. And until she had the evidence, she would keep her secrets.

When the letters blurred, she gave up. She carried a lamp into the bedroom and set it on the nightstand. Fully clothed, she eased into bed beside Dante. He stirred, rolled on his side toward her. She studied his sleeping face, warmed by lamplight. His color was good, his breathing steady. Full, dark lashes rested on his cheeks and his sensual lips were slightly parted. Free from tension, pain and his usual fierce expression, he looked younger. Vulnerable.

Tenderness softened her heart. She didn't believe he was a hard-core criminal, any more than she believed her father was a smuggler. Circumstances had put Dante in a difficult position, but he had the smarts and resolve to change his life. Whether pain, wine, or the combination had loosened him up, he'd finally opened a part of himself to her. Or maybe he'd finally begun to trust her.

"*Sogni d'oro,*" she whispered. They hadn't shared physical intimacy, but he'd given her the most valuable gift of all: emotional intimacy.

She smiled at Dante sleeping peacefully beside her. *Golden dreams.* It was a start.

ARIANA AWOKE EARLY. Her sleeping Roman god looked fine. Okay, he looked scrumptious. Pleased that he showed no signs of a fevered flush or rapid respiration, she slipped out of bed. She lit the fire and brewed a pot of coffee before she heard him moving around.

He prowled into the kitchen barefoot, a stubbled outlaw wearing nothing but jeans. His hair was mussed, his caramel espresso eyes languid with sleep. Acres of hard muscle rippled as he yawned and stretched. "*Buon giorno.* I missed seeing you when I awoke."

"How's your arm?"

"Stiff, but not enough to hinder me." He rotated his shoulder, flexed his forearm. "What is left for breakfast?

They consumed a hasty breakfast of canned peaches and plain oatmeal with honey for sweetener. Dante murmured appreciation as he spooned up his cereal. "I like this wild honey. It tastes like summer meadows and sunshine."

"What a beautiful description."

He actually flushed before returning his concentration to his cereal. Her tough guy didn't often show his sensitive side, though she'd caught intriguing glimpses before. He hadn't won her heart with charm and sonnets, but selflessness and courage. As she'd learned the hard way, sometimes charm could be faked.

But courage was proven under fire.

He hastily consumed his breakfast, telling her they were running out of time. He could feel the storm brewing and vowed to finish the boat this morning. Personally, she'd be fine if *Titanic II* never got done. Call her a coward, but she was leery about tackling the ocean in such a wreck.

The still air hung ominously in the courtyard, and tasted heavy with dampness. Gray-green clouds bruised the sky, and the ocean roared in restless anticipation. The goat and chickens huddled around the shed.

Dante had made good progress before he'd sliced his arm. They finished the hull repair and then slathered the bottom and sides of the boat with pitch. Her anxiety built with each brushstroke of the pungent sap, but Ariana kept her misgivings quiet. Dante knew how she felt, and she counted on him not to recklessly endanger her life.

He pondered the horizon for several moments after they'd completed the task. "I think the weather will hold long enough for us to reconnoiter the beach." He retrieved two fishing poles from inside the shed and rigged them with lines. "*And* secure more food." When he started to dig grubs from beneath a rotted log, she fled to the house to pack a lunch.

Worry weighted her shoulders as they descended the slope to the cove. The closer down the beach she trudged to the churning water, the more rampant her fear. How would Dante navigate to civilization? What if they got lost and died in an agony of thirst and starvation? Or another storm hit and swamped the boat? She shuddered. She'd be a huge liability to Dante, and he could die attempting to save her.

"My audacious librarian is too quiet." He propped the poles against a boulder and shrugged off the pack containing the food.

"And you're complaining?"

He caught her hand, tugged her close. "You are tormented by doubts."

She ducked her chin. "I'm scared."

"Yet I know you will step into the boat when the time comes. That is true courage." He wrapped his arms around her in a comforting hug. "Release your worries for now. Concentrate on catching our dinner."

"Dinner it is." She squared her shoulders. *Destino.* Worrying wouldn't help.

He impaled a fat, slimy grub on his hook, and she nearly lost her breakfast. "I don't think so." Clutching her pole, she backed away. "I'm not exactly a frontier gal."

"Cosa?" He chuckled. "I hadn't noticed."

"I'll try this, instead." She tore off a small piece of tinfoil she'd used to wrap their lunch and twisted it around her hook. "Fish like shiny things."

He grinned. *"Va bene.* We'll see how it works in practical application."

"Dare to put your money where your ego is, tough guy?"

"A wager?" His grin went wide and wicked. "How certain are you?"

She couldn't help but return his smile. "I'm not sure I like that evil glint in your eye, but I'm game. Are you willing to pull dish duty for the rest of our stay?"

"Non c'è problema." Long legs spread, he tilted his head and tucked his thumbs in his pockets. "And you, *bella?* Do you dare pay with a kiss?"

Well, she'd strolled into that trap. Her dismayed gaze shifted to his mouth, and her breath jammed. "I'd prefer something less costly."

His lips curled into a seductive smile. "Whose ego is bankrupt now?"

That smile and the knowing glimmer in his eyes fired her competitive streak. He thought she would back down? Wrong. She planted her hands on her hips. "Bring it on, *signore.*"

His confident laugh made her snatch up her pole and stride to the surf's edge. Ariana cast her hook into the foamy waves and scowled. He'd known exactly what he was doing. She'd snapped at his bait faster than a hungry sea bass, and he'd reeled her in.

He sauntered up beside her and flipped his hook into the water. "You can only be irritated if you think you will lose."

His teasing was impossible to ignore, his rare playful mood contagious. Over the next few hours, they fished—without luck—snacked on the last of the smoked pork and crackers and talked.

Dante ramped up his considerable charisma. If he was on a mission to boost her spirits, it worked. She delightedly discovered his childhood hadn't been all dreary, and he amused her with boyhood misadventures.

She was fascinated by the changing facets of Dante's personality. The enigmatic, guarded man she'd first met was the part of him that kept him alive when he worked in the shadows. But now he let her past his defenses, let her inside and showed her the humor, compassion and integrity in his heart.

And made her care about him all the more.

Neither caught a fish, in spite of their competitive rivalry. Dante theorized the sea creatures had gone deep to ride out the coming storm.

So, no fresh seafood dinner. She was relieved she wouldn't have to kiss him. At least that's what she convinced herself as she pulled in her line.

As Dante reeled in his line for the final time, it jerked. "I snagged one!"

She watched him reel in a small flopping fish and snorted. "A little minnow hardly counts."

He gravely examined his tiny catch. "I have heard size does not matter."

His overly innocent countenance made her laugh. She'd bet a *thousand* kisses he'd never had that said to him. "Converting centimeters to inches loses something in translation."

"It's enough to win." Grinning, he squatted and released his wriggling captive back into the ocean, then washed his hands.

"I'm not a welsher." She steeled herself. "You won, I pay."

His warm glance stroked over her. "Should I be insulted that you appear less than enthusiastic?" He chuckled. "I didn't say I required immediate payment." He gathered up their poles and the pack and strode toward the path.

She followed. *Wonderful.* Along with the approaching storm, she had a kiss hanging over her head. Her pulse sped. Kissing Dante on impulse was vastly different from anticipating his embrace.

He waited for her at the base of the hill and clasped her hand in his as they toiled up the incline. No matter how roughly the wind buffeted her, his touch made her feel safe. Anchored.

Almost to the top, she stopped to catch her breath and looked up at Dante. He'd set down the poles and pack and stood above her at the crest of the bluff, staring out to sea. The wind tugged at his dark locks and fanned out his long coat. A crack of lightning speared the horizon, chiseled his masculine profile in seductive shadow. Thunder rumbled, and he raised his face to the storm-clad sky, exposing the strong column of his throat. He spread his arms and leaned into the lashing wind as if he could harness the storm and ride it to freedom. Powerful and confident, Zeus calling down thunder and lightning.

Ariana's heartbeat pounded in her ears, and she forgot to breathe. He'd sprung from this untamed land. Wild and dangerous, he would hate being caged. Chafe against restraints. She tried to picture her dangerous outlaw in a suit, parked in an office or carpooling little girls to ballet practice—and failed wretchedly. Settling down would bore him into misery.

For him, his job wasn't only about money. Attempting to change him could destroy the man he was.

Dante looked down at her and gave her a smile of pure joy. He loved the risk. Realization slammed her, and pain exploded inside her, sending her reeling.

And she loved *him.*

His eyes glowed with fierce pleasure as he reached out his big hand to pull her into his realm. To experience the storm from his perspective.

Her heart lodged in her throat and she swallowed around the ache. She wavered, hesitant to leave the sheltered hillside and step into the gale's sharp teeth. The Fates had brought them together. To help each other. And possibly hurt each other.

So be it.

She placed her palm in his, and he lifted her up to stand at his side. His arm slid around her waist, tucked her close, and he grinned at the furious battle boiling toward them over the waves. "Magnificent, yes?"

"Yes," she whispered. And far beyond her control.

Utterly terrifying.

They stood together and embraced the storm. And instead of destruction, Ariana saw artistry. She cast aside fear and thrilled in the power of the wind and thunder and flashing lighting.

She lifted her face to the heavens, and raindrops sprinkled her skin with cool, glittering diamonds. Here was beauty. Excitement. An unstoppable force under the control of a spirit mightier than any mere human's.

Sparkling vitality surged through her, making her giddy. She laughed, reveling in the bliss of relinquishing control. She'd never felt more aware. More alive.

Dante turned his head and their eyes locked. His umber gaze burned brilliant with passion. She understood his need to challenge the elements. His exhilaration at defying life and death and destiny.

His desire to tempt the Fates.

She had always found security in planning ahead, foreseeing every detail. She didn't know if they would have a future. But they had today. Today was enough.

His arm tightened, swung her to face him. He lowered his head, and she read his intent to kiss her in his eyes. And surged up to meet him.

If she was going to get burned, she would at least savor the memory of one wild dance in the flames.

Dante tasted of rain…and his kiss devoured her. He drank from her mouth, consumed her. Yet he gave back more, filled her with sensation, emotions.

She needed him in a way that she had never needed anyone.

He thrust his fingers into her hair, pulled her closer and immersed her in the kiss. She wrapped her arms around his neck, yearning to meld with his hard body. A vibrating cannonade of thunder echoed the thudding of his heartbeat.

He kissed her until she was breathless and trembling. His soft lips cruised her jaw, and she tipped her head back, offering her neck. He claimed the sensitive spot just beneath her ear, then roved downward to nip at the taut cord where her neck met her shoulder. Blissful shivers sped over her skin.

Dante's fingertips feathered over her face, followed the line of her throat, then fisted in the collar of the sport coat and yanked it down her arms. He flung the coat aside, tugged her sweater up and stripped it off her. Her camisole followed, leaving her in her bra. *"Sei bella,"* he breathed.

You are beautiful. Awed desire flared in his eyes, and scrambled her pulse, flooded her with warmth.

He captured her mouth in another demanding kiss even as he shrugged out of his coat and it dropped to the ground. As wild and powerful as the storm crashing over them, he was no timid suitor. But she wasn't afraid. She welcomed the tempest. Gloried in it.

Ariana thrust her hands beneath Dante's T-shirt and slid her palms from his stomach to his chest, loving the play of heated skin and hard muscles flexing beneath her touch. She teased his flat nipples, thrilled when he hissed in a breath.

She grasped the hem of his T-shirt and peeled it up. The shirt followed his coat to the ground, and she returned his smile. *"Sei bello."*

Dante gave a husky laugh. His hands raced up her spine, tossed aside her bra. Her nipples grazed his bare chest, slick and wet with rain, and tingles zipped through her. He groaned. *"Dio, mi fai impazzire."*

"Oh!" She gasped when he dipped his head and his warm tongue licked a raindrop from her nipple. He was making her crazy, too.

Lightning blazed in the sky and in her belly as he bowed her over his arm and suckled hard, one nipple, then the other. Pleasure spiraled inside her, every cell taut and trembling.

She needed him so badly she ached with it. Ariana moaned. She was close…already. So fast. So close.

When she was quaking, teetering, when blinding need screamed inside her for release, he bent and kissed her stomach.

"Hurry, Dante," she panted. "I need you."

"And I, you." Breathing hard and fast, he unbuttoned her pants, shoved them down her hips. She kicked off her shoes, and he yanked her free of her pants. He swept her panties down and off, and she stood naked before him.

"Tesoro." He went to his knees as if to worship her. Looked up at her as if she were his most cherished possession. *"Ti adoro."* His fingertips reverently traced the damp curves of her body from shoulders to hip. He cupped her bottom in his hands, drew her toward him and then his mouth closed over her in the most intimate kiss of all.

Cool rain sluiced her skin while Dante's hot mouth ignited a molten inferno inside her. Her fingers tangled in his hair, and she threw her head back, trusting him to anchor her body while her spirit soared. His silky tongue drove her higher and higher. Lightning sizzled, thunder exploded.

Ariana's heart galloped, her body quivered. Gasping for breath, she would have fallen if Dante hadn't held her, taut and shaking on the edge of forever.

Then he pushed her over.

She flung out her arms, let go…and tumbled into ecstasy. Wave after wave of white-hot pleasure crested over her, and her knees crumpled.

Dante's strong arms supported her, bore her down to lie on his coat. "Ariana." Her name was a whisper of adoration as he rose over her, unzipped his pants. "Look at me." Cradling her face in his hands, he held her gaze and thrust into her.

Their connection was instantaneous, electric. The glide of heat sent a thousand aftershocks sparkling through her. He filled every empty place inside her body and her heart, and she uttered a cry, arched against him.

Dante's big body shook. He groaned. "I am undone."

His breathing ragged, he drove into her, murmuring to her in a soft, broken mixture of English and Italian. "Give me everything, Ariana. Let me give to you."

Bonded body to body, heart to heart, soul to soul, she looked into his eyes…and saw love.

Raindrops misted her face, mingled with scalding tears of joy. Sobbing for breath, clinging to his gaze, she let him take her up again.

This time when she leaped, she cried out his name. And he flew with her.

CHAPTER ELEVEN

SHELTERED BENEATH DANTE, Ariana trembled in the afterglow of pleasure, wreathed in bliss. The storm raged around them. The warmth of her tumultuous lover's rapid breaths tingled in her ear. The thudding of his pounding heart sang to hers.

He groaned and raised his head to look at her. "Are you cold?"

Ariana grinned at his dazed expression. She'd put that stunned look on his handsome face. She had a feeling she appeared pretty bedazzled herself. "There's steam rolling off us."

"Un momento." His unsteady chuckle was hoarse as he dropped his head back into the curve of her neck and snuggled in. "I do not think I can walk at the moment."

Their joined body heat quickly dissipated in the chilly rain, and he gently withdrew from her and zipped up. Amusement tickled her. While she was buck naked, Dante hadn't wasted the time to remove his jeans...or his boots.

He gathered their scattered clothes, then scooped her up coat and all and carried her toward the cottage.

When she started to shiver, he scowled. "I—"

She clapped her hand over his mouth. "If you apologize for what just happened, I'm seriously going to hurt you."

His obsidian gaze grew somber.

Regrets, so soon?

"I am not sorry for making love to you. Merely the time and place I chose."

"We didn't choose the time and place. It chose us."

"In either case, what's done is done." As her teeth began to chatter, he hugged her close and broke into a jog. "But I do not want you to catch a chill."

He kicked open the door, swept her inside the house and into the bathroom. He deposited her in the tub, stoppered the drain and cranked on steaming water. "This will warm you."

She leaned back, luxuriating in hot silky water flowing over her cold skin. Dante's touch had awoken every sensual nerve and tender emotion. Loving him had brought her to life.

While the tub filled, he tugged off his boots and prowled in damp jeans and bare feet, carrying in a lantern and hanging their clothes beside the fire.

"Dante," she called, "would you please hand me the soap?"

"Of course." He retrieved it from the sink, leaned over and held it out.

"Thanks." She grabbed his wrist and yanked him into the huge bathtub with her.

Hot water geysered, and he surfaced, sputtering. ".What the—"

She laughed. "You looked cold, too."

"I'm sitting in the bath wearing my pants," he muttered.

"Well, I know you only take them off when they're wet." He slanted her a wry glance, and she wiped her dripping face. "I have something important to tell you."

Dante went rigid, his gaze wary. He sat up and shoved his wet hair back. "I am listening."

Pain hitched in her chest, but she ignored it. She would get serious and think about repercussions later. "You, Signor Sexy, are yummier than any chocolate fudge cake."

His laughter shook the tub. Erotic intent gleamed in his eyes as he crawled up her body. "Then you won't mind a second helping."

After a tempestuous, breathtaking bath, Ariana accepted Dante's helping hand out of the tub. She was none too steady on her feet. She laughed at the water covering the tile floor. "At least this time I managed to get you out of your jeans, but you made everything sopping wet."

He gave her the innocent face. "*I* was not splashing and screaming."

She wrapped her tingling body in a towel. "I don't scream." When his eyes glinted, she relented. "Okay, maybe on special occasions. I might let you wager on that later." She rose on tiptoe and planted a kiss on his soft lips. "You were quite…ah… innovative."

His grin widened as he draped a towel around his lean hips. "*Sì*. Being in the water doesn't normally lend itself to—" Shock blanched his face. He flung out his hands and began to pace the bathroom, castigating himself in furious Italian.

"Dante?" She couldn't keep up with the turbulent swearing. "Slow down! What—"

"I cannot believe it." Temper blazed in his eyes. "I am *un idiot*," he fumed. "I only thought about having you. Not protecting you."

Her stomach bottomed out. If either of them had stopped to think, they wouldn't have made love at all. "Neither did I."

"I have *never*—" He swore again. "How could I forget?"

"Whoa. Cancel the reservations for the guilt trip." She grabbed his arm and swung him around. "I use a monthly patch, and I applied a new one right before you kidnapped me." She did a quick calculation. "We're probably fine."

"*Probably?*" His eyes narrowed.

Oddly, the idea of having Dante's baby didn't upset her. She filed the conundrum to her growing "ponder later" list. "It's a little late to worry about locking the stable door after the stallion has run amok."

He shot her an enigmatic look. He fought it, but his lips twitched. Then he snickered, and finally, he gave a crack of laughter. "Stallion?"

She patted his forearm. "Let's put a dry bandage on your stitches and go rustle up dinner."

Inside the pantry, she scanned barren shelves. "Not much. Canned tomatoes, dried pasta, cheese and herbs from the garden."

He peered over her shoulder, then planted a kiss on top of her head. "I will cook you something wonderful." He left and quickly returned dressed in the burgundy sweater, borrowed pants and his coat. And carrying the ax.

"What kind of dinner are you fixing with an ax?"

"Chicken cacciatore."

She cringed, but he strode out before she could comment. She knew where the food in the supermarket came from, but in-your-face reality was brutal.

Dante's jeans had taken so long to dry earlier, Ariana decided to wring them out and put them in a pan, which she slid into the oven on low heat. She put her cargo pants in with his, and hung their lighter clothing beside the fire. She slit the seam of a throw pillow from the settee to hide her iPod and notebook inside. It was the best she could do in the small cottage. She knew Dante the man. Trusted Dante the lover. But she wasn't sure about Dante the thief.

Soon, they would run out of food. She would have to reconcile herself to getting into a tiny ruin of a boat and rowing out to sea. Back in the real world, she and Dante would be forced into confrontation and she would have to leave him.

But not here, not now.

Ariana plaited her unruly wet hair into a French braid before donning the tight wool slacks and cream sweater once again. Since her underwear was still damp, she went commando.

She lit the candelier over the table, trying not to dwell on the drama happening outside. How long did it take to murder… no…butcher…

Finally, Dante blew in the back door, slamming it on the shrieking wind and lashing rain. He was dripping wet…and empty-handed.

She didn't know whether to be relieved or sorry. "You couldn't catch a chicken?"

"I caught one." She waited, and he shrugged. "The skinny, cocky little rooster reminded me of myself as a boy, scratching a hardscrabble living out of the dirt." He dropped his chagrined gaze. "I could not bring myself to kill him."

He didn't have the heart to kill a chicken. She ran to him, flung her arms around his neck. *I love you.* The words shimmered in her heart, trembled on her lips, and she bit them back. She'd seen Dante's emotions when they'd made love, but he wasn't ready to acknowledge his feelings. If she blurted hers, he would raise his defenses. She smiled at him. "That's okay, we'll have chickenless cacciatore."

He hugged her. "I appreciate your enthusiasm."

"Oh, I'm a new fan of improvisation, tough guy."

Laughing, he kissed the tip of her nose. He stepped back, and his admiring glance roamed her body, lingered on her unfettered breasts cupped by the tight sweater. "So I see." One glossy brow arched as his eyes fired. "I like the ensemble even better than before."

As if he'd touched her with the warm stroke of his gaze, her body tightened in anticipation.

Dante insisted on cooking, so Ariana set the table and poured wine. It wasn't long before Dante carried a skillet brimming with a spicy-smelling creation to the table.

As rain pummeled the roof and spattered the windowpanes, they discussed music, art, philosophies, and even politics, as if they were longtime lovers sharing a meal, not captor and captive in an isolated cottage on a rocky Greek island.

When she was finished, Ariana rested her fork across her empty plate. "That was four-star delicious."

"*Grazie.* You clear, and I will wash up."

"You won the bet. I should wash the dishes."

"*Tesoro mio,* you gave me a kiss." His voice was rich with innuendo. "And so much more."

Her skin tingled with passion. "It was freely given. No strings, no expectations."

He covered her fingers with his and gently squeezed. "Which makes the gift all the more precious."

Tears blurred her vision as she rose to clear the table. Their lovemaking hadn't been merely physical for him, either.

While Dante washed dishes, she investigated the gramophone, delighted to find recordings by Puccini, Donizetti and Bellini. She cranked the machine's handle, and the first scratchy strains of "*Lucia di Lammermoor*" floated into the air.

"*Bravo.*" Dante sauntered into the living area. "That opera was based on a true story, you know this?"

"Yes." She straightened. "And a tragic one."

His profile turned thoughtful. "Great passion often ends badly."

The reality of their own situation lurked beneath his words, and she pivoted to stare out the window into the howling storm.

"Ariana?" She hadn't heard him move, but he stood behind her now. "What is wrong?"

"Nothing."

"When a woman says *nothing* in that tone, she means *everything*." His hands settled on her shoulders. "Are you suffering second thoughts now? Regrets?"

"Absolutely not." Not about their intimacy. She leaned back against his solid warmth and nestled her head into the curve of his shoulder. "The weather must be making me jittery."

His arms enfolded her, wrapped her in his strength. "The gale cannot touch us here."

But they would not be here forever.

"No need to be afraid." His fingers slipped the fastening from her braid and stroked through her thick hair. "I hope you don't mind. I adore your beautiful hair."

The hard ridge of his arousal grazed her bottom, and her breathing quickened. "Dante, I'm not sure we should tempt..."

He nuzzled her nape, making her pulse leap in response. "Ah, *tesoro.*" The caress of his black velvet voice brushed her ear, feathered over her skin. "There are many ways of making love."

Her eyelids drifted closed. And he probably knew them all.

The music soared, drowned out the wind and rain. In one graceful movement, he grasped her hand in his, gave her a little push and spun her around to tug her into his embrace. "Dance with me."

She looked up and got tangled in the sensual smolder of his

smoky gaze and dazzling smile. The man could blitz her with charm. All of it genuine. "All right."

"You look sad, Ariana." He smiled at her as he took her in his arms. "Tell me about your dreams—if life were different, if you weren't a librarian, what would you be?"

She swayed in sync with his sinuous rhythm. No surprise, he was as magnificent at dancing as he was lovemaking. "I've always wanted to write an epic fantasy novel," she confessed. "I'd love to be the next J.R.R. Tolkien."

"So what is stopping you?"

"Good question." She mulled it over. "Dad encouraged my writing. There was a frustrated storyteller inside him. I think that's why he loved legends so much. Mom thought a steady paycheck with benefits was more valuable. Yin versus yang. I enjoy being a librarian, but in the end, practicality canceled daydreams."

"You cannot fill an empty belly with dreams." He dipped her dangerously low, held her suspended in midair. "Yet there are different kinds of hunger. It is as perilous to starve your soul as your body."

Awareness sizzled between them. Just when she thought he couldn't further amaze her, he gave her a deeper, more fascinating glimpse of himself. In centuries past, he might have been a brooding Italian composer. Armed with a warrior's spirit and a poet's heart, a rapier blade and even sharper wit. "What are your dreams, Dante?"

He swooped her upright. "My dream is to ensure that others get to live theirs."

Another cryptic message. Was he referring to his job brokering stolen goods? "What was your favorite subject at school?"

"Besides soccer and *signorine?*" He flicked her a dubious glance. "Don't laugh, but I adored art and music."

"I'm not surprised. But why? With few exceptions, the arts don't interest adolescent boys. Especially mischievous, macho types." She smiled at him. "No offense."

"Only a fool is offended by truth." He echoed her smile, then sobered. "I value traditions and art…things that possess heritage and history." He hesitated a heartbeat. "Because I…do not have a history."

She frowned. "I don't understand."

He hesitated again, so long she thought he'd decided not to answer. He drew her close, his body brushing hers. "No one knows who my father was. He deserted my mother when she discovered she was pregnant. My mother died giving life to me."

The sharp punch to her heart stole her breath. He was clearly ashamed and upset by the circumstances of his birth. Yet he had confided in her. "I'm sorry you never had a chance to know your parents, Dante. But you aren't responsible for what happened."

The tumult of the storm outside raged in his eyes. "I am a man without a past."

"Your past is part of who you are. It helped shape you into the man you became." Ariana gripped his fingers tightly. "Your past doesn't make me think less of you. I'm more concerned about your future."

He stiffened and his guard went up. "That is not for you to worry over."

She mourned his withdrawal. *Al contrario. I'm in love with you…and invested heart and soul in your welfare.*

Whether or not we're together.

She firmed trembling lips. "With your love of art and antiquities, have you ever considered a job as a museum curator, or maybe teaching?"

He smirked. "Can you picture me stuck behind a desk in a dusty museum? Or lecturing a classroom of sullen students?"

"Not really."

"Did you love him so much, then?" There was a slightly bitter edge to his voice. "I can never replace him."

Startled, she blinked. "Who?"

"Your professor."

She gasped. "You think I want to remake you into Geoff?"

His shrug failed to conceal the hurt. "You said you wanted me to teach."

"I want you to do something you love. For your sake, I'd like to see you…working on the right side of the law." He continued to stare down at her, waiting, watching, and she drew a steadying breath. "I'll admit, Geoff was good-looking, educated and clever. We got along well."

Dante's features hardened as hurt melded with undisguised jealousy.

"I'm not finished." She rubbed his taut back. "I loved the person I *thought* Geoff was. But we dated for over a year and he never let me see his true self."

"A sin of omission."

"Still a lie. You, on the other hand, are the most compelling man I've ever met. I've known you less than two months, but I already know you—and connect with you—far better than the man I thought I wanted to marry."

He jolted. A whirlwind of emotions chased across his features in rapid-fire succession. Astonishment. Pleasure. Terror. Anguish.

"It's all right, Dante, you don't have to say anything back." Ariana ducked her head so she wouldn't have to see his stricken face. "I just wanted you to know."

He went as still as a marble statue. Then his big body began to tremble. With his cheek pressed against her hair, she stood in his embrace, feeling the war rage inside him.

"I meant what I said." She gulped, battling stinging tears. She would *not* let him see her cry. "No strings, no expectations."

"San Gennaro, help me," he breathed in a hoarse whisper. He held her for another wrenching moment, then stepped back. "I will get more wine from the cellar."

He snatched up a lamp and bolted from the cottage, leaving her standing in the middle of the floor.

When the door slammed behind him, Ariana groped her way to the settee. She sank down and covered her face with shaking hands. Dante didn't back down easily. He wasn't a man accustomed to retreat. What had provoked his torment?

There was more to his situation than he was telling. Whatever he was hiding from her, whatever was driving him away must be bad.

She forced herself to sit upright and take slow breaths. She had to stay calm. Set aside spiraling emotions. Think things through.

She'd seen deep feelings in him when they'd made love. The fact that she'd told him she admired him wasn't enough to make him run. The obvious conclusion was that he was attempting to distance himself to protect her.

From what? From whom? Her stomach lurched. What kind of terrible trouble had forced him to kidnap her? Why was the Camorra blowing up yachts in order to kill him?

More importantly, how could she help?

She stared into the reckless orange flames. She didn't dare involve the authorities. As she'd told Dante, after butting heads with the FBI over her father's situation, she didn't trust the police not to make everything worse.

Another rush of tears threatened. She couldn't stay with him if he didn't want to go straight. He might not want her with him long-term, anyway. But even if she wasn't destined to be with Dante, she could not bear to see him die.

Ariana shot to her feet and paced the living area. Somehow, she had to convince him to confide in her. To trust her.

There was a way out for him. A safe way to start over. They only had to find it.

She retrieved her notebook and was scribbling theories and crossing out ideas when Dante exploded through the back door.

"Ariana, quickly *per favore!*" He ran for the ax. "Grab a lamp!"

Adrenaline spiked. She dropped her pencil and snatched up the nearest lamp. "What happened?"

Waiting at the door with the ax propped on his shoulder, he gestured. "You must see to believe it!"

CHAPTER TWELVE

ALEXANDRA'S DREAM had embarked on a final cruise around the Greek Isles before docking at Piraeus to prepare for the Caribbean leg of the voyage. Bernardo "Milo" lit a cigar inside the door of the cool, dim Emperor's Club. Quiet strains of slow jazz drifted on the smoky air. He waited for his eyes to adjust to the mood lighting, and then sauntered to where Father Connelly sat drumming his fingers. A glass of untouched soda water languished on the burnished table in front of him. Bernardo's life depended on discerning the contradictions between words and body language, and the man wasn't the affable, pious clergyman he attempted to portray "Ciao, Father."

Connelly looked up. He smiled, but his cool eyes warily assessed Bernardo. "Signor Milo. Hello."

Bernardo returned the gesture with an innocuous smile and a benign gaze that didn't betray the urgency gnawing at his gut. "May I join you?" His given name *was* Bernardo, but Milo wasn't his surname, and he wasn't a historical buildings contractor with a deceased son. Although anyone who checked would find solid evidence to the contrary. A mortgage, an obituary, a contractor's license, even clients who would highly recommend him.

He hadn't been in the game for years, but had slipped back into the guise that fit him as easily as his favorite baggy denims and battered brown leather jacket. He didn't wait for Father Connelly's assent before casually dropping into a plush chair next to him. "Would it be inappropriate to buy you a drink, Father?"

Connelly swallowed the bait as expected. He leaned back and

his smile warmed. "I'm off duty, so I'm sure it would be all right. Bless your generosity."

Bernardo rolled cigar smoke on his tongue. "I hear you had some excitement earlier on the voyage." He arched a brow at Connelly's fabricated blank expression. "People are talking about a missing librarian."

"Ah, yes. Our Miss Bennett. There's speculation she ran off with a lover." The priest's gaze shifted upward and to the left, indicating a lie. "I pray for her safety nightly."

"*Dio* will reward your devotion." *You fork-tongued* serpente. Bernardo clamped a lid on his anger, glad for the server's interruption to take their drink orders. First thing he'd done after boarding seventy-two hours ago was access voice messages left for Ariana. A professor friend in the United States had phoned to tell her the pottery chip she'd sent for appraisal was from a genuine Olympian vase. A message Ariana hadn't received, having been kidnapped before her call was returned. The vase had broken in the ship's library, where Ariana worked, and Father Connelly was in charge of the artifacts display.

Bernardo had the authority, means and damned good reasons not to spare manpower. He'd made discreet conversation with current passengers and crew, and every individual at his disposal was interviewing former passengers who'd attended the priest's lectures. Father Connelly had been observed flirting with women in a most unpriestly way and caught in a few slipups in his lectures on Greek and Roman antiquities. The discrepancies between Connelly's behavior and his priestly profession were multiplying faster than caged rabbits.

The drinks arrived, and he toasted the priest before sipping. As they engaged in small talk, he mentally sorted details. His second task had been to pick Father Connelly's lock and search his cabin. Art was Bernardo's specialty, and the Albanian triptych he'd discovered in a drawer had caught his eye. The icon was an excellent specimen for a supposed reproduction. The muddied colors looked genuine fifteenth century. It was an odd piece to add to a collection that consisted mostly of sculptures and pottery.

Bernardo had taken a miniscule scraping of the paint and messengered it to headquarters at the last port, and he'd sent a man to interview the employees at the chapel in the Vatican that housed the original icon. He expected both reports momentarily.

He had also examined Father Connelly's purchase receipt for the first century B.C. Hellenic Fish plate that was currently on display in the library…and if it wasn't a fake, he'd eat his boots. He had dispatched operatives to glean information from every port Alexandra's Dream had visited.

Giorgio Tzekas entered the club. The first officer was an oily little *ratto* with a furtive gaze and nervous habits. Body tense, he headed for the priest, noticed Bernardo and his steps faltered. Then he pasted on a fake smile and joined them at the table. Bernardo smiled back. *Interesting.* Had Father Connelly been waiting for Tzekas?

Bernardo finished his drink and puffed his cigar while half listening to the men's strained discussion about the early onset of stormy weather affecting sailing conditions. It didn't require a mathematician to put two and two together. Even the ship's Captain wasn't crazy about Tzekas. Nor was the security officer, Gideon Dayan. Bernardo saw disdain and suspicion in their eyes whenever they encountered the first officer. The background check on the crew had revealed Pappas was ex-Greek Navy and Dayan was ex-Mossad. They'd be top-notch judges of character.

Bernardo was positive the priest and Giorgio were smuggling artifacts and had been involved in Ariana's disappearance.

And the disappearance of Bernardo's best operator.

The question was whether Ariana was the duo's coconspirator, or their victim? It was no secret that Tzekas had been sniffing around Ariana, and people had noticed tension between her and Father Connelly. Her late father had been arrested for brokering stolen Etruscan jewelry.

Had Derek Bennett's daughter inherited his business?

He'd heard nothing from Dante since the yacht where the duo had been hiding had exploded off the Greek coast, over seventy-two hours ago. Ariana was Bernardo's only lead to Dante, which was why he'd boarded the ship and begun his investigation. Did she have anything to do with Dante being incommunicado? If Dante were able, he would have checked in.

Connelly and Tzekas stood and voiced excuses about wanting to stretch their legs on deck before retiring. They extended a half-hearted invitation to join them, which Bernardo was clearly expected to decline. He obliged. They left, and he snuffed his cigar, then slipped Father Connelly's empty whiskey glass into the bag lining his jacket pocket. The fingerprints would be invaluable.

He had contacts swarming the region. Had nearly unlimited resources and technology…and intense personal motivation. He was quickly gathering evidence to bring the smugglers down. His eyes narrowed in fierce determination. If the bastards had killed Dante, the man he loved like a son, they would pay.

GIORGIO PACED in front of the starboard railing. "Why were you talking to him again?"

"Don't get your shorts in a bunch, junior. He bought me a drink, is all. I've been running cons since you were in diapers. Give me some credit."

Credit. Giorgio scratched his neck. Credit was his problem. Money never seemed to get from his hand into his pocket. Even before payday, it was already spent. Between crappy cards and dud bets, he'd had a string of bad luck. "Did Megaera contact you about the Athens deal?"

"Yeah. We're all set."

"What artifact are we bringing aboard? What's the plan?" Desperation churned in his guts. When he'd lost an assload on the Grand Prix, he'd been forced to borrow funds, and not from the local bank. His father had made it clear he wasn't covering any more of his son's debts, and Giorgio's "loan officer" was getting antsy. The interest alone was draining him dry.

"Why, so you can shoot your wad early and screw it up? You'll know when you need to, and not before."

He clenched his fists. "I swear, O'Connor, if you're running a game on me—"

"You'll what, junior? Without me, Megaera won't get her merchandise. And you do not want to make her unhappy. So put up and shut up."

Giorgio watched his surly partner stride away. He looked out at the shifting waves, and not for the first time wondered what had happened to Ariana. He'd liked the thrill of the chase, and though she'd shut him down at every pass, he'd bet she'd enjoyed it, too.

But Ariana's questions had torqued the boss.

If Megaera found out Giorgio had made private deals on the side, she would... A shiver of fear racked him. He and Connelly had been promised a bonus after the Athens deal. He'd better step damn carefully.

If he crossed Megaera, or didn't get the money to pay back his loan, he would be the next person who disappeared.

ARIANA SPRINTED through the stormy night and jogged down the cellar stairs behind Dante.

When she reached the floor, she jerked to a halt. "Is that what I think it is?"

"*Sì.*" Dante hefted the ax.

Boxes littered the floor, the shelving unit angled outward from the wall and a crowbar lay on the bench. She peered at the small opening he'd hewed in the stone. "Secret rooms were common in Europe, especially during the World Wars. How did you find it?"

"I held up the light to see the wine bottles, and a draft wavered the flame. So I searched the shelves and found a hidden latch." He gestured at the rough hole in the wall. "The shelves disguised this partition. It's not as old as the cottage."

"I wonder what's in there?" She thrust her lamp onto the workbench beside his. She loved her father's tales of artifact discoveries, but had never experienced the thrill firsthand. "I can't wait to see!"

Dante grinned. "You won't have to wait long." He swung the ax in his powerful arms. Metal rang against stone and sparks flew as he hacked a jagged entryway.

Ariana rushed toward discovery and skidded on loose rock. Dante's hand shot out to catch her. "Watch your step, *cara*."

"We need light." Jittery with anticipation, she grabbed her lamp. She stepped around the debris and into the secret chamber, and her breath hitched. Wooden crates filled the large enclosure, stacked to the ceiling in places. "A vault of hidden treasure," she whispered.

Dante read the label on the nearest crate and snorted. "More like hot commodities, I'm thinking."

Her heart lurched. What had they stumbled into? "Get the crowbar to pry the lids off—"

A crash from upstairs trembled the ceiling and she jumped. "What was *that?*"

Dante swore and grabbed the ax. "Breaking glass. Stay put." He raced up the stairs two at a time.

"Down here, alone? Uh, no." She snatched up the crowbar and sprinted after him.

They engaged in a brief tussle amidst the driving rain. Since Dante was hampered by the ax and unwilling to toss her down the stairs, she managed to slip under his arm and away.

"Ariana," he gritted, "you must remain where it is safe."

"Where I'd be a sitting duck?" She brandished the crowbar. "Besides, you might need backup."

"At least keep behind me." Dante sighed. "And let's try to be quiet, in case it is intruders." Muttering dire laments beneath his breath in Italian about a mule-headed *signorina,* he stalked toward the cottage.

"I understood that," she whispered.

A low, frustrated male growl was the only reply.

The cottage's back door was closed and the area looked undisturbed. Dante motioned her to wait while he pressed his ear to the wooden panel. Silent as smoke, he prowled to her side beneath the shadowed eaves. "I hear rustling and things being knocked about." He gripped her arm. "I must trust you not to do anything foolhardy...or I will bodily return you to the cellar."

She nodded. "Absolutely." This was his territory, and she didn't want to endanger either of them.

"Follow me inside, then stay hidden in the pantry. If it *is* intruders, strike first, strike hard." His low voice was lethal. "Do not stop until you immobilize your opponent. Otherwise, you will be hindrance rather than help. *Capisci?*"

Her hands on the crowbar grew clammy. Suddenly hiding in the murky cellar didn't sound so awful. She'd seen Dante's ruthless side before, but was darned glad he was on her team. "I can do what I have to."

"It is not too late to change your mind, Ariana."

"No. I've got your back." Her fingers tightened on the cold metal. Had someone come for them? If it was the Greek and Russian, they were in for a fight. Megaera's hired thugs had almost succeeded in killing Dante before.

He eased open the door and they crept inside the darkened kitchen. She'd barely ducked into the pantry when she heard Dante's exclamation. "Ariana, come out."

"Who is it?" She rushed to the living area.

The wind had hurled a pine bough through the living room window. Four intruders ran around raising havoc amidst the wind and rain and broken glass. She giggled in surprise at the chickens who had sought shelter. "I don't think you'll need the ax."

Dante smirked. "Our chickens have come home to roost." He grabbed at the cocky young rooster whose life he had spared, and the chattering bird evaded him and flapped up to perch on the chandelier. Dante climbed onto a chair. "This is the gratitude I receive for not making you into dinner."

The rooster shrieked as Dante carried him to the window and tossed him out. Ariana chased a squawking hen who leapfrogged furniture, scattering pillows and white feathers in its wake. "What a foul job," she yelled at Dante over the clamor.

He shoved another wriggling, protesting hen out the window, then shot her a droll glance. "I need to get supplies from the shed and board up that window."

"How can I help?"

"You can stay out of my way. *Per favore,*" he added at her loud huff.

"Carpentry isn't my forte, anyway. I'll go back to the cellar and examine our find."

"Be careful." He was already striding out the door. "I will meet you there when I am finished."

She ventured into the storm once more. Only forbidden treasure could lure her down the shadowed stairs and into the spooky old cellar alone. One kerosene lamp on the workbench and another inside the secret chamber spilled two small puddles of light crowding back the oppressive darkness.

Ariana used the crowbar to pry open a crate. She sifted through shredded excelsior and lifted out a Villanovan spike-handled vessel. The cup dated to seventh century B.C. and was worth eight grand. Everything in the crate was Etruscan, and extremely valuable. The Etruscan period was one of her father's specialties, which enabled her to identify the pieces and gauge the cost. She reverently extracted each artifact and set them on the floor. Two hundred thousand dollars in merchandise from one crate.

Really curious now, she picked up the lid and read the shipping label. The postmarked date was eighteen months ago.

A cold chill crawled up her spine. The recipient was the Greek culture minister. His address wasn't the official one. Her breath panted out in short, choppy rasps.

It matched the address in her father's notes.

She examined labels on nearby crates. Different dates going back several years. Postmarked Milan. Barcelona. Istanbul. Cairo. All addressed to the Greek culture minister at the second dary address. All cities her father had visited in his business travels around the same time periods.

Nobody would suspect artifact shipments to the Greek culture minister were anything but legitimate. Then why were they hidden here? Dizziness assaulted her. *No.* This was circumstantial. There had to be an explanation, a paper trail. She needed to find insurance receipts. Customs forms.

Ariana shoved aside crates and found a locked metal file box in a corner. She smashed the lock with the crowbar, uncaring when she also smashed her knuckles.

She opened the box, leaving a red smear on the lid. Letters. Dozens of folded letters on scarlet linen paper, sans envelopes. Trembling, she unfolded the top sheet. It was written in Greek, and like the postmark on the first crate, dated eighteen months ago.

My Dearest Tasia, I hope this finds you well and happy. I'm sorry about the circumstances of our last parting, but you understand that I cannot leave home until everything is settled. Take good care of the latest investment I've sent toward our nest egg. Remember that I'm always thinking of, and living for the time we spend together, and long for the day when we'll be together forever. I'll phone you next week at the usual hour.

It was signed *Love Always,* with one bold, looped initial. *"D."*

The next half-dozen letters she scanned were similar in content, bore the same initial. Her mind screamed with denial, even as nausea surged in her throat. Ariana flipped the box and dumped the contents, unwilling to believe her stinging eyes, desperate to disprove her worst fears.

The damning letters rained down, each slap of paper on stone another spike into her heart. As the letters spilled into a crimson pool, several pictures fluttered free, and she slowly bent to pick up one.

A laughing man lounged on a sunny veranda with the Mediterranean sparkling in the background. He cupped a full wineglass in one hand and teasingly dangled a golden bracelet adorned with bloodstones from the other. Ariana recognized both the jewelry and the man. The bracelet was the one Megaera had been wearing.

The man was her father.

She forgot to breathe as a memory slammed into her. Herself at twelve, balking over attending summer camp, instead accepting her father's offer to work with him at the museum. She'd idly opened a box hidden at the back of a drawer inside his desk…and discovered the Etruscan bracelet. She'd tried it on, admiring the gleaming gold and scarlet stones. Her father's uncharacteristic rage when he'd caught her had shocked her. He'd snatched away the jewelry and ordered her out of his office. His later abashed apology explained that the bracelet was a priceless artifact for a special client.

Over a decade later, he'd been arrested in an unsuccessful attempt to barter a black-market deal for the matching necklace, using stolen jewelry from another dig site as collateral.

Rage scalded her, made her shake. Her father and his mistress Megaera/Tasia, had been stealing from dig sites and fencing antiquities through the Greek culture minister to finance Derek's plan to abandon Ariana and her mother.

The FBI hadn't destroyed her family.

Her own father had.

Moving in slow motion, she read letter after letter. The walls closed in, creating a prison of hot fury and pain. Hurt scorched her skin, and the truth writhed inside her, eating at her stomach, crushing her heart. Time ceased to have meaning, and everything blurred in the haze of grief.

Eventually one clear thought pierced the fog.

Find Dante.

Ariana didn't remember leaving the vault, but was suddenly outdoors.

She stumbled through the darkness, through the lashing wind and stinging rain, tears streaming down her cheeks.

Dante would help her. Dante would know what to do.

Lost in the storm, she tried to call out for him, but the horribly familiar smothering feeling locked her lungs. Panic seized her. She could not make a sound. She couldn't breathe.

DANTE HAMMERED the last nail into the boards covering the shutters. He hurried around the corner, anxious to get out of the weather and back to Ariana.

She slammed full tilt into him, and his arms automatically went around her. "Why the haste, *bella?*"

Her trembling hands gripped the lapels of his coat like a lifeline. She was shaking violently. Sobs wrenched her body and harsh breaths wheezed in her throat. Fear crashed over him. "*Ariana?* What happened?"

She swayed. Her fingers fell limply from his coat and her knees gave way. Swearing, he scooped her up and sprinted inside. He dropped to the settee in front of the fireplace, cradling her in his arms. Her face was bleached white, and her raspy, labored breaths terrified him, and clearly, her. "It's all right." He rubbed her back. "Ariana, you're hyperventilating. Slow your breathing."

Sobbing, she huddled against him as if she couldn't get close enough. He stroked her hair, kissed her temple. "You must listen to me, *tesoro*. You need to calm down. Do you understand what I'm saying?"

She jerkily nodded.

"Take a slow, deep breath. Can you do that for me?"

She nodded again and her body quaked as she struggled to comply.

"It's all right." He stroked her back in soothing circles. "Now another."

Her breathing eased, and she clung to him and cried. He ran his fingertips over her, checking for injuries. She winced when he picked up her left hand. It was bloody and bruised, and her right hand was blistered with burns. Dante's pulse ricocheted, and he stiffened. "You are injured. Did something attack you in the cellar? Tell me!"

She shook her head. He carried her into the bathroom and sat her on the counter. "What happened down there?"

"It hurts." She leaned on him and wept forlornly while he gently cleaned and dressed her wounds. His gutsy librarian had handled so many traumas without shedding a tear. She couldn't be falling apart over injured hands. His throat tightened. What had so badly wounded her heart?

He carried her back to the settee, murmuring soft comfort. "Ariana, you're frightening me. Tell me, *per favore*. I cannot leave you like this and go look for myself. And I cannot help if I don't know what is wrong."

Finally, he managed to coax the information from between choked sobs.

"It—it was all there in the letters. Their schemes and p-plans. Lists of goods they smuggled. Accomplices. M-methods."

The sinking feeling in his gut warned him he'd been correct all along, but he had to ask. "Who are you talking about? Who wrote the missives you found?"

"M-my f-father. The artifacts in the cellar were sent here by…my father. Using the Greek culture minister as a fence, he was stealing. Smuggling."

He rested his forehead against hers. "I am sorry."

"It gets worse." The anguish in her voice constricted his chest. "His mistress was Megaera. She was wearing a bracelet he gave her when she interrogated me on the boat. Her real name is Tasia. They were stealing to build a nest egg, because they planned to run away together."

That explained her mental and physical condition. When she discovered the truth, she must have been so distraught that she'd tripped trying to get upstairs to him and burned herself with the lamp. He hugged her tightly, let her pour out her torment.

"He wanted to leave us." She choked on sobs. "How could he throw our family away? How could he walk out on me and Mom?"

He didn't remember his own father's desertion, and still the hurt sliced to the bone. Ariana's suffering had to be far worse. His heart ached as he held her close and rocked her. "I wish I had an answer."

"We didn't mean anything to him. Nothing was real. Our life together was a fake. Concealed by a facade of lies."

Dante shook his head. "I know you don't want to hear this right now, but I believe your father loved you. You have a forgiving heart. You did not condemn me for being a thief. In time, you may be able to forgive him, too."

"As a little girl, I looked up to him. He was my hero. I've known who and what you are almost from the beginning. You didn't hide it from me. Didn't lie when I asked you. Didn't pretend to be something you're not."

Dante inhaled a stinging breath. He'd been lying to her from the moment they'd met.

He smoothed a damp tendril from her face. "You're hurt and angry now. Later, perhaps you will come to peace with this."

She shook her head. "I believed in my father," she sobbed. "I defended him to everyone. I wasted nearly a year of my life trying to exonerate him." She vibrated with hurt and fury. "How could I have been so wrong? About both of them...first Geoff and then Dad?"

His insides wrenched. He didn't want to be the next man on that list, the next to let her down. Yet he feared—no, he knew with a certainty that tore him apart—he would soon be forced to betray her. How could he make her understand? "Sometimes, Ariana, lies are necessary. Sometimes, circumstances *force* choices upon people. Sometimes lies cloak the truth, but do not invalidate what is real."

She jerked in his embrace. "Are you making excuses for what he did?"

"No. I am trying to help you see that nothing is completely black or white. Good people can make bad decisions."

"I just don't understand."

"You are upset, and you have every right to your feelings. You will need time to work it all out."

"Why?" Her voice dropped so low he could barely hear her broken whisper. "Why doesn't anyone ever love me back as much as I love them? Why am I never enough?"

His heart stopped, and then shattered. *You are enough for me, Ariana.* Ti adoro. *You are the only precious thing I want in this world.*

Ti amo.

But he was not free to say any of those things.

As if she sensed the feelings burning inside him, her mouth sought his in a desperate kiss. He tried to soothe her, but hot, bright passion exploded between them. He eased back. "Not when you are so distraught."

"Please, Dante." She wrapped her arms around his neck. "Don't reject me. Not now."

He kissed the tears from her eyes. Then he gently laid her down on the rug in front of the fire and made slow, tender love to her. With his kisses, he tried to tell her the hope and longing inside his heart.

With his body, he tried to show her the love he dared not speak aloud.

When she shuddered in his arms and cried out his name, he clung to her, poured himself into her, and prayed their union would be enough to bind her to him through all they had yet to face.

Afterward, he looked down at Ariana's sleeping face and ached with the pain of loving her. He'd been ordered to kill her. Instead, he had reluctantly taken an oath to protect her. She had started out as his hostage, but now his heart was her captive, a hostage to the Fates.

He would do anything to keep her safe.

Dante traced her face with his fingertips, storing away the memory of each delicate feature. Ariana filled the dark, lonely void inside him with light. Her sweet generosity washed away his bitterness. Her glowing spirit vanquished his pain. He did not want to let her go.

He gently kissed her lips, perhaps for the very last time. How he felt, what he wanted didn't matter. If he let his motives turn personal, innocent people would die. Ariana could die. He had to do right by her.

At all costs, he had to protect her.

Even from himself.

Dante buried his face in her silky, fragrant hair as the knowledge lodged like a knife in his heart. He had to follow through. He could not drop his mask of lies. His secrets had to be kept locked up, because the truth would destroy everything. Destroy her.

And after he did what he must…she would despise him.

DANTE WOKE before daybreak. He eased from the bed, as sore and battered inside as when he'd taken a beating on the yacht. He paused in the doorway and turned to look at Ariana's slumbering face. Her skin was white as milk and dark circles of grief bruised her eyes.

"Remember, *amore mio*," he whispered.

He stole from the room, quietly gathered his own clothes— dry, thanks to Ariana's ingenuity—and then dressed. He stoked the fire and donned his coat before grimly slipping out the back, careful not to wake her. Better if she slept through this part.

The storm had blown out, but mournful gray clouds masked sunrise in the chilly dawn. He reluctantly descended to the depths of the cellar to obtain proof of Derek Bennett's crimes.

Dante lurched to a halt inside the secret chamber. The artifacts were scattered. Two blackened, empty kerosene lamps sat on the floor, their globes shattered. Where there should have been letters, there were only piles of ashes.

Ariana had burned the evidence.

Stunned disbelief raged inside him. Even before she came to him last night, she had already chosen.

That made his decision both easier…and a whole lot tougher.

Confused, angry, and he admitted, scared, he loped up the stairs and strode across the courtyard. He bent to pluck a crinkled paper from the mud. The photo Ariana had mentioned, crumpled by her fingers and soaked with rain. Ruined. Useless.

Dante stalked into the cottage. She'd been writing in her notebook when he'd surprised her the night before. He crossed to the settee, knelt and flung aside pillows until he found the small book.

He didn't want to believe it, but there it was in her own neat script. Names, addresses, inventories. The most recent notations seemed to be brainstorming ideas for changing her identity and outwitting the Camorra.

The blade twisted in his heart. Had he been played? How could the past few days—her anguish and their lovemaking last night—have possibly been acting on Ariana's part?

Why? He'd confessed his criminal past. If her feelings for him were genuine, she should have had no reservations about telling him the truth. In fact, she should be begging for his help.

Unless she really was just about the money.

She'd claimed her family was nearly destitute after the FBI had confiscated their assets. Was this her way of striking back at the police and regaining her wealth? Money was a powerful motivator. He'd seen people do far worse for a lot less than the stakes in this scheme.

His glance snagged on her iPod, hanging halfway out of a fallen pillow. He snatched it up, plugged in an earbud. What sounded like Greek language lessons had to be encoded information.

"What are you doing with my things?" Ariana's appalled question spun him around.

She stood in the doorway, naked and beautiful. Anger shadowed her blue eyes. "Leave them alone. They're private."

Every cold word from her lips strengthened his doubts.

Watching her, he slowly set down the notebook and iPod. Even through the pain of her deception, his body hardened with wanting her. His heart still ached with loving her. And that infuriated him.

"Get dressed." He flung her clothes at her and strode toward the back door, gritting his teeth against hurt, bewildered words he would regret forever.

"Dante, wait!" She ran after him, grabbed his arm. "Why are you angry with me?"

He reluctantly turned. Ariana stood in front of him heedless of her nudity. Confused vulnerability shadowed her features. In his profession, a man ruled by his emotions didn't live long. Though he'd easily mastered his feelings for a decade, he struggled to leash his temper. "Let it drop."

"No." She was trembling, but held her ground. Held on to him. "I've let too many important things in my life go. We're going to talk this out."

He inhaled a deep breath. Her nudity could be calculated. She'd certainly proven her body could sway him. He eased his arm from her grasp. "Tell me, Ariana, is there a goddess of deceit?"

"Yes," she replied, obviously unsure of his tack. "Her name is Apate. Goddess of guile, fraud and deception. She was one of the spirits inside Pandora's box." She frowned. "Why? You think I've somehow deceived you?"

"Have you not?"

"Is this about my father's files on the iPod?" Her teeth worried at her lower lip. "I didn't mention them before because I wasn't sure about him *or* you. It's a moot point after last night. You know everything."

"Sì," he ground out. "Including that you burned the evidence."

She raised her hands and stared at the bandages over her knuckles. "I was…oh…God." She gasped. "I was hurt. Furious. I didn't think about— I just…wanted them gone. For a year, I've sacrificed everything in search of the truth. And the truth is so ugly."

She sank down, buried her face in her hands and burst into tears. "His betrayal hurt more than his death. I just wanted to destroy the words, the way they destroyed our family. The way they destroyed me."

Dante closed his eyes against the sight of her huddled on the floor. Tried to wall off his heart. Maybe she was playing him, maybe not. He swore. Perhaps he'd pay the ultimate price for being a gullible fool, but his heart wasn't made of granite. He couldn't bear to cause her anguish. Not over this.

Not when there was more to come.

He dropped to his knees and gathered her chilled, shaking body into his arms. "Shh. It is all right."

"I didn't mean to do anything wrong. I miss him so much. And I'm so upset. I didn't consciously decide to destroy evidence."

If her performance was staged, she was damn good. He didn't think she was lying to him, yet a bitter taint of doubt remained. He hadn't survived this long by easily giving away his trust.

Ariana clung to him, and Dante held her and stroked her hair. If they continued in this vein, he'd end up making love to her again. Which could be exactly what she wanted. He might not be the only one hoping their physical union would create a bond...but for very different reasons. He ground his teeth. For the first time, he hated his job. Despised the hard edge that had taught him to second-guess every word, every action.

His pulse pounded in his ears, and he eased away. "Ariana, you must pull yourself together and get dressed. We are leaving in the boat, and have to launch with the tide."

Her body trembled as she choked back sobs. "I'm sorry, I'm not usually an emotional wreck."

"No need to apologize, *bella*. Your father means the world to you. Of course you're emotional. You've been through hell in the past year. As you told me, it is healthier to release your feelings." He kissed the top of her head. "But we really must go."

She went silent for long moments, and then breathed a quivering sigh. "I'll be ready."

Her quiet bravery was almost his undoing, and he fought the temptation to throw his entire life away and carry her back to bed. He made himself get up and stride from the house.

Dante loped to the cellar, snagged a handful of antique coins and then stuffed the swag into his coat pocket. He'd be back for the rest later.

He ripped the tarp off the rowboat to examine the reinforced hull. Ariana wouldn't balk over getting into the boat, but she'd be terrified. His stomach tightened. Her life was in his hands, and he would give up the entire treasure for one life jacket. He glanced out to sea to assess the tide.

And saw a yacht bobbing on the horizon.

It wasn't Megaera's, and since the woman had kidnapped them from beneath the mob's nose, the Camorra had no idea where they were. "Ariana!" he yelled. He charged through the back door. "A yacht! Light the signal fires!"

She hit the courtyard on the run, buttoning her shirt. They doused the woodpiles with kerosene and ignited a trio of fires. He finished first, and flashed the mirror at the horizon.

"They see us!" Ariana rose on tiptoe as the yacht turned. Sudden worry creased her brows. "That's not Megaera's ship, is it?"

"Her yacht was trimmed in red. This ship is white and green."

She tossed him an unfathomable look from those forget-me-not blue eyes. Uneasy silence loomed between them as they hurried into the cottage. He killed the fire and snuffed lanterns while she stuffed her iPod and notebook into her pants pocket and yanked on the sport coat.

They rushed back outside to see a small speedboat slide onto the rocky slice of beach.

Four men jumped from the boat. Dante frowned and his heart slammed against his ribs. Four men brandishing pistols.

Men swarmed the hillside, and Dante swore. "I recognize one of them." Too late to remember his warning to the Greek and Russian on the beach. To realize his impetuous shout that first night had borne poisonous fruit. Word of the bounty on him and Ariana must have traveled. The thugs would have collected a fortune for betraying Megaera and revealing his and Ariana's location.

Adrenaline blasted through him. He grabbed Ariana's hand and towed her toward the cottage. "Move! It is a Camorra hit squad!"

CHAPTER THIRTEEN

DANTE TORE INTO the cottage and snatched up the ax.

Ariana panted beside him. "They're blocking the path to the beach!"

He ran back out to the courtyard and scanned the area. "The rear trail is useless, we'd be trapped on the other beach. The island is too small to conceal us for long, but hiding is our only choice."

As he clasped her hand and bolted toward the woods, her glance flew in the direction of the men boiling up the trail. "Can we buy them off with the loot in the cellar?"

He was torn between love and distress. His librarian was quick in a crisis. And too damn devious. She thought like a criminal. He shook his head. "They'll take it and kill us, anyway."

Dante reached the tree line and the only viable conclusion at the same time. He dropped Ariana's hand and gave her a push. "*Run.* Hide. I will face them alone. I'll tell them I killed you to keep the food and artifacts for myself."

"They'll kill *you.*" She whirled on him, face aghast. "I have another idea."

He could knock her out and hide her, but she would fight him. Assessing the stubborn line of her jaw, he scrapped the idea.

The sound of men's voices and hurried footsteps scraping on rock grew closer. "Talk fast. We are about to have company."

Admiration warred with dismay as she explained.

"Risky plan," he said when she'd finished.

"I used to watch the kids in my neighborhood do it with cardboard boxes." Though trembling with apprehension, she still managed a credible imitation of his shrug. "Better than hide-and-seek with a firing squad."

No argument there. Her shrewd brain could save both their lives. Dante tossed the ax. "Let's move."

They tore back to the courtyard, then flipped the rowboat and bulldozed it to the edge of the bluff. Even with their hearts and minds at odds, their teamwork was perfect.

The timing had to be exactly right, and there was still a possibility they would get shot. He'd take the chance over facing down mob hit men. One ax against four semiautomatics was shitty odds.

They waited until the first assassin's head crested the top of the bluff. Ariana jumped into the bow and Dante shoved the rowboat over the edge.

He gave the boat a running start, pushing with every ounce of strength. He steered toward a trajectory between boulders and leaped in behind Ariana.

Men hollered, and bullets screamed through the air as the rowboat tobogganed down the slope.

"Duck!" Dante yelled. He covered Ariana with his body during the teeth-jarring downhill hurtle.

Shale scraped beneath them and branches flung out skeletal fingers to snag the hull. The shuddering rowboat held together and rocketed toward the bottom. Then the boat careened onto the beach…and skidded in sand.

Shouts and gunshots roared overhead as their scrambling pursuers floundered back down the trail.

Dante didn't wait for the boat to lurch to a stop before he bailed. He hauled a stumbling Ariana from the bow, and hand in hand they sprinted to the speedboat. A hailstorm of bullets whined past and plowed into the water.

Ariana yanked up the dripping anchor while Dante hot-wired the speedboat's starter. He grinned fiercely as the powerful motor roared to life. A new personal best. So much for a misspent youth.

He shoved the throttle wide and sped out to sea, swerving

wildly to avoid exploding gun shells. Their pursuers were left swearing and stranded on the beach.

Ariana's face was ghostly pale and she clutched her seat. "That was…interesting."

Dante didn't have time to offer solace. He gripped the wheel, fighting to keep the boat from foundering. Since he had no idea where in the Mediterranean they'd been stranded, he attempted to hail help on the radio.

He eventually reached the Hellenic Coast Guard and the dispatcher directed him to the closest port using GPS.

Dante avoided the main dock—too many questions—and slipped into a side cove. Having worked in the region for years, he knew how to bypass customs. He convinced Ariana to stay aboard and lie low with the argument that it would be easier for him to evade detection by the Camorra alone. He kept the speedboat in sight through the window while he made several covert phone calls from a small taverna.

Twenty minutes later, he met his contact and handed over the coins he'd taken from the cottage in trade for a black Lamborghini Diablo, a wad of cash, a cell phone, a Glock 20 concealed in his back waistband, a backup Glock 26 strapped around his left ankle and two hundred rounds of ammo.

Outside, glowering clouds and a leaden sky reflected Dante's dire mood. The orders he bore were a far heavier burden than the artillery.

Dread weighed his chest like a Kevlar vest as he retrieved Ariana from the boat. "We're a short distance from Piraeus."

She gasped. "The port of Athens! What day is this?"

"October thirteenth."

"*Alexandra's Dream* is due to be docked here this week before the Caribbean leg of the voyage!" She smiled. "Is this serendipity or what?"

"*Sì. Destino.*"

"I meant luck, not destiny." Worry smothered her smile. "What's wrong?"

"Nothing."

"When a man says *nothing* in that tone, it means *I don't want to tell you, for your own good.*" She gripped his arm. "Did the Camorra find us?"

"Not yet. I would like you to stay in a safe place until the area is secure." He steered her toward the taverna's parking area, already anticipating her answer. But he had to go through the motions. Play his part. Do what she expected of him to squelch her suspicions.

"I'm going back to the ship." She held up a hand. "There's no way you can force me to stay, and I know you won't hurt me."

"As you wish." This time she was wrong. Dead wrong. "I confiscated your money, identification and passport when I first kidnapped you in case you attempted escape. They have been safely stored. I will messenger them to you." He clenched his jaw so tightly it ached as he led her to the car. "Your ship is on the other side of the port."

"*Diablo.*" She read the logo emblazoned between the taillights of the Lamborghini. "The name certainly fits." Her eyes widened. "Is this yours?"

He silently opened the passenger door, and she ducked inside. He slid behind the wheel and fired up the ignition, and her eyes grew larger. "How fast does it go?"

"Three hundred and fifty kilometers per hour."

"Planning on leaving in a hurry, are you?" Thick silence suffocated her joke. He wheeled the powerful car out of the parking area, and anxiety sharpened her lovely features. "Dante, please talk to me. What's the matter?"

"Nothing." It was a short drive. He maneuvered through traffic and bustling tourists, and pulled into a spot fifty yards from the mammoth cruise ship. If he could survive the next few moments, he'd be all right.

Keep lying to yourself. Whatever it takes to get through this.

He forced himself to stride around and open her door. Ariana climbed out and looked up at him, making his heart hammer painfully against his ribs. "Dante?" Her teeth caught her lower lip. "Will you call me?"

Afterward, she wouldn't want him to. "I don't know."

"You can leave a message." She blinked away the moisture glistening in her eyes. "I just need to be sure you're all right."

The sad uncertainty in her tender gaze and the hitch in her voice stole his breath.

He grasped her shoulders, shoved her against the car and captured her mouth in a desperate kiss. Dante battled back despair. He didn't want to send despair with her. With his kiss, he offered both promise and apology. Hope and regret.

Ariana's arms slid around his neck, and she pressed against him. She returned his kiss with desire. With love and longing.

Love slammed into him. His hands drifted down her body one last time, memorizing her soft curves. His heart ached to speak the words she wanted to hear. Words he needed to say.

She'd wanted to know his dream. Ariana was his dream.

And he couldn't have her.

He was panting from the strain when he gently pulled away. She reluctantly released him, and he rested his forehead against hers. "Go in safety."

He was shaking. She reached up and touched his cheek. So was she. "There's so much… I wish…" Her lips trembled and she inhaled a quivery breath. "If you need anything…any help, you know where to find me."

He forced his words through a throat so constricted he could barely talk. "Stay strong, Ariana."

She spun and stumbled through the throng, and a sharp pang of loss cut into him. His job was his life. He'd lived for his work with no regrets. Until now.

He was giving up everything for his job. Giving up everything for duty. For honor.

He hoped honor would warm him during the cold, lonely nights to come.

Gritting his teeth against the pain, Dante watched the woman he loved walk away from him. He had to live the life he'd chosen, rather than the life he wanted. He could not tell Ariana who he was. And he would not, *could* not, compromise her safety more than he already had. Not to mention the shredded remnants of his integrity.

And it had only cost him his soul.

At the last moment, she turned and looked back at him. He pressed an unsteady hand to his lips and then waved, shoving aside the vision of her hurt face when she learned the truth.

She disappeared from sight, and a tall, lanky Italian separated from the crowd and followed her aboard. Dante closed his eyes and leaned against the car. She was stronger than any woman he'd known. But his betrayal would shatter what remained of her faith.

What could have been—what could never happen—between himself and Ariana would haunt him to his last breath.

"Forgive me, *tesoro mio,*" he whispered. And though he hadn't cried since he was a boy of twelve, Dante couldn't stop a tear that silently slid down his cheek.

A SHAKEN ARIANA wiped away hot tears as she trudged aboard ship. The shocked security officer at the crew gangway had recognized her and waved her through. She was free. She should be happy. Instead, sorrow and frustration churned inside her. Along with overwhelming worry for the man she'd left behind. What would become of Dante?

Misery sat like lead in her stomach. Would she ever hear from him again? She glanced up at the huge white smokestack. The circular logo of glittering stars always brought to mind the Roman goddess Fortuna, guiding the wheel of fate. But fate was capricious. Fortune spun her wheel at random, bestowing blessings…and disaster.

Fate had brought her to Dante. Ariana fought to squelch her tears. After her stint on *Alexandra's Dream,* maybe she would return to the Mediterranean. She stared at restless waves reflecting a steely sky. And do what? If Dante didn't want to be found, she would never find him.

She climbed stairs, avoiding the elevators to allow time to collect herself. Dante hadn't pulled that pricey car out of a hat. Likewise the gun she'd felt beneath his coat when they'd kissed. Her heart gave a sickening lurch. He cared about her, but did he care enough to give all that up?

Or had he already sold his soul?

She wiped the sport coat's sleeve across her eyes. Though terror for Dante's safety screamed inside her, there was nothing she could do. Fortune only ruled one half of men's fates. The other half was their own free will.

If Dante wanted to be with her, he would have to surrender his life in the shadows. He had to come to her, ready to start over.

He had to make the choice.

She walked past the children's wading pool. A few noisy kidlets splashed in the heated water. Her hand tenderly covered her abdomen. If she was carrying Dante's baby, she would cherish the child, whether Dante was with her or not.

If she were having his baby, would he want to know?

Ariana swallowed hard. She didn't have to wrestle with that decision until a baby was a reality, not a daydream.

She'd had her wild, beautiful dance in the flames. Time to pay the piper. She braced herself as she toiled up the last set of stairs to the security office.

Gideon Dayan, the security officer, recovered quickly from his astonishment. Ariana assumed, from the fierce flash in his eyes at her statement that she'd been kidnapped, and his intense inquiry about her welfare, that she looked as ravaged as she felt.

Gideon took her to the bridge to report to the Captain. When they entered, every officer on deck turned to stare. Shocked beats of silence ticked past, and then Captain Pappas surged from his seat. "Miss Bennett!" His eyes narrowed in concern at her tear-stained face. "What happened to you? Are you all right?"

She self-consciously smoothed her tangled hair. How to

answer that question? Her entire life had changed and she would never be the same. "I…was…kidnapped outside of Naples."

"Gideon," Captain Pappas barked, "notify the Athens police and Interpol. And phone the ship's physician."

Obviously, they suspected she'd been assaulted. A natural assumption, given the circumstances. Out of the corner of her eye, Ariana saw Giorgio Tzekas, the first officer, slip away. The playboy had been putting the moves on her since day one. How uncharacteristic of him to show some tact.

Ariana let their assumptions stand. The kid-glove treatment would give her room to think. "I'd like to go to my cabin, call my mother and clean up before I talk to the police."

Captain Pappas nodded. "Officer Dayan and I want to be present when you're questioned, but neither of us can leave for a lengthy procedure. I'll request a police officer come to the ship, and use every means at my disposal to influence their decision."

"Thank you, Captain." She knew he and Officer Dayan were concerned about her…but also about the cruise line's reputation. Nevertheless, she appreciated it. She'd rather not have to endure Athens traffic and hours of interrogation at a foreign police station in her raw emotional state.

Captain Pappas surprised her into speechlessness when his gaze softened and he patted her shoulder. "Don't worry, Miss Bennett. You're safe with us." Then he abruptly turned away to pick up the phone. "I'll notify you when the police arrive."

Gideon escorted Ariana to her cabin, and gently advised her not to change clothing or shower until after she'd seen the doctor and police. She declined his offer to wait with her.

Inside, she leaned against the door. Her heart yearned for Dante, logic and the law be damned.

She swallowed the aching lump in her throat and willed herself to stop trembling. Dante's final words echoed inside her. *Stay strong.*

What was she going to tell the authorities? Dante *had* kidnapped her. But he'd also saved her life…multiple times. And he'd voluntarily released her. She hadn't been harmed.

A knock sounded behind her, and she sighed. She opened the door expecting the doctor…and was stunned to see her mother.

"Ariana!" Sadie threw her arms around Ariana and burst into tears.

"Mom?" Ariana hugged her, suddenly vulnerable and bereft and as glad to see her mother as if she were ten years old again. A fresh rush of tears hit. "I was just going to call you. What are you doing here?"

Sadie cleared her throat, gave a little shake and composed herself. "Sit down. You must be exhausted. And you've lost weight."

Ariana sat cross-legged on the bed while her mother marched to the phone. Chic and pretty in charcoal pants topped by a sage sweater, Sadie ordered coffee and food, firmly insisting on immediate delivery. Then her mother commandeered the lone chair in the cramped quarters. "When I couldn't get straight answers from *anyone* after you went missing, I decided it was high time to board the ship. I wasn't about to give up until they found you."

Ariana stared at the confident, take-charge woman. "Where's the pod, and what have you done with my mother?"

"I *have* changed." Sadie smiled wryly. "We have a lot of catching up to do."

Ariana dreaded the coming conversation.

Sadie studied Ariana's face. "You seem different, too. Somehow…older. And my girl is sad." Her mother's pale blue eyes misted. "Was it so very terrible, honey?"

Terrible *and* wonderful…and she didn't regret one moment with Dante. "I'm fine, Mom. I wasn't mistreated or hurt."

"Something happened."

"I…I can't talk about it yet." She might never be able to mention Dante. He was a precious jewel she might have to keep hidden inside her heart forever.

"I'm here when you're ready." Sadie rose and patted Ariana's shoulder. "I have something important to discuss with you, too. However, now isn't the time."

Ariana blinked. Normally, her mom would hover and ask anxious questions. Instead, Sadie briskly greeted room service.

Ariana watched her mom set plates of sandwiches on the nightstand and pour coffee. Once the police arrived, details would come out about Megaera. Ariana didn't want Sadie hearing about Derek's infidelity from a stranger.

It was now or never.

"We should talk while we can. Once the authorities arrive, we might not get another chance for hours." Telling her mom about her father's infidelity would be as painful as stitching Dante's arm. And, she sternly reminded herself, just as necessary.

Buying time to settle her emotions, she reached for a turkey sandwich she had no appetite for. The conversation would be hard enough on Sadie without Ariana falling apart. "If you have important news, why don't you go first?"

"Are you sure you're up to this?"

"Absolutely," she lied.

"Yes…you'll probably hear through the ship's grapevine any way. It's better if I simply come out with it." Sadie smoothed nonexistent wrinkles from her slacks. "I'm… At my age, I hate to use the term *dating*. But I'm seeing someone."

Ariana nearly dropped her plate. *"What?"*

"I'm seeing a wonderful man." Sadie clasped nervous fingers together. "And it's serious."

"Wait a minute." Ariana set aside her food. "You're *serious* about another man?" She stared at her mother. "Dad hasn't even been gone a year."

"I know it's a shock, honey. It shocked me, too." Her mother scooted to the edge of her chair. "It wasn't something I went looking for. I traveled halfway around the world to find you, and found Elias."

"Elias?" Ariana shook her head. "*Elias Stamos,* the tycoon who owns this entire cruise line?"

"Yes. You've met his lovely daughters Katherine and Helen, and his granddaughter, Gemma. Elias also has a son, Theo, from another relationship. You might have seen him around. He operates a tour company that offers shore excursions to cruise passengers."

"How did this happen?" She struggled to process her mother's startling revelation. "When?"

"We met when Elias came aboard after you first went missing. He was kind to me, and terribly concerned about you. We grew extremely close."

"But you doted on Dad."

"Yes, I loved your father—you and I both did. I still miss him. But the world keeps turning. And I've found something with Elias that I didn't even know I was missing. I don't know how to explain it."

Ariana could completely relate. "At the risk of overstepping...I know your marriage wasn't exactly...fraught with passion." She slowly exhaled. "You and Dad had affection for each other, like Geoff and me. But in the end, you needed something more. A man who makes your heart pound and your knees shake. A man who makes you feel as if you can't breathe when he's not there."

"Yes." Sadie gave her an odd look. "That's it...exactly."

Ariana could hardly begrudge her mother a chance at happiness. "He obviously makes you happy. You're glowing."

Sadie's anxious expression smoothed out. "Shinier than I've been in decades."

"Then I'm glad for you, Mom." She smiled. "For both of you."

"Elias had to leave to attend to business, but he reboarded the ship last night." She looked up, blue eyes wide. "I'd like very much for you to meet him."

Ariana nodded. "I can't wait to meet him."

Sadie jumped up and hugged her. "What a relief! I was worried sick about breaking the news to you, especially with everything you went through after your father's death. You always looked up to your father like he hung the moon and stars."

"About that." Ariana patted the bed, and her mother sat beside her. "There's something I'm not anxious to share. Something tough to hear, Mom."

Sadie squeezed her hand. "Nothing could be harder to hear than the news that you'd gone missing."

"Trust me, this won't be easy." She inhaled a fortifying breath. "I've stumbled across information about Dad." She bit her lip. Which bullet to deliver first? "You don't know the real reason I took this job."

"You wanted to visit the ports your father had, hoping to somehow prove his innocence."

Ariana sighed. She hadn't given her mother nearly enough credit. "I found a CD hidden inside one of my journals. It was filled with Dad's files encoded in ancient Greek. I've spent months transcribing notes, searching dig sites, talking to his contacts." She swallowed. "But Dad didn't leave the CD in my journal for me to find. He just thought the police wouldn't look there. He...he was guilty. I can't tell you the details until later. He did broker that stolen necklace...and a lot more."

"Oh, Derek." Sadie closed her eyes, silent grief etching her face. "That's where the money came from to pay all the medical bills when you were younger. He said he'd cashed bonds."

Ariana was shaking. "I'm sorry, Mom. I should have listened to you and left well enough alone."

"No." Sadie opened her eyes and gently kissed Ariana's cheek. "You don't really believe that, and neither do I. I'm sorry you got dragged into the middle of it. I'm proud of you for revealing the truth, no matter how ugly."

Tears welled. "Brace yourself, okay? Because it gets uglier. Dad had... He was involved with another woman. For a long time."

Her mother didn't speak for a span of heartbeats. "I see."

Ariana watched her calm profile. "You *knew?*"

"I suspected." Sadie sighed. "Not the criminal activity. I never would have turned a blind eye to stealing! But about another woman...yes. As you mentioned, things weren't as they should have been between us. There was a separateness to our lives. He was gone so much."

"Why didn't you say anything? Why did you stay?" Ariana gasped. "Was it for me?"

"Honey, no! Don't blame yourself. It was *my* choice. I didn't want to face the truth. Didn't want to shake up the safe world I'd created around my child and home and my charity work." Sadie hung her head. "I loved Derek, and didn't want to lose him. So I let him keep his secrets.

"I don't understand." Ariana clasped her mother's cold hand between her own. "How could you continue to love him after he lied to you? Cheated on you? Betrayed you?"

"My sweet girl." Sadie's eyes swam with tears. "You don't pick the person you fall in love with. You can't switch love on and off." She patted Ariana's cheek. "The heart loves, flaws and all."

"How could I have been so blind?"

"Your father had his faults, but he loved you dearly." Her mother turned toward her. "Nothing he did negates his love for you. Never doubt that. It's why he stayed as long as he did. Derek was obviously torn, kept from the woman he wanted to be with. Now that I've met Elias, I honestly feel sorry for Derek."

"Then you're a stronger and more forgiving woman than I am."

Sadie smiled ruefully. "You're young yet. It takes two people to make a relationship work…or fail. I should have confronted Derek instead of clinging to him. I should have let him go. If I'd set aside my own selfish needs, maybe we would have all been happier." She smoothed Ariana's hair. "If I'd been strong and forgiving enough to do what was best for him, maybe your father would be alive right now."

"Don't, Mom!" It was Ariana's turn to sweep her mother into a hug. "It's not your fault. Dad lived and died by his own choices."

Her mother's eyes welled again. "We all do, sweetie."

Ariana's tears spilled over. Clinging to each other, the two women quietly wept for the man they'd both loved.

CHAPTER FOURTEEN

SADIE LEFT, instructing Ariana to rest before her ordeal with the police, and to phone her when she felt up to talking. Ariana forced herself to eat half a sandwich and chugged coffee. How much should she reveal about Dante? The thought of both the Camorra and the police hunting him down like an animal made her sick.

The knock rapped on her door long before she was prepared. Ariana steeled herself and swung open the door.

"Giorgio?"

His glance skittered over his shoulder. "I have to talk to you."

"This isn't a good—"

"The cops have just boarded, and they'll talk to Gideon and the captain first." His voice dropped to a murmur. "I have a message from a mutual acquaintance."

Her heart leaped into her throat. Had Dante sent him? "Come in."

He sidled inside and raked his fingers through his dark hair.

"Well?" she prompted.

"If you want retribution for what happened to your father, and if the police give you trouble, Megaera will help you."

"You're working for her?" Stunned, she assessed him. Was this a police trap? "What if I don't want her help?"

"She…ah…said if you decline her offer, it will be her pleasure to remove any obstacles blocking your cooperation. Such as the Napoletano." His glance slid away. "She wants you to know if you're concerned about Dante's welfare, you won't talk to the police. About anything."

Fear rocketed through her. "She threatened Dante's life?"

"Hey, I'm not involved with any death threats." Giorgio shoved his hands into the pockets of his white uniform. "If you keep your mouth shut to the cops, she'll meet with you. Says she has an offer to make."

"All right." She'd strike a bargain. Stall for time. Whatever it took to protect Dante. "When and where?"

"Soon. I'll let you know."

Giorgio slunk down the hallway, and she closed the door. Until she could somehow contact Dante and warn him, until she could speak to Tasia, she had no choice. She had to make a temporary end run around the police without perjuring herself, so she could eventually come clean.

The million-dollar question was *how?*

She ignored the inner voice whispering this was exactly what she wanted. A reason not to turn Dante in.

"Miss Bennett?" Gideon Dayan's voice and accompanying knock gave her a guilty start. She counted to five and opened the door.

Dayan brought her to the captain's office, saying many of the crew had been worried about her and would be glad to see her. They joined Captain Pappas and a stern Greek police officer named Inspector Zahakis. Zahakis grudgingly introduced a striking brunette with intelligent green eyes as Agent Esposito from Interpol. The ship's physician, Dr. Latsis, was also present. The cool, competent blonde apologized for not being immediately available and she offered to examine Ariana after "the interview."

Inquisition seemed a more fitting word. Ariana was directed to a chair between Gideon and the doctor. A discussion ensued about who had jurisdiction. No one knew for certain. Ariana was an American citizen, but employed by a foreign cruise line, and she had been kidnapped in Italy, but released in Greece. The closest international FBI office was in Rome, with no FBI agents immediately available for a nonemergency.

Since Interpol had posted the missing-person notice on Ariana and coordinated interagency communications, Agent Esposito was present as a liaison to collect information. Interpol's files would be shared with all involved law-enforcement agencies.

Inspector Zahakis questioned Ariana in accented English and noted her date of birth, social-security number and employment details before barking out the scary questions. "You claim you were kidnapped outside of Naples over five weeks ago?"

"Yes."

"Can you describe your kidnappers?"

Down to the golden highlights in his eyes and the sensual curve of his lower lip. "I was so terrified…" She inhaled a wobbly breath. "I have memory gaps." True. She had been scared at times, and didn't remember every detail.

"You cannot even recall your kidnappers' appearance?"

Dr. Latsis spoke up. "Memory lapses are common in victims who have suffered trauma. Especially over a long period of time."

"Miss Bennett." The inspector's sharp hazel eyes bored into hers. "When you disappeared, there was speculation that you willingly left with a lover. If the affair ended badly, there is no shame in admitting this. You need not to concoct a kidnapping."

"I'm not making it up!" The walls in the crowded room closed in on her. "I did not willingly leave Naples!" But she *had* taken Dante as a lover. And would have stayed with him if he'd asked. She had to get out of here before she did anything that would cause Megaera to hurt him. She couldn't trust the authorities to protect him. She was the only one on Dante's side. The only one who could help him now.

The doctor leaned toward her. "Miss Bennett? Are you all right?"

Guilt and fear smothered her until she could barely breathe. No, she was suffocating! The seed of an idea sprouted. "I…I'm sorry." She didn't have to fake her tremors. "I want to cooperate." Again, true. "I don't understand why you're blaming *me*. I'm…confused and…and scared."

"Relax, Miss Bennett." Captain Pappas leaned forward. "No

one is accusing you. Simply tell the truth. You have nothing to be afraid of."

Wrong. The truth would get Dante killed. "I'm in a foreign country, and I don't want any…miscommunication." Ariana forced herself to hyperventilate. "I'd…like to…speak to someone from the American Embassy, get a translator and…an attorney." Tears were still so close, it was easy to make them surface. "Please. I don't want any trouble."

"She's hyperventilating." Dr. Latsis surged to her feet and turned to Gideon. "Do you have a paper bag?"

The doctor searched cabinets as Zahakis and Captain Pappas clashed. The Inspector was all for hauling her into Athens and detaining her. The Captain insisted Zahakis didn't have probable cause and vigorously defended his employee.

The doctor bent over Ariana, instructing her to breathe into a paper motion-sickness bag as the argument escalated.

Finally Gideon rose. "Enough!" he declared. "We aren't accomplishing anything. We not only have Miss Bennett to protect, but the cruise line, as well. Honoring Miss Bennett's request for an embassy representative and a lawyer will accomplish both. And I'd prefer to have the FBI involved from the beginning."

Inspector Zahakis resisted, and Ariana feared the men might come to blows before Gideon and the Captain prevailed. Zahakis stomped to the door, snapping orders to Ariana not to leave Athens without permission. He declared he'd be back as soon as she had contacted the embassy and acquired an attorney.

As Agent Esposito passed Ariana on her way out, she slipped her an empathetic smile and her card. "Ring me if you need assistance," she murmured. "I can put you in contact with the FBI office in Rome, and possibly help you locate a more reasonable local official."

Ariana let the doctor monitor her vital signs and told her she hadn't been assaulted. She returned to her cabin, amazed at how well her plan had worked. She'd never been a good liar. But then she'd never had the motivation.

No matter how valid the reason, she still felt tainted. Craving a long, hot shower, she peeled off her shirt. She slid her hand into her cargo pants pocket to retrieve her iPod and notebook. She'd been in turmoil since the moment she'd left Dante and hadn't even thought about them.

Her breath caught. They weren't there.

Don't panic. She had buttoned them in. They couldn't have fallen out. Maybe in her rush to leave the cottage, she'd forgotten which pocket. She thrust her hand into the left pocket.

Unwilling to believe what her screaming mind already knew, she stripped off her pants and frantically searched every pocket.

Empty.

Realization staggered her. That last soul-searing kiss. Dante's clever hands skimming down her body. Dante the pickpocket had stolen her iPod and notebook with the same ease and stealth as Dante the thief had stolen her heart.

Why? Why had he taken her father's files? Did he plan to sell the antiquities and take over the smuggling ring? Bewildered hurt whirled inside her, and she paced the cabin.

Had he fabricated everything? His empathy; his kisses, the poor, starving orphan story? Had it been a calculated lie to serve his selfish ends?"

No. She didn't want to believe that. But how much evidence did she need?

Once a thief, always a thief.

And she'd just lied to the police to protect him.

Her chest ached, heavy with grief. Every man she'd loved had betrayed her. The one man she'd believed in, the one she'd thought she could count on, had turned out to be the worst of all.

He'd asked her about the goddess of deception. She should have remembered Apate had a male counterpart—Dolos, the demon of trickery and wiles. Dolos gained people's trust and fed them falsehoods mixed with bits of truth, so the lies were harder to see. Dante had pretended to sympathize about Geoff and her father, while preparing to stab her in the heart. She wrapped trembling arms around herself. How could she have been so gullible? She'd fallen for the oldest con known to womankind.

She'd invested her body and soul in Dante. Invested her hopes and dreams in something she'd thought unique and wonderful. But his love had turned out to be a cruel forgery, cleverly crafted to seem real. A pretty illusion.

And like all fakes, alluring but worthless.

She'd given him everything, and he'd used her.

She stumbled on the carpet and sank to the floor. Tears would be a welcome release, but the pain cut too deep.

She was empty.

LESS THAN TWENTY-FOUR HOURS after Dante had thrown Ariana to the wolves, he sat alone at a table inside a smoky taverna in Athens.

Back to the wall, gaze on the door, he tuned out a raucous backgammon tournament. Between concern for Ariana's safety and ramping the job to full speed after his enforced absence, he'd barely slept. He gulped from a bottle of Peroni and made himself eat the souvlaki.

He scrubbed a hand over his unshaven face. He had to be at peak. Not staying on top of his game could cost Ariana her life.

The door opened, letting in a leaden slice of drab daylight and a tall, hard-as-nails Italiano in his midfifties. Ancient jeans bagged on his lanky frame, topped by a dark green shirt and weathered brown leather jacket. There was more salt in his thick salt-and-pepper mane than when they'd last met. Dante was responsible for the majority of that seasoning.

The man sauntered to his table.

"Ciao, Bernardo."

"Ciao, Dante. In trouble again, I see."

"Been in worse." Dante's booted foot kicked out a chair. "Have a seat."

"Not from what I hear." Bernardo sat across from him, his expression fierce. "The Camorra and the mystery woman, Megaera, both want your head on a platter."

"Nothing I can't handle."

"The way you handled Ariana Bennett? I saw you kissing her at the dock. What the *hell* are you doing?"

Fury flared. "The way I conduct business is my call."

"Kissing a mark in broad daylight for God and the world to see isn't smart business, *amico mio.* Not when you could end up forfeiting everything you've worked so hard to gain."

"Again, my worry."

The barmaid bustled over, and Bernardo ordered a beer. The men waited in taut silence while she delivered it and left. "Don't forget time, money and more lives than your own are at stake."

"Not for one second." Or he would have pulled out long ago. Dante took another swallow of beer, mostly to cool his temper. Anger only clouded things. "What do you have for me?"

"You won't like it."

"I have despised this assignment since I was ordered to kidnap Ariana and babysit her for weeks."

Bernardo slid a manila envelope from inside his jacket and passed it to Dante. "See for yourself."

Dante grimly flipped through time-stamped photos of Giorgio Tzekas entering Ariana's cabin. He'd visited her within an hour of her reboarding the ship. The food soured in his stomach. "So?"

"Tzekas spent a lot of time with Ariana before her inopportune appearance at the dig site in Naples."

Dante fought to keep rage at bay and his hand steady as he passed the damning pictures back. What he wanted to do was rip them to shreds. "Socializing with a coworker isn't a crime."

Bernardo tucked the envelope away. "She told the Greek police nothing. Claimed she had 'memory gaps.'"

Dante's heart stumbled. She was protecting him. And maybe her father. He shrugged. "Possible. She has been through a lot."

"*Che cazzata.* And you know it."

"I did not want to involve her to start with, *you* know that." He shoved his plate aside. "Leave her out of this!"

"We can't. Signorina Bennett may be involved up to her pretty blue eyes. Weeks ago, she sent a chip from a 'reproduction' vase to a friend in the States for analysis. Turns out it's part of a genuine artifact, missing from a dig site."

"The vase was broken in Ariana's library, and an insurance appraisal could require analysis."

Bernardo's heavy brows lowered. "Ariana speaks Greek like a native, yet she requested a translator from the police. It could be a stall tactic while her cohorts transfer the goods."

"Or perhaps she is being prudent." Dante had finally heeded his own warning to Ariana to listen to intuition, and knew she hadn't played him. Her distress over her father was genuine. As were her feelings for Dante when they'd made love, and her grief when he'd abandoned her at the dock. "You still have no information on this Megaera who kidnapped us and was Derek Bennett's mistress?"

"Only a first name and no face complicates matters."

"She is the brains of the organization. You have someone watching the island?"

"Sì. The Camorra picked up their men, but no one has retrieved the antiquities yet."

"Then Ariana has not spoken to Tasia, either." Dante scowled. "If she were working with her, she would have made contact."

"There are…concerns about you at the top. Doubts about which side you are truly on." Bernardo's weathered face creased in warning. "If Ariana Bennett is running Derek's business, she'll drag your career down with her."

Dante's fingers tightened around the bottle. "Screw my career." He believed in Ariana. Perhaps too late, he'd realized that he loved her more than duty, more than anything in this world… or the next.

"You would throw it all away?"

"Paintings, jewelry, sculptures—everything I have devoted my life to protect are merely things, Bernardo. They have no heartbeat. No soul."

Bernardo assessed him closely. "What has happened to you?"

Dante looked at his friend and mentor and admitted the truth. "Ariana happened to me." He needed to be with her, but he couldn't go to her with stains on his hands. Finishing this was his only way to keep her safe. "I will stake my life on her innocence."

"Your job has been everything to you." Bernardo rubbed his chin. "If you would risk your future, your very life, for this woman, you're in so deep you can no longer distinguish fact from fantasy."

"I know what's real." And it wasn't the dark realm he'd inhabited the past fifteen years. Ariana wasn't just any woman. She owned his heart. She might be carrying his baby. He didn't care how much she hated him when this was over. When he was free, he would *not* abandon his woman or his child as his father had done. He slammed his bottle down. "I hate using her! If she is harmed, there will be hell to pay."

Bernardo frowned thoughtfully. "I have not seen this reckless fire burning inside you since before you went to jail."

Dante battled for control. "If Ariana is hurt, those responsible will see more than my temper. No matter whose side they are on."

"Ah. It's finally happened." Bernardo's frown deepened. "I knew if you ever fell, it would be hard. I hope she's worth it."

Dante leaned forward and dropped his voice. "This is the last time, Bernardo. I no longer have the stomach for lies. After this, I am done."

"Be very careful. You are swimming in dangerous waters, Dante. I do not wish to see you drown."

He shrugged again. "My funeral."

"I fear so, *amico mio.*" Bernardo sadly shook his head and passed over a thick envelope. "Here are data, photos, everything you need. A cache of stolen antiquities was discovered when *Alexandra's Dream* was docked in Livorno, but nothing came of the investigation. Giorgio Tzekas has a gambling habit his salary can't support, and the only reason he has a job is because his father knew Elias Stamos. One of our operatives has ascertained that a man matching Giorgio's description attempted to buy a black-market amphora from a dig site near Naples."

Bernardo paused to drink. "Movement of black-market anti-quities has occurred wherever Giorgio Tzekas and the ship's priest have visited, and the pair has been seen engaged in in-tense discussions. We suspect they're front men for something much bigger."

"A cruise ship is a perfect base of operations for a smug-gling ring."

"*Sì.* I took a sample from a triptych in 'Father Connelly's' room. Analysis shows it's fifth century. It belongs to a small order of Albanian monks who reside at the Vatican. The operative I sent there reports the gardener had spoken to a foreign priest about six weeks ago, and his description sounded like Father Connelly. Their conversation stuck in his mind because of the severe storm that caused the two men to seek shelter inside the chapel, and because the father's blessing of him had seemed rather jumbled. He couldn't positively identify Patrick Connelly from a photo. The chapel had been dim, and the priest was wearing a cassock."

"Convenient."

"But a bartender in Alghero, Sardinia did recognize Father Connelly's photograph as a man who had been drinking heavily in his establishment—in civilian garb. The man paid in American dollars, and the bar doesn't see many Americans."

"Connelly is not a priest."

"Not even close. Fingerprints ID him as Mike O'Connor, bit actor and con artist. His description fits a man who romanced Contessa Valerio in Rome a few years ago and absconded with her diamond earrings. The Contessa said she and O'Connor visited the chapel and he took dozens of pictures of the icon."

"So he could have had a forgery made and slipped it in place of the real item."

"You can connect the dots as well as I can. Stolen antiquities aboard *Alexandra's Dream* with tension running between 'Father Connelly,' Giorgio and Ariana. Ariana's appraisal of the broken vase. Ariana's investigation of one of her father's known dig sites causing both of you to be kidnapped by Megaera. Derek Bennett and his lover, the same mysterious Megaera, stealing the antiquities you found on her island. What's the common denominator?"

Ariana. Dante's throat tightened. He'd only wanted to keep her safe. Instead, he'd sent her directly into the lion's den. Into mortal danger. "O'Connor and Tzekas are working for Megaera."

"That's what we need to prove. I have enough to finish off 'Father Connelly,' but we're not settling for a minor player. I want him and Giorgio to lead us to the boss. I want to put Megaera out of business." Bernardo paused. "I'm sorry, Dante. If your Ariana is involved, we must take her out, too."

Dante slowly laid the envelope on the table. "And now, *amico mio,* is when I must ask you for something that will put me forever in your debt."

ARIANA TOWELED DRY after her shower and then donned brown slacks and a copper silk blouse. As she slid her feet into short brown boots, a knock rapped on her door.

She accepted her breakfast tray from the steward. A bulky padded envelope sat to one side, and he nodded. "That was delivered for you this morning. And the switchboard operator says there's a phone message for you. It came while you were…uh…gone."

She thanked him and he strode away. Heart pounding, she set the tray on the nightstand and picked up the envelope. Her name stood out in bold, slanted script. She tore open the flap, and dumped out her passport, wallet, keys and cell phone.

Disappointment washed over her. She was silly for wishing for something more than the impersonal package. Dante had returned her things, as promised. What did she expect? Considering what he'd already stolen from her, she should be glad he'd followed through.

She flipped open her wallet. ID and credit cards present. As was her cash. She swallowed hard. And something that *wasn't* there before. A white slip of paper tucked between the bills.

Her hands trembled as she unfolded the note. It was in Italian, written in the same bold script emblazoned on the envelope.

Ariana, *mia cara,* please forgive me. When you think back, you will know I spoke the truth. I did what I must. Now you must do what is right for you. I hope that some day, you will again believe in the magic of fairy tales.

There was no signature. There was no need for one.

Ariana buried her face in her hands and burst into tears. She missed him with every breath. Even now, she still wanted to believe in him.

What was *wrong* with her?

Sorrow swamped her, and she cried for all she'd gained in the past five weeks…and for everything she'd lost.

She hated what Dante had done to her. But she couldn't hate *him.* She sobbed out her heartbreak. Her mother was right. You couldn't switch love on and off.

Ariana had admired Geoff's solid pragmatism, the very trait that had made him overly cautious. She had adored her father's imagination and penchant for dreams, which had steered him toward a doomed romance. Her father had made foolish choices, but he wasn't a bad person. He'd been a good father. Had always loved her. He'd stayed with his family and treated them well, though his heart was elsewhere.

Ariana better understood her father's choices now. Understood taking risky chances for love. How easy it was to rationalize veering from your moral compass for your soul mate. She had crossed way over the line for Dante.

And no matter how much she protested, she still loved her tough guy. She loved his intelligence and courage and wry humor. His passion and strength. She loved the lonely, hungry boy inside him that tempted him to seek the thrill and false security of stealing.

Did that make her weak and stupid? Or merely human?

The heart loves, flaws and all. Like mother like daughter. Sadie had loved a smuggler and a thief, as did Ariana.

She reread Dante's note, and her emotions calmed. He'd warned her on the island that she'd experience doubts. Had cautioned her to use intuition to discern the truth. An undercurrent had often hummed beneath his words. Unspoken subtext, as if he wished to convey thoughts he couldn't say out loud.

I hope that someday, you will again believe in the magic of fairy tales.

In the myth she had related to him, both Eros and Psyche believed the other had betrayed them, when in reality, they loved one another. Ariana inhaled sharply. Was Dante telling her that his betrayal wasn't what it seemed?

When you think back, you will know I spoke the truth.

She'd seen sorrow and regret in his eyes when he'd released her. Had heard raw pain in his voice. She gulped. Or maybe her imagination was working overtime because she didn't want to admit she'd fallen for a con man.

She slowly set the note on the bed. Dante had sent her things back, as promised. He'd followed through on every promise he'd made. He had taken a brutal beating trying to protect her from the Greek and Russian. He'd stepped between her and a lethal viper. He'd shared his body heat, his food, his tender concern.

Dante had always put her welfare ahead of his own. He had kept her safe.

Her heartbeat roared in her ears. Was it possible Dante had sacrificed himself to stop her from trying to help him, to keep her out of danger? Had he made some sort of bargain with Tasia to ensure Ariana's well-being?

Her tough-but-tender guy was all about selfless sacrifice. He had been willing to give his life for her. Nearly forty days of loyalty to compare with one seemingly traitorous betrayal.

His deep voice rang in her thoughts. *Sometimes, Ariana, lies cloak the truth, but do not invalidate what is real.*

She and Dante had shared friendship and philosophies. She had seen love in his eyes, felt love in his touch when they'd shared their bodies. "Yeah, tough guy," she muttered. "Words can be twisted. But your actions don't lie."

Only a sociopath could pull off a convincing pretense of human emotions. Dante was the opposite of a cold, selfish predator. If he were only interested in saving himself, he would have made an immediate deal with Tasia on the yacht and left Ariana to die.

Sometimes, Ariana, lies are necessary. Sometimes, circumstances force choices upon people.

Dante had run from her in the cottage with a burden too heavy, too dangerous to share. He'd denied himself to protect her. Perhaps…taking the files was another way of protecting her. Did he think she'd be safer if she wasn't in possession of dangerous information? That she'd halt her investigation if she had no leads?

I did what I must. Now you must do what is right for you.

She reached out an unsteady hand and traced the bold script. Neither her father nor Geoff had been the men they appeared on the surface. Dante might be a thief, but he was kind and decent. He'd acted with infallible integrity toward her. Had treated her with consideration and care. His gentle lovemaking and tender words were evidence of his true feelings.

She didn't even know his full name, yet she loved him with every cell of her being.

Dante had secrets he didn't feel safe divulging. Perhaps he was working things out so they could be together. The note was a message. A promise.

And Dante always kept his promises.

In the end, it came down to choices. Though she'd derided Psyche as a fool, Ariana would reject reason and cling to hope. Though her decision might bring her grief and pain, she would choose to trust Dante. Choose to believe he loved her as much as she loved him.

It was too late for her father. Her mission now was to save Dante. Ariana wrapped her arms around herself.

But how?

CHAPTER FIFTEEN

GIORGIO SCUTTLED down the stairs to the crew's quarters. This was his second errand since yesterday for Megaera, and uneasiness churned inside him. She usually contacted O'Connor, but he wasn't answering his phone. Giorgio had caught him schmoozing a buxom blonde in a secluded corridor the night before. The bastard better not be holed up in his room indulging his libido, because they were supposed to acquire another antiquity today in Athens.

He stopped in front of Ariana's cabin. How was Ariana involved? She'd arrived back on the ship looking like something the cat dragged in, claiming she'd been kidnapped. He and Mike had talked it over, and Mike was so unsettled by the news, he'd made Giorgio call the boss. Megaera had been furious when Giorgio had phoned her to report it, and demanded he immediately deliver a message to Ariana's cabin. Clearly, Ariana had escaped the boss's custody.

His hand trembled as he knocked on the door. Megaera was in a rank mood, and when she was pissed, everybody paid. But now she was offering Ariana a deal? It felt as if the boss was rapidly losing her grasp on the situation, and Giorgio was growing increasingly nervous about putting his future in the hands of people who couldn't care less if he lived or died.

Ariana warily asked him inside, and he cleared his throat. "The meeting is set. In two hours, disembark and take the metro to the Monastiraki flea market. A white Kia Picanto will be parked in a side street beside a used bookstore called *Rubáiyát*. The keys and a map will be inside the glove box."

If the message startled Ariana, she didn't show it. She coolly showed him out, and he hurried down the hallway. How much did she know? Getting involved with Megaera didn't seem like a good move for a smart broad. People who played games with Megaera always lost. He wasn't sure whether the boss wanted to reward Ariana's cleverness for escaping by offering her a job…or if she wanted to teach her a lesson. And he didn't want to know. Smuggling was one thing, but he didn't want any part of kidnapping or murder.

He reached O'Connor's cabin and raised his fist to pound on the door. If he wasn't there, Giorgio would personally search every inch of this friggin' ship. The panel swung open, and he swore. The sonofabitch had left in a hurry, not even latching his door completely closed. The closet and bureau gaped open, clothing and papers and a few reproduction antiques strewn everywhere. His stomach pitched. Many of the antiquities were missing. The real ones.

No wonder O'Connor had insisted on moving the real ones from the case in the library to "refresh" his display. Giorgio backed out of the cabin and sprinted to the crew gangplank. Panting, he skidded to a stop and addressed the security officer on duty. "Have you seen Father Connelly today?"

Officer Barnes nodded. "He left about a half hour ago."

"Did he mention where he was going?"

"He was carrying a large duffel bag full of reproductions. Said he was guest lecturing at the Athens Cultural Center."

Damn it all to hell. Obviously, O'Connor didn't want any part of kidnapping or murder, either. The sewage was circling the drain, and Mike had bailed out rather than go under. What did he know that Giorgio didn't?

Giorgio swallowed choking fear. When Megaera found out, she would kick ass and take names. And his ass wasn't gonna be first on the list.

"Thanks. I…uh…he forgot something."

He raced to the library and snatched up the one remaining

piece of value, the Hellenic fish plate, wrapped it in the daily newspaper, then ran back to the crew gangway. "I'd better get this to him right away." He stumbled down the gangplank. He barely had enough cash to ride the metro to where his boyhood pal Aetos tended bar in the Gazi district. But six Euros was all he needed to save his life.

ARIANA FINISHED scribbling her letter and thrust the pages beneath her pillow. If something happened to her, the police would have a signed affidavit detailing the past six weeks.

No loose ends.

She picked up the phone to access her messages. Maybe Dante had called. She could warn him and wouldn't have to meet with Megaéra. *Please let him have called.*

One message. She listened as Professor Riley informed her that the vase sample she'd sent for analysis was genuine. It should have shocked her, but she'd had suspicions. Father Connelly was disguising genuine artifacts among reproductions. No wonder he'd behaved so oddly the day she'd run into him in that antique shop back in Alghero...sans collar.

She sank down on the bed. Megaéra was a smuggler. Giorgio worked for her, and Connelly, his coworker, was smuggling artifacts. Not a coincidence.

She glanced at her watch. Ninety minutes before she was supposed to leave to meet Megaéra. Ariana planned to go to the meeting, intending to find out Megaéra's identity and how her operation worked, then tell the FBI. Without involving Dante.

But the fact that crew aboard *Alexandra's Dream* had used the cruise line for their smuggling operation changed everything. Not just her own neck was on the line. Captain Pappas, Gideon Dayan and Elias Stamos, the man her mother loved, were all at risk. The criminals' activity extended further than she'd imagined.

And Dante? Her heart stuttered. Surely he didn't realize how far the operation reached, either. If he was attempting to wheel and deal with Tasia, he could be caught in the fallout.

Her mother's words rang in her ears. *If I'd set aside my own selfish needs, maybe we would have all been happier. If I'd been strong and forgiving enough to do what was best for him, maybe your father would still be alive.*

She started to tremble. Perhaps her father hadn't died in vain. She knew what she had to do. Oh, God, it was so dangerous. So risky.

But risk, no matter how much it hurt, was part of really living. Truly loving. If she were to crawl back into her safe shell now, she might as well have died on Tasia's yacht. If anything happened to Dante, she would never forgive herself.

At least this way, he stood a chance.

She would give up everything for Dante, including her life. But she could not put innocent people at risk. She picked up the phone and shakily dialed Yvonne Esposito at Interpol. Agent Esposito was understanding and sympathetic to Ariana's plight. Ariana asked to be connected to the FBI office in Rome and clung to the receiver through a clicking series of switchboard holds and transfers. Finally, she reached a man who identified himself as FBI Special Agent Davis. The conversation that followed was long and painful.

Tears stung her eyes as she disconnected. Dante had declared after she'd stitched his arm that sometimes you had to do what was best for a person, even if it hurt them. She could only pray that by doing what was right, she would do what was best for him. Dante had made his choices. Now she had to stick by hers.

In order to save the man she loved, she had to let go of him.

MIKE O'CONNOR SHIFTED gears and stomped the gas pedal in his rented Fiat. It would be a punishing drive to Rome where his cousin Paulo lived. Especially once he finally reached the winding, obscure mountain roads that bypassed border checks. Paulo had helped him steal the Albanian triptych. Mike grinned. His shiftless cousin was unaware of that fact, of course. Paulo had connections with many of Rome's less reputable citizens, and had obtained false ID for Mike and slipped him into the Vatican. The wad of money he'd given his cousin had squelched pesky questions.

If anyone could help him convert the duffel bag of "investments" in the backseat into fast cash and get him out of Europe pronto, it was Paulo.

The hair on the back of Mike's neck had been prickling since Ariana Bennett had returned to the ship. He'd reported Ariana's presence at the dig site to Megaera right before the girl had disappeared, which made him an accessory to her kidnapping. The FBI would be swarming all over, and even if Ariana didn't know anything about the boss's operation, she had taken the shard from the vase in the library. She had to know by now Mike was smuggling artifacts aboard the ship. It felt too dangerous.

It felt all wrong.

He'd tried to hang in there for the big payoff. Had tried to drown his screaming instincts inside a bottle of Jameson and a luscious blonde, but when that hadn't exorcised his jitters, he'd known it was time to jump ship. He'd survived two decades in the business by listening to his gut, and he wasn't about to turn a deaf ear to blaring warning sirens.

He glanced in his rearview mirror at a blue sedan a comfortable distance behind, and exhaled a relieved breath. He was five miles out of Athens, and traffic had thinned. He'd make better time.

He lowered the window partway and lit a cigarette from the pack he'd purchased at the petrol station. The heady buzz of nicotine flooded his system. He'd had to sacrifice the smokes for his priestly cover. Father Patrick Connelly had plodded into a men's room in the Athens Cultural Center and Mike O'Connor had strolled out, his hair dyed chestnut brown and a false beard and mustache hiding his face. The good father had faded into history, never to be seen again.

That little screwup Tzekas could take the brunt of Megaera's fury and the heat from the law. Mike had a hefty haul from this job, and there was always another scam on the horizon.

He checked his mirror again. The blue sedan had caught up and pulled out to pass. He slowed, allowing it to whiz by as he switched on the radio. Humming, he glanced up, and swore as the sedan abruptly braked. Idiot must have won his driver's license as a prize in a cereal box.

Without warning, the sedan's emergency flashers blinked on. The car swung diagonally across the road and blocked both lanes, forcing Mike to slam on his brakes. The violent curse had barely exploded from his lips before a tall, lanky man leaped out and strode toward him, gun drawn.

Mike recognized the guy with the gun. His guts twisted painfully and he fought the urge to puke.

"Colonel Bernardo Moretti, Guardia di Finanza." The man Mike knew as Bernardo Milo from *Alexandra's Dream* flashed a police badge with one hand and pointed his pistol at Mike's head with the other. "I'm the commander of a smuggling investigation task force with multinational jurisdiction. I've been tailing you since you disembarked from the ship. Keep your hands in sight and exit the vehicle."

Mike climbed out, his knees shaking like a little kid's, and Moretti made him lean on the Fiat with his arms outstretched and legs splayed. Cars began to stop behind both sides of the roadblock. Humiliation burned up Mike's neck and into his face as the passengers gawked at him spread-eagled on the car while Morietti patted him down and cuffed his hands behind his back. The entire ordeal took maybe two minutes. The longest two minutes of his life.

Colonel Moretti extracted the duffel bag from the backseat, grabbed Mike by the arm and marched him toward the waiting sedan. "Michael O'Connor, you're under arrest for smuggling stolen artifacts."

THUNDER SNARLED OVERHEAD, and a damp slap of wind scattered pebbles across the pavement as Ariana climbed inside the small white car and studied the map Tasia had left for her. After she'd spoken to FBI Special Agent Davis, he had contacted the task force in charge of smuggling investigations in the area. Ariana was awed at how quickly they'd formed a plan and phoned her back with instructions. A female undercover officer posing as a store clerk had met her in a fitting room in a busy Athens mall midway to the flea market. A microphone the size of a matchstick was clipped inside Ariana's bra, and her car was being discreetly tailed by undercover officers.

Before the end of the day, Megaera was going to jail.

The map led her thirty miles along the rugged coastline to a small cove. She exited the car and stared at the private dock where the yacht was moored. If she boarded that boat and it sailed, the FBI wouldn't be able to immediately follow. She scrubbed clammy palms on her slacks. If she didn't board, Dante would never be free.

She squared taut shoulders and marched down the dock. A man greeted her, said he was the captain and led her below to a huge stateroom with opulent Moorish decor. The room was overly warm and redolent with Megaera's perfume. Ariana shrugged off her suede jacket and draped it over the arm of a plush chair as the ship's engines started and the craft set sail. Where was her father's mistress?

The door opened behind her. "Hello, Ariana."

At the familiar voice, Ariana turned. A stunning brunette with flawless olive skin, dark eyes and a sultry mouth regarded her with practiced ease. Either the woman was younger than Derek, or she'd aged extremely well. Her camel tailored slacks and cashmere sweater hugged her lithe figure to perfection. The Etruscan bracelet winked at the edge of her sleeve like a cruel taunt.

"Hello, Tasia." Ariana feigned calmness. "Where are we going?"

"Just for a little sail."

Not helpful to the FBI agents listening in. Ariana's glance strayed to the bracelet on Tasia's wrist. While attaching the hidden mic, the FBI agent had coached her on how to elicit information. Starting with what the women had in common.

"You're still wearing the bracelet my father gave you. Either you admire fine jewelry, or you and Dad really cared about each other."

"Does that disturb you?"

Tasia hadn't affirmed or denied. Ariana knew this game. "Should it?"

"Actually, you're the reason Derek sought me out. Once you were born so ill and weak, Sadie didn't have time for anyone else. Derek was lonely, at loose ends."

Ariana nearly surrendered to the sick clutch in her belly before she steadied. This woman would not exploit her weaknesses. "My mother loved my father. And he knew it."

"Yet, I'm the one who suffered." Bitterness sharpened Tasia's tone. "I waited years for him, listened to countless, irritating excuses. I spent every holiday alone while he was with his family."

Rage stung Ariana. "Common hazards of an affair with a married man."

"Touché." Tasia surprised her with a husky laugh. "You're refreshingly honest."

If you only knew. "Why did you ask to see me?"

"You survived the island, outwitted the Camorra and turned the Napoletano to our cause. You manipulated the cops and secured incriminating data." Tasia slanted her a smile that seemed almost fond. "*And* cleverly destroyed...sensitive information. You're your father's daughter."

A compliment to her father's duplicity. How had she lived with him her entire life and not recognized his dual nature? Ariana inhaled a quivering breath. *Wait a minute.* How could Tasia possibly know she'd burned the letters? Had she been back to the island and taken the antiquities—taken the evidence of her crimes?

Ariana's breathing sped up as the full import of Tasia's statement sank in. *You turned the Napoletano to our cause.* "How—"

Tasia raised her hand in a gesture to wait and picked up the phone. "Come to the main stateroom."

Moments later, Dante strode inside. He was dressed in his usual head-to-toe badass black. His sculpted face was shadowed with stubble, his beautiful eyes wary. Tired lines bracketed his mouth.

Ariana smothered a gasp. *Oh, no!* Dante had come to make his own deal with Tasia. To protect Ariana. He'd martyred himself for her, she knew it as well as her own name. "Dante," she breathed.

Shock flashed in his eyes before they darkened. His nostrils flared with anger. Then his face went as hard and cold as the mirror above the bar. "Ciao, Ariana," he drawled as indifferently as if he'd never kissed her, never held her, never made love to her. His aloofness was so convincing, a chill crawled up her spine. "Here on business?"

She fought a momentary battle with uncertainty. Surely Dante wasn't a real traitor? Surely he didn't think she was?

No. She believed in him. Believed in his promises. He was playing his part, just the way she was. Now he'd be caught in the surprise arrest. If he resisted, he could get badly hurt.

Well, she'd be damned if she'd let him.

"Ciao, Dante." She sent him a silent plea, while striving for the same cool tone. His spoken words often had subtext humming beneath. She hoped he would discern her true meaning. "I assume we're here for the same reason."

He shot her a barbed glance, his eyes chips of black ice. "Money."

Tasia nodded as if satisfied. "Now we can proceed."

Ariana declined champagne and caviar. She accepted coffee only to give her nervous hands something to do.

Their hostess popped champagne and filled glasses at the far end of the room, and Dante bent to growl in Ariana's ear. "Why in the hell are you here?"

She held his gaze. His features were edged with stress and fatigue. "You thought you'd scared me off and I'd be curled in Mommy's lap, whimpering?" she murmured.

His eyes narrowed. "I underestimated your stubbornness."

"You don't know the half of it." She gripped his forearm, his muscles steely beneath the supple leather. "Grab a Zodiac, life-boat, whatever, and *leave!*"

Fury tightened his chiseled face. "What are you up to?" he managed to yell in a whisper. "You will get yourself killed!"

"I'll be fine. Make an excuse and go!"

"If you think I would leave you here, you have underestimated me. San Gennaro, help us both."

He visibly stifled his ire as Tasia returned with two filled flutes and sank gracefully onto the maroon velvet love seat. She handed a glass to Dante and patted the cushions beside her. When he sat, she leaned so close her breasts brushed his arm. "A toast." She slid her palm intimately up his thigh. "To a mutually beneficial partnership."

Ariana's fingers curled with the urge to commit violence, and Dante's sardonic glance said he knew exactly what she was thinking.

Dante set his glass on the coffee table. "What exactly do you want from us?"

"Beautiful *and* practical." Tasia crossed her long legs. "I had an important buy arranged in Athens today, and my brokers are incommunicado." Anger flared in her eyes, and she took a deliberate sip of champagne. "Dante, I've learned that you're a skilled broker. I'd planned to ask Ariana to help me slip on board *Alexandra's Dream.*" She took another sip. "But since I am unable to reach my contacts, I've reconsidered. I won't risk myself if anything happens to be…askew. However, I do have another job for Ariana."

"What kind of job?" Ariana asked, remembering the FBI agent's admonition to lure Tasia into discussing specifics.

"Since my contacts have left me adrift, I need you to take some papers aboard *Alexandra's Dream.*"

"I won't courier anything blind."

Tasia smiled. "You'll make an excellent business associate."

Dante rested his elbows on his thighs and spread his legs wide. The aggressive male gesture not only displaced Tasia's hand, but commandeered maximum space on the love seat, crowding Tasia into the corner. "And I don't deal without knowing what my associates are involved in," Dante added. "Are you connected with the Camorra? What is this about?"

"Wise of you to steer clear of the mob. I pay well to do the same." Tasia watched Dante over the rim of her champagne flute, making Ariana chafe with anxiety. She needed him gone when the police arrived. Provided the FBI could find the yacht.

"I do adore a thorough man," Tasia added. She stared at Dante for a lingering moment before strolling to a small wall safe and extracting a stack of papers, which she handed to Ariana.

"Invoices for antiquity purchases…by Elias Stamos?" The surprise in Ariana's voice was genuine.

Tasia sat and regarded Ariana. "Have you ever been betrayed by a lover?"

Ariana went still. Her apprehensive glance flicked to Dante. "I'm female and breathing, aren't I?"

Dante's brows lowered, and Tasia laughed. "I knew you would understand." Her mouth hardened. "As a young woman working in my parents' taverna on Corfu, I fell in love with a patron. He was wealthy and came from a good family."

Ariana fumbled with her cup and hot coffee stung her leg. Tasia was involved with *Elias Stamos!* Were they using *Alexandra's Dream* to smuggle antiquities? Fate couldn't be so cruel to Sadie.

Tasia passed her a linen napkin. "When I became pregnant, he walked away. He didn't think me worthy of his name, though I bore his son."

Dante's disconcerted gaze sought Ariana's. She swallowed a lump in her throat and stared into her coffee, the same rich brown as Dante's eyes. Was he worried about the possibility of becoming a father?

He frowned at Tasia. "Elias Stamos abandoned you and his child?"

"Oh, he provided financial support, through his lawyers. He thought he'd bought me off, like a common prostitute. He left us on our own and married another woman, better suited to his station. They had two daughters before he was widowed." Tasia nodded at Ariana. "I hear he's sniffing after your mother."

She blotted her pants so she didn't have to look at Tasia's cruel smile. "You want revenge on Elias."

"I imagine that makes you happy, as you were so devoted to your father. It will be a double blow to Elias to discover that Sadie's daughter works for me." Tasia's eyes glittered. "After his wife, Alexandra, died, I swallowed my pride and went to him again, begged him to acknowledge Theo. There was no longer a reason not to, but he refused."

"I'm…dismayed he would shun his only son." *And isn't that what you asked my father to do to me?*

"Eventually, Elias agreed to meet him…if Theo initiated it. They've developed a sort of relationship." Tasia snarled. "Far too little, too late."

"From what I've read of Elias, he came from wealth," Ariana said carefully. "But he built his cruise empire on his own, with hard work and strong ethics."

"Elias had every advantage, but *I* built *my* empire from nothing! I've studied hard, worked harder and planned carefully. Now, it's all in place. Tomorrow, Elias will be arrested for smuggling." She offered Ariana another napkin as coolly as if she weren't plotting to torpedo a man's life. "The fact that he's only guilty of possessing a massive ego makes it all the sweeter."

"Theo condones your revenge against his father?" Ariana crumpled the stained linen, attempting to hide her horror. Not only would Elias be devastated, but so would Sadie, along with Elias's daughters and granddaughter.

"Theo is too honest to trust with this. He knows nothing." She shrugged. "He's only met his father recently, and will get over his duplicity."

Dante angled his body toward Tasia. "You're a patient woman, and very clever to wait so long. No one will suspect you. How have you arranged this?"

"I knew there was much more to you, Napoletano, than a gorgeous face." She glided scarlet-tipped fingers down Dante's cheek as Ariana fumed. Where was the FBI?

Tasia glanced at Ariana. "Remember the vase in the ship's library, Ariana? Before it got broken, it was assumed to be a reproduction. My people planted many stolen artifacts aboard. Some are on display as 'reproductions' and some secreted inside the ship Elias named after his precious lamented Alexandra. Today's purchase was to be the pièce de résistance. An almost perfectly preserved fourth century bust of Aristotle discovered during the excavations to build the new Acropolis Museum. Elias contributed generously to the museum fund. Possession of a stolen artifact regarded to be one of the truest representations of Aristotle ever found will earn him not only a prison sentence, but the hatred of his countrymen."

Tasia scowled. "Police investigators will receive an anonymous tip. They'll find the invoices Ariana took aboard, along with recent deposits to Elias's 'secret' bank accounts. I had planned to watch him be arrested, but with my contacts at loose ends, I'll have to settle for hearing about it from Ariana."

She poured another serving of champagne. "Elias is treated like a god in Greece because of his pride in his heritage and large contributions to Greek cultural institutions. But not even his money will prevent his beloved cruise empire—and his prized reputation—from imploding after he's arrested for bastardizing antiquities."

"Hell hath no fury," Dante muttered drily.

Tasia caressed her bracelet. "After Elias is in jail, Dante will help me broker the antiquities from the island—my retirement fund. For a generous payment, of course."

The stateroom phone trilled, and Tasia rose to answer it.

"Stay calm," Dante warned Ariana. "Don't do anything rash."

Tasia hung up after a brief conversation. "The captain requests our presence on deck to meet a visitor."

Ariana held her breath. Hopefully, the cavalry. Tasia led and

Ariana hung back, forcing Dante to slow behind her. As Tasia ascended the stairs, Ariana turned to him. "I'm expecting the police," she hurriedly whispered. "I'm wearing a wire, and I hope they heard everything. I've negotiated a deal for you with the FBI. In return for our joint cooperation and testimony against Tasia's ring, you'll serve less than a year. Then your record will be wiped clean."

Stunned amazement flashed in his eyes. "Why do men fool themselves into believing they can control women?" he muttered.

"Listen," she hissed. "I had the agreement faxed to me at the ship's library in writing. I had arranged for you to voluntarily turn yourself in later, but I didn't know you'd be here. Don't resist arrest."

Tasia called down the stairway. "What's the delay?"

"Sorry," Ariana answered. "I forgot my jacket." She cupped Dante's warm, bristled cheek. It might be the last chance she'd have to touch him for a very long time. Her throat tightened. "If you go straight, I promise I'll be there when you get out. I promise I'll wait for you."

Ariana turned and hurried up the stairs, smothered by foreboding. Dante would have had a choice if he'd been given the option to turn himself in. Would he hate her for bargaining away his freedom? What if he tried to escape? Her heart lurched. Dante was intelligent enough to accept the chance for a new life.

Up top, the wind shoved Ariana forward, and the deck pitched under her feet. She staggered and gripped the railing. The yacht was now anchored in a secluded cove, surrounded by lashing gray waves. Distant rock formations jutted from the choppy sea. There were no signs of civilization. Or visitors.

Dante covered her hand with his, gave her fingers a reassuring squeeze. "No matter what happens, trust me."

What was he going to do? Ariana turned to face him, and saw Agent Esposito boarding from a speedboat moored at the stern. The Interpol Agent's right hand gripped a big black pistol.

Ariana frowned in puzzlement, even as Dante released her and went rigid. "The Interpol agent," she murmured. "What's she doing here?"

Tasia boldly stepped forward to challenge the new arrival. "What is this all about?"

Agent Esposito smiled, but there was no humor in the gesture. She trained her gun on Ariana. "If you'd pick up your damn messages, you'd know. Wake up, Anastasia. You're harboring a traitor. She inclined her head toward Ariana and Dante. "You two, don't move. And keep your hands where I can see them."

Dante swore, and fear surged in Ariana like a cold, choking wave. "W-hat? But you work for Interpol."

Tasia's accusing gaze locked on Ariana. "She's also been on my payroll for years. And I pay better."

The blood drained from Ariana's head, making her dizzy. "Can't I trust *anyone?*"

Tasia sighed. "Explain, Yvonne."

"How do you think I've supplied you with information all these years? I have the phone lines monitored. Daddy's girl spilled her guts to the FBI." Esposito scowled. "She negotiated a deal for handsome here and sold you out."

"I'm so disappointed, Ariana. I liked you." Tasia shook her head. "We women always make the wrong choices when it comes to men."

Agent Esposito shrugged. "I'm afraid there will have to be a drowning accident. Poor Miss Bennett was already distraught over her father. Then the alleged kidnapping and suspicions about her own culpability pushed her into complete instability."

Ariana's heart hammered against her ribs as Dante subtly shifted. He was preparing to defend her, no matter the cost. Trapped, terrified, she knew who she could trust, more than anyone. Her tough guy.

Keeping the gun pointed at Ariana, Esposito moved closer to Tasia. "Everyone in the security office saw her breakdown. When she disappears from the ship and her body is found floating not far away, a tragic fall overboard will be easily accepted."

Dante's stance went combat ready, his level stare fixated on the women. "So far, your crimes only warrant jail time. Don't cross the line into murder."

"Killing her seems rather drastic." Tasia looked at Agent Esposito. "As Derek's daughter, her life does have some sentimental value. She's quite attractive. I have associates who would pay top dollar for her...services. She'd never be heard from again."

A low growl rumbled in Dante's throat, and Esposito shook her head. "Too chancy. With Derek gone and his evidence in our hands, the girl isn't connected to us. We'll never be caught." She motioned Dante aside with the gun. "You can still prove your usefulness. Be smart and step away from her. Or you can choose to join her. Nobody will miss you."

Ariana started to protest, but Dante spoke over her.

"Wrong," he said calmly. "I am an undercover police officer, working for a multinational task force. For obvious reasons, I don't carry a badge or identification, but my supervisor will confirm when provided with a code number."

Ariana reeled. "You're a *cop?*"

Dante's gaze didn't waver from Agent Esposito as both women stonily assessed him. "Headquarters knows about Giorgio and the priest. They have copies of the intel on the iPod and notebook, and coins from your island stash are in their possession. I'm wearing a tracking device and have already signaled an extraction team. You are surrounded. You'll never get away with killing us. *You* be smart, and surrender. There's no way out."

The Interpol agent's eyes narrowed. "Nobody knows about *me.* And nobody will."

Ariana's heartbeat thundered in her ears as she stared into the bore of the gun. Stared into the eye of death. "Wait! I'm wir—"

Esposito's finger tightened on the trigger. A flash seared Ariana's vision, a roar echoed. Dante shoved her down, threw his body in front of her as three blasts fired in rapid succession.

Dante jerked with each explosion. His blood sprayed the deck and then the force of the bullets slammed him over the railing, into the sea.

CHAPTER SIXTEEN

"DANTE!" Ariana screamed. A splash resounded and water geysered up.

She didn't think. Didn't hesitate. She tore a life preserver off the railing and jumped after him.

The icy slap of water ripped away her breath, and she floundered. One hand death-gripped the life preserver and she flailed with the other. She grabbed Dante's hair and yanked him to the surface. "Breathe," she yelled. He didn't move, didn't respond. "Dante, breathe!"

He coughed weakly, and her heart leaped. He was alive!

Even with the flotation device, their combined weight pulled her low into the roiling waves, and she choked on brine.

Dante coughed again. Blood streamed from his shoulder, more blood streaked his face. There was blood everywhere. He struggled against her. "Let me go. Too heavy."

"Stop fighting me!" Panic screamed inside her, but she stubbornly clung to him. "I'm not letting you go."

Bullets pocked the surface, ploughed into the waves. She kicked toward a rock formation that looked miles away.

Though weak and injured, Dante kicked also. "You can't swim."

She gritted her teeth against a surge of hysteria. "Just move!"

The hail of bullets stopped. Esposito probably figured they were doomed, and the shark had escaped.

Sharks. Dante was bleeding profusely. If they didn't drown first... Ariana thrust aside crippling fear. "C'mon tough guy, a little farther."

The ocean slammed her against the rock formation, knocking the breath from her again. She dragged Dante into a gap between boulders. Freezing water pummeled her. She held fast to Dante, battling terror. His face was as colorless as the murky sky. The sea around them churned red with his blood. She had no way to stem the bleeding or prevent shock. "It'll be okay, Dante. The cavalry is coming, right?"

"Jacket," he mumbled. "Kevlar panels. Heavy. Get it off."

Buffeted by pitching waves, she tried to brace against a boulder so she could comply. She needed to keep him alert. "Why didn't you tell me you were a cop? I'm furious with you."

He merely groaned.

"Hey, tough guy. You passing on a fight?"

"Tesoro," he whispered. "Forgive…" He went slack.

She shook him. *"Dante?"* Helpless despair clenched her insides. "If you die on me, I will *never* forgive you, do you hear me?"

She was trying to alternately beg and bully him back to consciousness when helicopter blades thwacked overhead, whirling wind and water into a stinging tornado. Speedboats roared up and frogmen rappelled from the chopper and splashed from boats.

Men surrounded her. In the melee of shouted questions and grabbing hands, they determined she was unhurt and took Dante from her. Her heart lodged in her throat as she watched his limp, bleeding body being winched up to the helicopter. The chopper sped away, and she was hoisted into a boat. Someone draped blankets around her and led her below, out of the wind.

It seemed only minutes before they reached the port of Piraeus, but Ariana had lost all sense of time. The officers bundled her into a police car and drove her to the hospital, where she was locked inside a small exam room with two cops guarding the door. A nurse brought her dry scrubs and a pair of paper surgical booties. The woman took her vitals, dabbed ointment on her scrapes and then departed.

Nerve-racking minutes later, the door swung open. "Signorina Bennett." A lanky Italian with graying hair, craggy features and wise brown eyes extended his hand. "I'm Colonnello Bernardo Moretti, with the Guardia di Finanza. I'm commanding the task force that is conducting this investigation. I apologize for the hasty transfer, but your safety was our utmost concern. I'm told a doctor will be available to see you soon."

"I don't need a doctor." Ariana didn't care that she sounded desperate. "There was a man with me—he was shot. His name is Dante. I need to know how he is. *Please.*"

Worry etched deep lines in the steely officer's face. "I'm Dante's lifelong friend, his mentor and his boss. He was rushed into surgery. The best way to help him right now is by telling me everything you know. I have no intention of leaving him, so I'll be taking your statement here. My report will note that you needed to be observed by the medical staff after your ordeal. The moment we're done, we'll go to Dante."

Her insides churned at the delay, but she was grateful the colonel had the position and influence to allow them to stay at the hospital. "All right. May I call my mother, first?" She phoned Sadie and asked her to bring dry clothes and check on Dante's progress when she arrived. She arranged to meet her mother in the surgery suite.

For the next ninety minutes, Ariana recited details for Colonel Moretti, answered questions and anxiously watched the clock.

Finally, the colonel nodded. "I have what I need."

Ariana accompanied him to the surgery suite, attempting to reconcile herself to Dante's bombshell. She'd known Dante lied for a living. If he had told her he lied on the law's side, she wouldn't have worried about saving him from the Camorra or Tasia. Then again, she wasn't thrilled with undercover cops, and probably would never have confided in him. "How long have you known Dante?"

"Since he was a boy."

Dante had insisted he'd spoken the truth to her about his past. She frowned thoughtfully. "The mentor reference. You arrested him, right? Gave him the 'scared straight' treatment?"

"He *told* you?" Colonel Moretti threw her a startled look. "He never reveals his history. He must completely trust you."

Her lips trembled. Had she profaned Dante's trust and failed him? If she hadn't interfered and called the FBI, he wouldn't have been shot.

Tears welled in her eyes, and Moretti's glance sharpened. "And you love him."

Ariana nodded. "More than life." She only prayed she'd have the chance to tell her tough guy how much he meant to her.

"Then he is very fortunate."

Sadie met Ariana accompanied by a handsome older Greek man she recognized as Elias Stamos.

"Mom, how is Dante?"

Sadie hugged her. "No one will tell us anything."

Her breath caught. That couldn't be good.

Colonel Moretti left to fax Ariana's statement to the police station and elicit information about Dante. Sadie introduced Ariana to Elias. He warmly clasped her hand. "I'm so sorry for your troubles. I've arranged a private waiting area where you can speak to your mother."

Ariana trudged into the room, her shoulders heavy with dread. Sadie drew Ariana down beside her on a sofa. "Honey, are you all right?

Ariana sighed. "Everything's gone to hell, Mom."

"It will be all right, honey." Sadie gently kissed her cheek. "Now, who is this Dante you're so concerned about?"

"He's an undercover officer." She related a censored version of the past six weeks. Certain things you just didn't tell your mom. "We grew very close. He protected me." Her voice caught. "The bullets they're removing from his body were meant for me."

"He must have an iron will." Sadie patted her hand. "Such a strong, brave man will make it through this."

"He has to," Ariana whispered. She couldn't bear to think otherwise.

Elias entered with a tray of coffee mugs. Ariana saw Moretti behind him and surged to her feet. "What did you find out?"

"Nothing new. We'll be informed when Dante is out of surgery." The colonel shook his head. "He was already in position on the yacht when the FBI arranged Ariana's meeting. A hazard of interagency undercover operations."

An hour later, his cell phone rang and he strode outside. He returned smiling. "That didn't take long. Giorgio Tzekas was picked up attempting to sell a Hellenic fish plate in a gay bar in Gazi. Sniveled like a baby when he was arrested." His smile broadened. "We used Ariana's deposition to threaten him and Father Connelly—Mike O'Connor—with accessory to attempted murder, and they sang louder than Pavarotti. Yvonne Esposito and Anastasia Catomeris are going to prison for a long time."

Anastasia Catomeris. The final piece of the puzzle fell into place. Since there was no *C* in ancient Greek, Tasia was the *A/K* mentioned so often in her father's notes.

Elias started. "Anastasia is involved?"

"She was framing you for smuggling artifacts aboard *Alexandra's Dream*." Ariana refused coffee. She couldn't swallow anything past the fear. Why didn't anyone know Dante's condition? "She claimed you'd taken advantage of her and was furious that you never publicly acknowledged Theo."

"I don't suppose she mentioned she calculatedly got pregnant in order to marry into my money?" Elias sighed. "I made mistakes where Theo was concerned, but he and I have reached an understanding. I hate to see him hurt like this." He glanced at Colonel Moretti. "I should be the one to break the news to him about his mother."

Moretti nodded. "That will be arranged." He inclined his head at Ariana. "The head nurse offered the staff's locker room for you to bathe. We could be here a while, and you'll be more comfortable."

Ariana hesitated, then decided she could worry as easily in the shower. And if…no…*when* Dante came to, she wouldn't smell like bargain day at the fish market.

A nurse led her down the hallway. Ariana rushed through her shower holding sorrow at bay. Her last words to Dante had been *I'm furious with you.* She hadn't meant them, but he didn't know that. What if—

Don't think like that. He'll be okay. She hastily donned the gray slacks, sapphire blouse and black flats her mother had brought.

She hurried back, still braiding her wet hair. Colonel Moretti stood in front of the nurses' station talking to a nurse in blood-spattered surgical scrubs. The nurse offered him a clear plastic bag. "Here are his effects."

Ariana stumbled to a halt in the corridor. *Effects?* A familiar watch was in the bag with a wallet and a gun.

Moretti grimly accepted the package.

Her heart lurched, and she broke into a run. "Colonel? What's happened to Dante?"

Colonel Moretti jerked his gaze up. "Ariana. Come with me." He put an arm around her and guided her into an empty room. "I'm so sorry, *bella.*"

Oh, Dante. Pain squeezed the breath from her lungs. *No.* She couldn't bear to hear this.

Moretti closed the door, then turned and grasped her shoulders. "Let me explain. We had to tell everyone, the press, the staff, that Dante was dead. We had to make them believe it. You weren't supposed to overhear."

Fragile wings of hope fluttered inside her. "What are you saying?"

"Dante has worked inside the Camorra a long time. He was checked into the hospital under his cover name. The mob must not doubt he's dead. Then he'll be safe."

"But he's...*alive?*"

"*Sì.* We've moved him to a secret location where he'll be monitored by trusted medical personnel."

The smothering weight dropped off her chest and a swoop of relief weakened her knees. "I want to be with him."

"I expected as much." Moretti nodded. "I apologize for unintentionally causing you distress. I had planned to bring you to Dante after we relocated him."

She explained the situation to her mother, and then Colonel Moretti drove Ariana to a private clinic outside the city. The doctor there told her Dante had grazed his head during the fall and sustained a superficial scalp wound. His Kevlar-reinforced jacket had blocked two bullets to his chest, and one bullet had lodged in his upper arm. There was no major muscle damage and he would regain full range of motion. His wounds were not serious, but he needed to sleep off the sedatives.

She hurried into Dante's room. He was pale, but his chest rose and fell with strong, rhythmic breaths. Humbled and grateful for the miracle, she reached out shaking fingers and gently touched his hand.

Ariana watched over him as he drifted in and out of sleep, only leaving him for a short visit to the lab. She was glad, and yet at the same time a little upset by the results of her pregnancy test. How would Dante feel about it?

When she got back to his room, she phoned Sadie with an update on Dante's condition, and her mom concurred she should stay with him.

She tenderly brushed his thick, dark hair back from the bandage at his forehead. As if she was going anywhere.

Rain started to fall sometime during the night. Cold and shivering in the dark, she carefully crawled into the hospital bed on Dante's uninjured side. She curled up next to him and tumbled into an uneasy sleep.

"HO FAME." Dante's hoarse mutter startled Ariana awake.

His sooty lashes fluttered and she looked into alert but puzzled brown eyes. She sat up and smiled. "You're *hungry?* That's a good sign."

"Ariana?" He glanced warily around. "Where are we?"

"Private clinic. Do you remember what happened?"

He hesitated. Blinked. *"Sì."* Anger flared, and he looked away.

When he focused on her again, his expression was guarded. "You were not injured?"

Her heart wrenched. Was he angry with her? "I'm fine, thanks to you."

"How long was I out?"

"A little over twenty-four hours." Hours of waiting and worry. "By the way, you were admitted as Vincenzo Liberatore."

"I am getting up." He threw back the covers.

"No!" She pressed the call button. "Ask the nurse first."

He swung his legs over the edge of the bed and grimaced at his hospital gown. "Where are my clothes?"

"Between seawater and blood..." She faltered, and his gaze narrowed. "They were wrecked." She removed a bag of clothing and personal care items from the cupboard and set them on the bed. "Bernardo brought you these."

"Va bene." He ripped off the tape from his IV and yanked the needle from his arm.

"You can't do that!" She ran for the door. "Help!"

A dark-haired pixie hurried into the room, and Ariana waved at Dante. "Tough guy jerked out his IV!"

The nurse strode up to Dante. "Get back into bed and I'll check your vitals—"

"I've had enough rest." He picked up his clothes. "I'm going to shower and shave. Then I am leaving." He stalked into the bathroom and shut the door.

"Seems steady enough." The nurse turned to Ariana. "Is he always that...ah..."

Ariana wrinkled her nose. "Uh-huh."

"I wish you luck." The nurse left to prepare discharge papers.

Ariana paced the room. She needed every ounce of luck. Dante had awakened as grumpy as a grizzly after hibernation. He'd said, *I am leaving.* Not *we.*

No longer forced to babysit her, was he about to tell her to get lost? Her chest tightened. Not that she would blame him.

She heard the shower stop. Dante called out a request for a

dry bandage for his arm. Her attempt to convince him to ring the nurse was unsuccessful. He insisted his stitches looked fine and opened the door a crack to accept the bandage.

Minutes later, he emerged from the bathroom amidst a cloud of laurel-scented steam. He was wearing snug, faded jeans and a white button-down shirt rolled over his tanned forearms. His silky hair was damp and tousled, his chiseled face clean-shaven. He looked gorgeous, and capable and still murder-ously angry.

He sat on the bed and pulled on socks and brown boots. If he was in pain, his abrupt movements didn't show it. "What is hap-pening with the case?"

"The cops arrested Giorgio and Father Connelly, who sold out Tasia, who then sold out Esposito. Antiquities were recovered from *Alexandra's Dream* and the island and the authorities are investigating all of Tasia's dealings."

He stood and shrugged into a brown leather jacket. "It is over, then."

"Is it?" She gulped. "Over?"

He held her gaze, his beautiful eyes unreadable. "We have much to discuss. In private."

That sounded ominous.

They ate a quick, silent breakfast of eggs, toast and coffee in the room. Then Dante had a behind-closed-doors consultation with the doctor and signed himself out.

Ariana barely clung to her faltering composure as a cab ferried them to a nearby hotel. Dante checked in as Roberto Serrano and paid with cash. How many aliases did this guy have?

The luxurious room on the sixth floor was an elegant blend of sea-and-sand colors. She walked to the window and stared out at wet terra-cotta roofs and wind-lashed trees. "Are you Vin-cenzo, Roberto, Dante...or none of the above?"

He strode up behind her. "I didn't lie to you about my name."

"I wasn't accusing. Just asking." She turned and saw him re-moving his jacket. He leaned to toss it onto a chair, and the V of his shirt gaped, revealing a dark bruise. Ariana gasped. "What caused that?"

He looked down, shrugged. "Bullets slamming into Kevlar."

She stepped close and unbuttoned his shirt, shoving aside his blocking hands. "No, let me see."

She parted the placket. Two huge purple bruises mottled his bronzed skin. One was on his left pectoral muscle. With shaking fingers, she gently touched the other—directly over his heart. "I'm sorry," she whispered. Tears welled up, spilled down her cheeks.

"Shh." Dante gathered her into his embrace. "Don't cry."

"This is my fault."

"What are you talking about?"

"It was my fault you were shot. Then I thought you were dead," she sobbed. "It was all to deceive the Camorra, but I thought you were dead."

He swore. "*Mia cara,* I am sorry."

"You nearly *died* for me."

"I was fully aware of my actions." He held her, rocked her while she cried. "I will not let you accept liability."

"You were pulled off duty because of *my* investigation, and it ruined your cover inside the mob. I put your career and your life at terrible risk." She choked back sobs. "Believe me, I understand the resentment of having your life shanghaied by forces beyond your control."

He tensed. "Exactly. It infuriated me, as it did you."

Enveloped in Dante's warm strength, in his scent, wrapped in his arms, realization hit. She'd botched his case, jeopardized his career and his life, and he was mad. Rightly so. But she'd spent six weeks telling him how much she hated being lied to. How much she hated cops. He was leery because he also thought she was angry with *him.*

She inhaled slowly…and leaped without a net. "Dante, the reason I turned you in to the FBI is because I wanted what was best for you. Because…I love you."

He went absolutely still. *"Che cosa?"* he asked hoarsely.

"When I thought I'd lost you, it was the most horrible moment of my life." She looked up into his wary brown eyes. "*Ti amo,* Dante. I love you."

"I think… I need to sit." He walked to the bed and dropped onto the edge of the mattress.

She knelt in front of him, nerves jittering. Was his reaction good or bad? "Are you all right?"

"I don't know anymore." He scrubbed his hand over his face. "I am furious, *bella.* But not with you. With myself." Anguish swam in his gaze. "Every man in your life has lied to you. Betrayed you. I have lied to you since the moment we met. How can you say you love me after I caused you great pain?"

She rested her palms on his knees. "Dante, you have also given me the greatest joy."

He stared at her in disbelief. "All these years, I have lived only for my job. A job you despise. I have nothing to offer you. No ancestry, no history, no family." He swallowed hard. "Not even a legitimate name."

"Wrong, tough guy. You possess many priceless treasures. Integrity. Courage. Loyalty. Honor." She touched his cheek. "You're everything I want. Everything I need."

His breath caught. He took her hand and pressed a kiss into her palm. "Come." He drew her up to sit beside him and gently wiped the moisture from her cheeks. "There are things I must say."

Her stomach cramped. He hadn't said he loved her back.

His big hand enveloped hers. "When we separated at the ship, Bernardo was aboard, watching the others, and you. Not just for surveillance, but also because I asked him to personally guard you."

"Why does that not surprise me?"

"I was under strict orders not to tell you anything, though it damn near killed me. Because you were asking questions, talking to your father's contacts, you were not only a protected witness, but also a suspect."

"Oh." She held his somber gaze. "So when you and I…on the island…you risked your case and your entire career."

"*Sì*. Sleeping with a suspect or witness is grounds for termination. And can taint court testimony." He squeezed her hand. "I was assigned to protect you. Ordered to kidnap you from the Camorra and obtain information. I resented you at first."

"I didn't like you much, either."

He leaned closer. "I did *not* make love with you to get information. I did not deceive you about that. I didn't mean for it to happen, but I couldn't stop it. As you said, my will was shanghaied."

"I know." She rubbed her thumb over the back of his hand. "And the loss of control freaked you out."

"It unsettled me. I have never lost control before. Never become personally involved in a case. But I don't regret it."

Tenderness curled inside her. She wasn't the only one who had taken chances. "When I found out you'd taken my father's files, I thought you had betrayed me. But your meaning came through loud and clear in your note and I figured out what you'd done."

"I hated having to treat you cruelly." He scowled. "I wanted to convey the message for you not to give up on me. I didn't think you would try to help me." He shook his head. "Let alone negotiate a deal with the FBI on my behalf. I will never again make the error of underestimating your stubbornness, intelligence or loyalty."

She smiled. "I do my best."

A wry smile banished his scowl. "It was Zia Ines who reported me for being a thief and errand boy for the Camorra. When the authorities were too lenient, she insisted I serve some time as a deterrent. In many ways, you remind me of her."

"Thank you." The ultimate compliment. "I wish I could have known her."

"She would have adored you." He toyed with a tendril that had escaped her braid. "Zia introduced me to Bernardo Moretti, the police officer son of a friend. He told me people who think like criminals make the best cops. If I stayed clean until I was eighteen, he would guarantee me a job with as much excitement—on the right side of the law."

She nodded. "They saw what I see. They believed in you."

"And except for brief doubt right after you burned the letters, I believed in *you*. Some of my superiors thought you guilty, and my strong defense of your innocence made them question my judgment. I *had* to finish the case. To clear us both." He kissed her now-healed knuckles. Zia told me something I have never forgotten after I got out of jail. *'Un uomo senza onore non ha niente.'"*

"A man without honor has nothing," Ariana said softly. "Yes, I understand."

"*Sì*. You understand why I couldn't compromise my honor, because you are a woman of honor. You…love me…" He blinked, clearly still wrestling with the concept. "But when you thought I was breaking the law, you turned me in. Thank you for calling the FBI."

Bittersweet emotion tightened her chest. "Don't thank me for almost getting you *killed*."

"You had no idea Agent Esposito was a traitor. Your report proved your innocence to my superiors. Proved your integrity." His voice went ragged. "You saved me. You jumped into the ocean to rescue me, though you cannot swim."

"After you took three bullets for me." Her heart fisted. "Please, accept my apology. I ruined your career and endangered your life trying to clear my father, who turned out to be a criminal."

"In both instances, you did what was right for someone you loved." He stroked her hair. "Whose father was the worse criminal, *cara?* Yours, who stole antiquities? Or mine, who stole my past. Stole my childhood." He trailed a fingertip down her cheek. "You have done nothing for me to forgive. But I ask your forgiveness for the lies. The hurt."

"No." She tucked her knees under her and rose level with his face. "Dante, I'm *glad* you didn't betray your honor and reveal your identity or information about the case."

Hurt and grief glinted in his eyes. "It was the hardest thing I have ever been forced to do."

"You are the most trustworthy person I've ever met." She cupped his face in her hands. "I know I can trust you with *every-*

thing. I can trust you not to betray me. To do what's right, even though it costs you dearly."

"It nearly cost me the only thing that matters. You, *tesoro mio.*" He wrapped his arms around her and drew her close. "*Ti amo.* I love you, Ariana."

Her heart stopped, and then sped into a jubilant flutter. Brilliant happiness sparkled inside her, exploded into joy.

This was the moment she'd waited for her entire life.

Laughing, she touched her mouth to his in a gentle kiss. "Right back at you, tough guy."

"My audacious librarian." He growled and tumbled her backward onto the bed. "I am crazy for you."

"Dante! Your arm!"

He grinned wolfishly. Wrapping his good arm around her, he rolled, putting her on top. "I have two."

She captured his mouth in a long, intoxicating kiss, her hair falling around them in a silky curtain. When he groaned, she drew back. "Too much?"

"Not enough." Desire fired in his gaze. "I need you, Ariana. Make love with me."

"Dante, your injuries—"

His grin flashed again. "You will be gentle with me, yes?"

She laughed. "Very." Scooting down his legs, she removed his boots and socks and bared her own feet. Then she crawled back up, watching his eyes go heavy-lidded and dark with passion.

She straddled his hips and carefully removed his shirt. His bandaged arm and bruised chest came into full view. "Are you sure you're up for this?"

His sensual lips curled in a slow smile. "You are sitting on my lap. You tell me."

"The southern province is having a heat wave. But your arm has to be sore." Ariana leaned down and kissed one bruise then the other. "And these must hurt."

"Mmm." Dante closed his eyes and spoke the truth. "When you are touching me, I feel only pleasure."

"Then let me make *everything* better." He heard the smile in Ariana's voice as she kissed the scrape on his forehead, his eyelids, his cheeks.

Their teamwork skills came in handy as they playfully removed each other's clothing. Ariana's hair trailed over Dante's skin like silken licks of flame. Delight winged through him, and he floated in a haze of rapture as Ariana covered his body with kisses, bathed him in her love.

In the misty morning, raindrops drummed on the roof and sang on the windowpanes. Their breaths mingled. His heart beat for her, and hers for him. Mouths fused, hands stroked, both leading and following in the long, slow waltz of rhythm and warmth.

He needed this woman, her touch, her taste, her fire. But more, he needed her generosity and courage and her unshakable spirit. He needed her love. His hands glided over her smooth skin, teasing, tantalizing until she was panting and breathless. "You fit in my heart," he murmured.

Her beautiful blue eyes smiled into his. "And you in mine."

Holding his gaze, she rose above him, and he trembled as she slowly took him into her. As their bodies melded, moved in heat and pleasure, he told her all the things he had never been able to say before. How much he loved her. Needed her. Cherished her.

Joy and awe played across her lovely face, and lit up his soul. Warm light banished the darkness. For the first time in decades, he stepped out of hiding. There were no more shadows between them. No more secrets.

Ariana's eyes locked on his and she whispered his name like a prayer. That radiant light expanded, surrounded them and burst into colors.

And Dante gloried in the sure knowledge that this was where he belonged.

A long time later, when his heartbeat slowed and he could breathe again, he gently withdrew and kissed her damp temple. "Ariana?"

"Hmm," she mumbled. "One minute. Then I'm good to go."

He laughed, even as his body twitched in response. "I thought we might talk first. I am leaving the force."

"What?" She jerked her head up to stare at him. "Why?"

"The reality of a cop's life is not pretty."

"I know exactly what it's like. I've had an up-close-and-personal view the last few weeks." Her heartbeat galloped against his. "I don't want you to give it up on my account."

"I would do anything to make your fairy tale come true," he declared fiercely. "Teach, run a museum, whatever makes you happy. I already told Bernardo I'm done going undercover."

She gasped. "Do you want to completely quit the force?"

"I no longer wish to lie for a living. But—" he refused to be a shade less than honest "—I would like to stay on as a detective tracking down stolen antiquities. Though even their hours can be long and unpredictable."

"I'll be plenty busy finishing that novel I've always wanted to write." She watched him carefully, as if trying to discern his thoughts. "You're a good cop, and you love it. Whatever your dream is, I want you to have it."

His heart turned over. "There is a poet who said it best. 'I, being poor, have only my dreams,/I have spread my dreams under your feet;/Tread softly because you tread on my dreams,'" he quietly quoted. "My dream, Ariana, is you. I want to make love to you every night and wake up beside you every morning." He cupped her face in his hands, watched her eyes go wide and vulnerable. "Would you do me the great honor of becoming my wife?"

"Oh, Dante!" Tears sparkled like jewels in her sapphire gaze. "Yes! *Sì!*" She hugged him.

Happiness soared inside him. He smiled, even as moisture stung his own eyes. He'd never dared to hope he would be worthy of such riches. "How long is your commitment to Liberty Line Cruises?"

"Four more months. We're sailing to the Caribbean next."

"As soon as I'm back on my feet, I must tie up this case…but

I will visit you in every port. Would you like to have the wedding aboard ship in the Caribbean?" He started, and his heart pounded furiously. "Unless...we need to marry sooner?"

She shook her head. "I had the clinic do a blood test. I'm not pregnant. At least not as of—" she leaned over to glance at the clock and smiled "—two hours ago."

Relief and disappointment tangled inside him. "I would not have been unhappy." He kissed the tip of her pert nose. "But is it selfish of me to want you to myself for a while before the bambini arrive?"

"No, I felt exactly the same." She hesitated. "However, I require a very important disclosure before marrying you."

Was she worried about events in his past? Something for which he might not have an answer? "I will explain the best I can."

She grinned. "What's your last name?"

Laughter rumbled out of him. Life would never be dull with Ariana by his side. "Dante Rafaele Colangelo, at your service." He sobered. "I promise, Ariana, I will never again lie to you. About *anything*."

"I trust you with my body, heart and soul." She kissed him. "When everything and everyone I believed in turned out to be false, I embarked on a quest for the truth. And I found you. I don't want fairy tales. I want the real deal—*you*, Dante Rafaele Colangelo."

He warmed with contentment, at peace for the first time in his life. "And I went searching for others' valuables, and was gifted with a priceless treasure of my very own." He smiled. "The Fates took us on a wild ride, but they knew what they were doing, *amore mio*."

"*My love*." She wrapped her arms around his neck. "I'll never get tired of hearing you say that."

"In that case..." He glided his fingertips down her spine. Her heart leaped against his, and he reveled in her response. "I will say it to you every day, *amore mio*."

Grinning, he rolled her beneath him. "For the next fifty years."

EPILOGUE

The crew bar aboard Alexandra's Dream
Two days later

ARIANA HAPPILY PROFFERED her left hand to show Patti Kennedy, the cruise director, her engagement ring.

"What beautifully burnished gold! Is it an antique?" Patti reverently touched the stone. "And the huge sapphire matches your eyes."

"That's what Dante said." Ariana smiled. "Yes, it's an antique Greek piece. The delicate wings carved into the band represent Eros, the god of love."

"You're so lucky." Patti sighed. "Dante is sooo romantic."

"I agree, on both counts." Low music swirled in the background, and the room brimmed with laughing, chatting people. Patti had summoned the couple to the crew bar and surprised them with an engagement party.

Ariana looked across the room where Dante and her mother were serving themselves from the sumptuous buffet. After protecting Ariana with his life, Dante didn't have to try to win Sadie over. He and Sadie had immediately bonded, and her mom had joyously welcomed him into the family.

Dante caught her eye and winked, then wove through the throng to her side. He offered her the filled plate. "Hungry?"

She grinned. "Did you bring olives?" He laughed, and her heart leaped. No longer forced into the role of brooding smuggler, he was the warm, teasing companion from their fishing expedition. And the caring, passionate lover.

Captain Pappas arrived with Helena Stamos at his side. Sadie had been right. The meaningful glances and knowing smiles said clearly the couple were in love. "Congratulations, Signor Colangelo, Miss Bennett."

"Thank you. *Grazie*," Ariana and Dante said in perfect unison, and everyone chuckled.

Gideon Dayan stopped to offer his best wishes. Katherine Stamos, Elias's oldest daughter, gave Ariana a hug and then laughingly hugged Dante, also. As head of public relations for the cruise line, Katherine had flown in from her home in England to deal with media inquiries. Bernardo Moretti was also there, thrilled at being asked to stand in as Dante's best man. He introduced his vivacious wife Giovanna to Ariana.

Theo Catomeris waited until Dante and Ariana had a moment alone before he approached. "I…just wanted to say I'm sorry—"

"No apologies." Dante slid his arm around Ariana. "A smart woman once told me that we aren't accountable for our parents' actions."

"I know that better than anyone," Ariana said gently. "No one blames you, Theo." Her smile returned. "Eventually, we're going to be family, and I couldn't be more thrilled."

"May I have everyone's attention, please." Elias Stamos moved to Sadie's side near the front of the room.

Elias had offered Dante a complimentary luxury cabin to recuperate during the crossing. Dante would fly from Miami to Italy to finalize the case before eventually rejoining *Alexandra's Dream* in the Caribbean. Elias had arranged helicopter transport to the mainland for party guests who weren't staying aboard.

Elias cleared his throat. "My deepest gratitude to Dante and Ariana for their courage and sacrifice to solve a crime that would have cost me dearly."

Everyone murmured approval, and Elias continued. "We've had quite the adventure so far." He looked down at Sadie and smiled warmly, then smiled at Dante and Ariana. "Congratulations. I wish you many happy years together, many children and many blessings."

He raised his glass and his gaze swept the crowd. "And to each of you…smooth sailing ahead."

* * * * *

MEDITERRANEAN NIGHTS

*Join the glamorous world of cruising with the guests
and crew of* Alexandra's Dream—*the newest luxury ship
to set sail on the romantic Mediterranean.*

*The voyage continues in February 2008
with CABIN FEVER
by Mary Leo.*

Becky Montgomery has been mourning her husband
for two years, and knows it's time to move on,
maybe start dating…but not yet. Not during a cruise aboard
Alexandra's Dream with her two children and a demanding
mother-in-law. Then she meets charismatic Dylan Langstaff,
the ship's diving instructor, and she can't stop thinking about
him. Dylan is also drawn to Becky—and her family.
Something about her is changing the way he wants to live….

Here's a preview!

"THERE'S THIS GREAT broccoli salad you should try," a voice said just behind Becky's right ear.

Becky turned to see Dylan's tanned face smiling down at her.

"I saw what you did for that choking woman," Becky said, ignoring his suggestion. "You were incredible. How is she doing?"

"She's fine. Resting in her stateroom."

"You saved her life. That was amazing."

"Thanks, but she was the amazing one. She never put up the least resistance. That's what saved her."

"I'll remember that the next time I'm choking."

His grin widened. "Good idea."

There was a moment of awkward silence while Becky searched for something to say. "Where is that salad?" she stammered at last.

She loved broccoli, but ever since Ryder had died, she'd found herself eating more and more comfort foods, like pasta and homemade breads. She'd put on about ten pounds in the past two years, even though she still worked out with weights. But the strange part was, she didn't seem to care about the added weight. Or maybe she simply didn't have time to think about it.

"On the other side of this station," he said, his eyes shimmering like pools of sea-green water and with a smile that could make a girl swoon. But she wasn't going to be one of them. Nope, not her. She knew better. Besides, she wasn't ready for romance, especially with this type of guy. His interest had to be all PR. It couldn't be real. Could it?

She didn't want to reflect on that. She had her kids with her, for heaven's sake. What would they think of their mother swooning over some man who would sail off again at the end of their cruise. The whole thing was ridiculous. She needed to stop these crazy thoughts right now, before her fantasies got completely out of control.

And she'd start with broccoli.

"Never mind. I'm not really that fond of broccoli," she said, without flinching at her little white lie, which was meant to prevent him from accompanying her to another buffet station.

"I would have thought you were."

"Is there a broccoli type?"

She was sure there was a teasing glint in his eyes. "Well, actually, there is," he said.

"And just what would that be?" He had her smiling now. She liked how easy it was to talk to him.

"She usually has an athletic body, strong arms and an equally strong opinion on matters that count. She eats whole grains, avoids most carbs and never eats anything with hydrogenated or trans fats. But she loves gelato, all flavors, though she only has it when she's on vacation. By the way…Artemis deck, Just Gelato. Best on the ship."

Becky turned back to the cornucopia of steaming food and added a square of lasagna to her plate. She considered lasagna the perfect food, at least lately. "And you've done research on this broccoli-woman theory, have you?"

"It's just an observation. You can tell a lot about a person from the foods they eat."

He followed her down the line as she added scalloped potatoes to her plate, then some kind of stuffing with thick, creamy gravy. She figured this would do the trick. He was looking for a broccoli babe, and right now she was a carboholic.

"And what if a person doesn't eat vegetables? What does that say about her?" She stopped and turned to him. He looked down at her plate, which was now a mess of carbs swimming in brown gravy. She felt a little of the gravy drip off her plate and onto her toes.

He gave her a sly smile, reached over, swiped the dripping gravy from the side of her plate and licked it off his finger.

"They make the best beef gravy on this ship," he said, wearing a pirate's smile. Then he turned and walked away.

Becky watched him for a moment, angry at his audacity, but charmed by it at the same time.

She spotted a waiter, apologized and handed him her dripping plate. Then, wearing her own pirate's smile, she went in search of the broccoli salad.